"Thank you ... **ur hand,"** he s...

"Sometimes a simple human touch goes a long way in giving people courage, in letting them know they're not alone."

Samantha stared at Brad. She had faced her greatest crisis alone, so she knew what he meant. A simple caring touch, a choice offered in compassion, would have made a world of difference to her once. It could have changed her whole life, in fact.

Her throat constricted and she squeezed Brad's hand. "You're not alone," she said softly, her voice uneven. Then she tried to smile, forcing a lighter note into her tone. "After all, what are friends for?"

He gazed at her speculatively. "You know, Sam, I think..."

"You think what?" she prompted.

Brad cleared his throat. He'd been about to say that at the moment friendship was the furthest thing from his mind.

Books by Irene Hannon

Love Inspired

*Home for the Holidays #6
*A Groom of Her Own #16

*Vows

IRENE HANNON

has been a writer for as long as she can remember. This prolific author of romance novels for both the inspirational and traditional markets began her career at age ten, when she won a story contest conducted by a national children's magazine. Presently, her editorial position in corporate communications—as well as penning her heartwarming stories of love and faith—keeps her quite busy.

Irene finds writing for the Love Inspired series especially rewarding because, "Inspirational romances allow me to focus on the three things that last—faith, hope and love. It is a special pleasure for me to write about people who find the greatest of these without compromising the principles of their faith."

The author and her husband, Tom—"my own romantic hero"—reside in St. Louis, Missouri.

A Groom of Her Own

Irene Hannon

Love Inspired™

Published by Steeple Hill Books™

STEEPLE HILL BOOKS

Steeple
Hill™

ISBN 0-373-87016-7

A GROOM OF HER OWN

Copyright © 1998 by Irene Hannon

Printed in U.S.A.

Ask, and it shall be given you; seek, and ye shall find; knock, and it shall be opened unto you.

—*Matthew 7:7*

To Tom
My Perfect Valentine

Chapter One

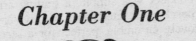

"Well, kiddo, this is it." Sam Reynolds gently edged the door closed behind Laura Taylor's mother and turned to face her best friend.

"Oh, Sam, I can't believe it's really happening!" Laura's eyes glistened suspiciously in her radiant face, and Sam felt her own throat contract. If anyone deserved a happy ending, it was the woman standing across from her. Sam wouldn't have laid odds on it, though. After trying mightily—but unsuccessfully—for years to find a man for Laura, she'd practically given up hope of ever seeing her best friend walk down the aisle. But in the end Laura surprised her by finding Nick Sinclair on her own—with a little help from fate.

"Well, I'm your witness. Literally," Sam said with a grin. "It's real, all right. And you look absolutely beautiful. I don't think I've ever seen a more radiant bride."

"Do you really think so?"

"See for yourself." She put her hands on Laura's shoulders and turned her to face the full-length mirror on the far wall.

Laura gazed at the woman in the reflection, hardly recognizing the image as her own. Her peach-colored tea-length gown highlighted her slender curves and accentuated her femininity. The satin underslip softly hugged her body, and the lace gown overlay, with short, slightly gathered sleeves and a sweetheart neckline, had a quaint old-fashioned air that suited Laura. She wore her strawberry blond hair loose and full, the way Nick liked it, pulled back on one side with a small cluster of flowers and ribbon. Her bouquet was simple, a trailing arrangement of ivory and peach roses intertwined with ivy and wispy fern. It was a lovely ensemble, perfect for a second wedding, and she was grateful to Sam for helping her find it. But what she noticed most as she gazed in the mirror was her face, glowing and content and happy.

"Oh, Sam, is that really me?" she whispered. "I look…well…pretty."

Sam moved beside her and placed an arm around her shoulders. "Honey, *pretty* is a gross understatement. Try *ravishing, drop-dead gorgeous* and *fantastic,* and you might come a little closer." She shook her head and chuckled. "Wait'll Nick gets an eyeful!"

Laura reached for her purse and fished out a tissue. "I'm so happy it's almost scary," she admitted, dabbing at her eyes.

"Hey, hey, hey, no tears!" Sam said. "Your mascara will run and you'll look like a racoon. Not a pretty picture, let me tell you. You can cry after the reception—although by then I think you'll have better things to do," she said with a knowing wink that brought a blush to the bride's face.

A discreet knock sounded on the door, and Laura's brother, John, stuck his head inside. "Ladies, it's your cue."

Sam gave Laura's hand one more squeeze. "You'll knock their socks off, kiddo," she whispered. "And if you don't believe me, just watch Nick when you walk down that aisle."

She moved toward the door, pausing in front of the mirror to cast a quick, discerning glance at her own reflection. The pencil-slim skirt and short-sleeved peplum jacket of her pale sea green brocade suit showed off her fashionably slender figure to perfection, and the color complemented her shoulder-length red hair. She adjusted the peplum, smoothed down a few stray strands of hair and gave her expertly applied makeup one final inspection. Then she turned and winked at Laura encouragingly. "Okay, here we go."

Sam stepped into the vestibule and took her place behind the double doors that led to the church. She heard the organ music pause, then change melodies, and a moment later two of the ushers pulled back the heavy doors.

As Sam made her way past the sea of smiling faces in the small church, she was struck by the romantic ambiance. The deeply fragrant scent of rubrum lilies filled the air, and wispy greenery anchored with white bows trailed from the ends of the pews. Late afternoon light illuminated the stained glass windows, which in turn cast a mosaic of warm, muted colors on the rich wood floor. It was a beautiful and appropriate setting, Sam thought appreciatively.

The icing on the cake, of course, was Nick Sinclair. She looked at him as she moved down the aisle, and he smiled at her. Tall, handsome, charming—those words accurately described him. But he was also a patient, caring, decent man. In other words, exactly what Laura deserved. She smiled back with a small, approving nod, which he acknowledged with a wink.

Nick's best man and business partner, Jack, met her at the altar and offered his arm. As they took their places, the organ music faded and an expectant rustle filled the church as the guests turned for their first glimpse of the bride.

When the doors opened and Laura and her brother stepped forward to the majestic strains of "Trumpet Tune," Sam glanced again at Nick. The tenderness and love she saw in his eyes made her throat constrict. What must it be like to be loved like that? she wondered, turning to look back at Laura, whose gaze was locked on Nick's. Clearly they had eyes only for each other. For the eleven years she and Laura had been friends, Sam had never seen such peace and joy and confidence on Laura's face. Little wonder, considering the trauma she'd had to overcome. But with Nick's help, Laura had found the courage to put her past behind her and look with hope to the future. Sam was happy for her.

What surprised Sam was the tangle of other emotions that suddenly overwhelmed her. Sadness, for one. In the excitement of the last few weeks she'd had little time to reflect on exactly what this marriage meant to *her*. Now, as she watched Laura walk down the aisle and take her place beside Nick, she realized that while their friendship was solid and would endure, change was inevitable now that Laura was becoming Nick's wife. Laura wouldn't need Sam as much anymore, and that knowledge brought with it an unexpected sense of emptiness.

She also discovered that she was jealous, and that jolted her. She certainly didn't begrudge Laura her happiness. It was just that she longed for her own happy ending, futile as that wish was. She wondered if Laura ever stopped to think how odd it was that Sam, the vivacious partyer with more dates than she could keep track of, had never remarried. What Laura didn't know, of course, was that Sam's life-style was a sham, a pretense, a way to keep the loneliness at bay—not an attempt to find the right man, as she always claimed. Because there was no right man for her.

Sam glanced around at the small group clustered in the chancel. Nick and Laura now had a lifetime to look forward to as a married couple. Jack, the best man, was happily married, with a lovely wife and children. Her gaze moved to the minister, an attractive man with sandy brown hair touched with silver, who looked to be in his late thirties or early forties. Even he had a ring on.

Suddenly Sam felt more alone than she had in years. Alone and lonely and empty. Laura would find that hard to believe, she knew. Through the years Sam had made no secret of the fact that she led a very active social life. By entertaining Laura with tales of her various dates and dragging her into the singles scene, Sam had hoped to convince Laura that *she* needed a social life. But Laura never bought it. With her faith providing a solid foundation, she'd found her own quiet way to deal with loneliness.

And maybe her way was better, Sam thought dispiritedly. Because while Sam's frenzied social life kept her busy, it didn't ease the deeper loneliness. If anything, it left her feeling lonelier than before. The men she dated were out for a *good* time, not a *life* time. Which was fine, of course. It was safer to avoid dating the kind of man she might want to settle down with—stable, not afraid of commitment, caring. Because she might fall in love, and she didn't deserve someone like that. At the same time, she wasn't willing to settle for anything less. Which meant, bottom line, that she would spend her life alone.

Unaccustomed tears of self-pity welled up in Sam's eyes, taking her off guard. She usually kept her emotions in check, hidden beneath the brassy, irreverent veneer that had been her protection for more years than she cared to remember. She closed her eyes, willing the tears to evaporate, then blinked rapidly, struggling for control.

Suddenly Sam realized that the minister was looking at her.

"The ring," he prompted softly, in a tone that indicated he'd made the request more than once.

Sam blinked again and removed the ring from her right pinkie, where it was hidden by her bouquet. As she moved forward and handed it to him, he looked at her questioningly.

"Are you all right?" he asked in an undertone.

She felt Laura's concerned eyes on her and somehow managed a shaky smile. "I'm fine."

Sam stepped back, her face flushed, embarrassed to have caused even a slight glitch in what was otherwise a perfect ceremony. She forced herself to focus on the moment, listening intently as the minister spoke.

"On behalf of Laura and Nick, I want to welcome you here today to witness their declaration of love and their pledge to spend the rest of their earthly days together," he said. He had a pleasant voice, mellow and soothing, and Sam felt calmer just listening to it. "I know it means a great deal to them to have so many friends and family members here to share this very special day. Their marriage is indeed a joyful event that we all celebrate.

"Witnessing a wedding is always an honor. It is an event marked with hope and love and commitment, and there are too few of those in today's world. But witnessing this wedding is a special honor for me. As many of you know, Laura and I share the same hometown. Her brother, John, and I are good friends, and through him I became acquainted with the whole family. So while I've been Laura's minister ever since she came to St. Louis, some fifteen years ago, I was her friend long before that.

"Through the years my respect for Laura as a woman and as a Christian has continued to grow. For all of us who are fortunate enough to know her, she is an inspiring example of what it means to lead a Christian life. I know that she will also be an inspiring example of what it means to be a Christian wife.

"I've known Nick for only a few months, but I have come to realize that he is a fine and caring man. I know he will love and honor Laura with a commitment and a steadfastness that will add richness and dimension to both of their lives.

"I think it's appropriate that Laura and Nick chose today—the first day of spring—as their wedding day. For both of them it marks a new beginning, a new life, a season of beauty and growth and hope, a new direction in their earthly journey. And that journey will hold challenges. Because as all of us know, the road of life isn't always easy or straight. We make wrong turns, we take detours, we hit roadblocks, we have flat tires. But as long as we keep our eyes focused on the destination, and as long as we are willing to listen to the Lord's direction, we can find our way home.

"Laura and Nick know their ultimate destination. They know the Lord will always be there to guide them. They've known that, individually, all of their lives. But now, as man and wife, they will have an earthly partner to help when the journey gets rough, as well as a friend with whom to share all the moments of joy and beauty that the Lord blesses us with along the way. I know that all of you join with me today in wishing Nick and Laura Godspeed on their journey as a married couple. And now let us pray...."

Sam stared at the minister, mesmerized by his rich, well-modulated voice and the words he'd spoken. His remarks were the most insightful, moving and comforting she'd ever heard in a church—a far cry from the "fire and brimstone" sermons she remembered as a child. For the first time Sam looked—really looked—at his face. He was actually quite handsome, she realized. And appealing in a way she couldn't exactly pinpoint. He seemed to radiate an innate character and kindness that spoke of trust and integrity. She frowned as she tried to recall his name. Laura had introduced them at the rehearsal the night before, but Sam hadn't been paying that much attention. It wasn't a "religious" name, she remembered that. Bill? Brent? Brad! That was it. Brad Matthews. Before the day was over she would find an opportunity to compliment him on his talk.

As it turned out, Sam didn't have a minute to herself until hours later. After the ceremony there'd been pictures, then the drive to the reception, then more pictures, a re-

ceiving line and finally dinner. All of this was followed
by the bride and groom's first dance, the wedding party
dance and the cake cutting. But finally the ceremonies and
rituals were over. Maybe now she could find a quiet spot
for a moment and take a deep breath, she thought hopefully.

Except that Laura's cousin intercepted her as she was
searching for just such a spot. Sam tried to be polite, tried
to focus on what the woman was saying, but she was suddenly bone weary, tired of smiling and plagued once again
with the feeling of emptiness that had overwhelmed her
during the ceremony. The melodic strains of Gershwin's
"Our Love Is Here to Stay" drifted through the room, and
she glanced at the dance floor to find Laura and Nick in
each other's arms, moving as one to the music. The tenderness in Nick's eyes as he gazed at Laura was suddenly
too much for her, and with a mumbled apology to Laura's
cousin, Sam fled toward the terrace. Maybe some fresh air
would help chase away the blues. At least it was worth a
try.

Brad Matthews jammed his hands into the pockets of
his slacks and leaned against the wall, breathing deeply of
the chilly air. It had been a nice wedding, and he was
happy for Laura and Nick. They made a wonderful couple,
and he knew that their life together would be full and rich.
He prayed that they would be blessed with the children
they both wanted and that the Lord would give them a
long and happy life together. They deserved it.

But so had he and Rachel, he thought sadly. They would
have made good parents, he was sure of it. And their love
would have endured, standing as an example for others in
this day of quickly forgotten commitments. But the Lord
had other plans for them.

For the first time in a long while Brad allowed himself
to remember his own wedding day. Rachel had made a
beautiful bride, he recalled with a tender smile. She had

been absolutely radiant as she'd walked down the aisle to meet him. Theirs had been a union of kindred spirits, firmly based on a strong Christian faith and the ability to find joy in the simple pleasures of life. They had eagerly looked forward to starting a family and creating a legacy of love for their children.

Brad's smile faded. Even after six years, the pain of Rachel's untimely death still made him feel physically ill. Not a day went by that he didn't miss her lovely smile or her musical laugh. His work usually kept him too busy to allow time for self-pity, but occasionally something would trigger memories that made him feel his loss as keenly as if it had happened yesterday. Laura's wedding had done that.

But it had done something else as well. For the first time since Rachel's death, Brad acknowledged that although his work was fulfilling, something was missing. No, he corrected himself, make that "someone." Because Brad had enjoyed such a wonderful marriage, he knew what it was like to share the day-to-day joys and sorrows with another person. And he missed that.

Would it be possible, he wondered, to find love again? Could there be someone else like Rachel somewhere out there? And what would Rachel say about it? Would she be hurt? Would she think he was being disloyal if he remarried?

Brad had never asked those questions before. Even when Rachel was alive, they'd been so young that they'd never discussed the subject. Death had seemed like such a remote possibility. But how would he feel were the situation reversed? he asked himself. Would he want Rachel to live the rest of her life alone? The answer was simple: Of course not. To deny her the chance to give expression to her bountiful love, to condemn her to living a solitary life just because he didn't want to share her with someone else, would be selfish. And he suddenly knew with absolute certainty that if she could speak to him, she would tell him that she felt the same way, that it was time for him to move on.

Yet Rachel still felt like such a part of his life. How did a person let go? As a minister, Brad knew he was supposed to have those kinds of answers. But suddenly he didn't feel at all like a minister. He just felt like a very lonely man.

As Sam stepped onto the dimly lit terrace, she realized that the late-March air had cooled considerably with the setting of the sun. Unfortunately, the short sleeves and sweetheart neckline of her suit didn't offer much protection from the chill. She shivered and wrapped her arms around her body for warmth. It was silly to stand out here and freeze, but she couldn't plunge back into the festivities just yet. For someone who was usually in control, the unexpected whirlwind of emotions she'd been experiencing all day was disconcerting, leaving her feeling off balance and confused, and she needed to regain her equilibrium. She sniffed, struggling once more to hold back the tears, and groped in the pocket of her jacket for a tissue.

"Excuse me...is everything all right?"

Startled, Sam gasped and spun around. Brad Matthews stood in the shadows, a few feet away, watching her intently. She had no idea how long he'd been there, but it was apparently long enough for him to realize that she was upset. Embarrassed for the second time that day, Sam turned away, struggling to compose her face, grateful for the dim light on the terrace.

The voice moved closer. "I'm sorry if I startled you."

Sam took a deep breath. "It's okay. I just didn't expect anyone else to be out here. It's pretty chilly."

Sam heard fabric sliding over fabric, then felt a jacket being draped over her shoulders. It still radiated body warmth, and she gratefully drew it around her even as she protested. "I shouldn't take this. You'll freeze."

"I'll be fine," he assured her. "You seem to need it more than I do."

This time Sam successfully retrieved the tissue and dabbed at her eyes. She was struck by the man's insight. When he'd realized she was cold, he hadn't suggested going back inside, as many people would have done. He seemed to understand that she needed some distance from the festivities, and had instead offered her his coat. She found that touching, and once again her eyes blurred with tears.

Brad frowned as he stared at the back of the woman in front of him. Laura often talked of Sam, and Brad had formed what he'd assumed was a fairly accurate picture of the bride's best friend. Physically, he was pretty much on target. Sophisticated makeup, svelte figure, striking hair. Not quite as tall as he'd expected, though. She was a good four inches shorter than he, with heels, and he was just under six feet. He thought she'd be statuesque. But it was the demeanor and personality that really surprised him. Laura always talked admiringly of Sam's composure and self-confidence, described her as the strong, invincible type who was never thrown by anything and never at a loss for words. But the woman who had nearly gone to pieces at the wedding and who now stood silent and shaky an arm's length away didn't fit that image at all.

Brad debated his next move. Should he discreetly disappear or, as was his nature when people were in trouble, offer his help? The decision was easier than he thought, because when she sniffed again he spoke automatically.

"I'm sorry if I'm intruding, but…is there anything I can do?" he asked gently.

She shook her head. "I'm fine, really," she assured him, but she knew her shaky voice belied her words. Desperately she tried to think of a reasonable explanation for her teary state. "I'm just a sucker for happy endings," she offered, grasping at the first idea that came to her.

Brad didn't quite buy that. The Sam he'd heard about

from Laura might be moved, but she'd hide it behind a flippant remark. She wouldn't cry. There was something else going on here, but he was a stranger to her, and the best he could do was empathize.

"I know what you mean. You know, I think we witnessed a real miracle today. I honestly wasn't sure if Laura would ever risk that kind of commitment again."

"Me, neither," Sam agreed with a sniff. "But I knew if she met the right man she might, and I sure tried to get her into circulation."

The minister chuckled. "So I heard."

Sam wiped her nose and turned to stare at him suspiciously. "What exactly did you hear?"

"She told me about a few of the singles dances you dragged her to. I just can't picture Laura at one of those things."

"She never did feel comfortable," Sam agreed, and he saw the ghost of a smile flicker across her face.

"You know, I realize we were introduced last night at the rehearsal, but it was all pretty rushed. So how about if we start over?" He held out his hand. "I'm Brad Matthews. And you're Sam Reynolds. It's very nice to meet you."

Sam took his hand. It was firm and strong, yet there was a warmth and tenderness in his touch that she found appealing.

"It's nice to meet you, too." She paused, and he sensed that she was searching for words, an experience that was obviously foreign to the usually glib Sam. "You know, ever since the ceremony this afternoon I've been wanting to tell you how wonderful I thought your talk was," she said slowly. "I've never heard anything quite that moving in church before."

"Thank you."

"I really mean it," she said earnestly, reaching out to touch his arm, wanting him to know that her words weren't just an empty compliment. For some reason, that was important to her. "I've never been much of a churchgoer, Reverend, but if there were more ministers like you I might have been."

Brad took her hand between his, engulfing it in a warm clasp. She had small, delicate fingers, and again he was struck by this woman's unexpected and touching vulnerability. "I appreciate that, Sam," he said with quiet sincerity.

For a moment there was silence, and the strains of "Till There Was You" drifted through the slightly ajar door. For some reason, Sam felt less lonely now. Maybe it was the way this man was holding her hand, his touch conveying caring and warmth and compassion. It had been a long time since a man had touched her like this with something other than sex on his mind. And it felt good. Very good. Too good. It was going to make her teary eyed again.

Reluctantly she withdrew her hand and slipped his coat from her shoulders. She'd monopolized enough of his time, anyway.

"Thank you for the loan," she said, holding the coat out to him. "It certainly came in handy. But I really should let you get back inside. Your wife is probably looking for you by now."

There was a moment of silence, and she could see even through the dimness that he was frowning. "My wife?"

Now it was Sam's turn to frown. "I noticed in church that you were wearing a ring and...well, it looked like a wedding ring," she said uncertainly.

"Oh." He glanced down and touched the gold band. Then he sighed. "Yes, it is. But my wife died six years ago."

Sam stared at him, her eyes growing wide. "I'm so sorry," she said softly.

"Thank you." He looked down again at the ring, and his face was deeply shadowed when he spoke. "The ring confuses a lot of people. I suppose I should take it off, but

I've never seen a reason to. Rachel is still part of my life, even though she's gone.''

"It sounds like you have wonderful memories,'' Sam said wistfully. Then she turned away, and when she spoke again there was a trace of bitterness in her voice. "I couldn't get my ring off fast enough.''

"Laura mentioned you were married, once,'' he said carefully.

"Yeah.'' She gave a mirthless laugh. "I always used to tell her we married two losers. Randy was a rat, plain and simple. He just walked out on me one day after only five months and never came back, even though...'' She cut herself off sharply, shocked that she'd almost revealed a secret she'd never shared with anyone, not even Laura! What was wrong with her today?

Brad waited a moment, and when it became apparent that Sam wasn't going to continue, he spoke. "Weddings can be an emotional time—for the guests as well as the bride and groom. They stir up lots of memories, good and bad,'' he remarked quietly.

Sam looked at him again, struck once more by his insightfulness and empathy. But unlike her memories, she was sure his were happy.

"Well, life goes on,'' he said. "Laura should be an example to us. She finally found the courage to stop letting the past control her future, and look at the happiness she's found.''

"Not everyone is that lucky, Reverend,'' Sam replied sadly, turning away once more to stare into the darkness.

Brad knew that Sam was close to tears again. He also sensed that whatever troubled her was a deeper issue than could be dealt with tonight. But at least he could try to cheer her up. "I'll tell you what,'' he said. "Suppose you stop calling me Reverend and start calling me Brad. Then maybe I can ask you to dance.''

Sam's head snapped around and she stared at him. "Dance?''

"Ministers can dance. It's allowed," he teased.

Sam found herself smiling. "I appreciate the offer. But you don't have to do that. I'm fine."

"Don't you like to dance?"

"Well, yes, but..." Her voice trailed off.

He grinned. "But not with ministers?"

"It's not that," she said quickly. "Actually, I've never danced with a minister."

"Well, if I promise not to preach while we polka, will you give it a try? Because, to be honest, I've been wanting to ask you all night but I just didn't have the nerve."

"Are you serious?" she asked incredulously.

"Would a preacher lie?" he asked solemnly. Okay, so he'd stretched the truth a little. He *had* hoped to have the opportunity to speak with her, though, considering how upset she'd been in church earlier in the day. But the invitation to dance was a spur-of-the-moment idea.

"Well...if you really want to, sure, that would be great."

"I wouldn't have asked if I hadn't wanted to. Let's catch the next number. Maybe it will be a nice fox-trot."

Brad pushed the door open and guided her inside, his hand at the small of her back. Sam liked the nonthreatening and protective feel of it. It was...nice.

As they reached the dance floor, the band swung into "In the Mood," and Sam turned to Brad with a grin. "So much for your fox-trot. That's okay. We can skip. But I appreciate the offer." She started to turn away, but he grabbed her hand and she looked around in surprise.

"You're not getting off that easy. Is this number too much for you?" he challenged with a smile, his eyes twinkling.

"No, of course not," she stammered. "It's just...well...fast. It's a swing number," she pointed out.

"I know. I'm game if you are."

Sam grinned and shrugged. She was beginning to really like this preacher. "Okay."

By the time the number ended, Sam was gasping and laughing all at once. "You are really good!" she said. "Where did you learn to dance like that?"

"I haven't always been a minister," he reminded her. He looked around and then dropped his voice conspiratorially. "Can I tell you a secret, Sam?"

She leaned closer. "Sure."

"Ministers are really just regular people. For example, even though you may think I dance divinely—no pun intended—I can't carry a tune in a bucket. My sister inherited the voice in the family. But I love to sing, and it drives Rose, our choir director, crazy. She just hasn't figured out a way to diplomatically tell me to shut up. She thinks ministers are specially blessed or something and she'll incur the wrath of heaven if she insults me. So if you ever meet her, don't let on that I'm just an ordinary guy."

Sam giggled and shook her head. "I've never met a minister like you."

"I'll take that as a compliment." He paused as the band struck up the opening notes of "As Time Goes By," and then he smiled. "Now there's our fox-trot. And that song is too good to pass up. How about one more dance before I call it a night?"

"Are you leaving already?" Sam asked, suddenly disappointed.

"I'm afraid so," he replied regretfully. "I've got an early service tomorrow. Shall we?"

He held out his arms, and Sam moved into them. The last dance had been exhilarating and loud and fast. This one was slow and…different. Brad held her close—closer than she expected for a minister—as they moved to the romantic melody. She could smell the scent of his aftershave, feel the slight stubble on his chin against her temple. She felt…strange. But good. He was a nice man. And it was nice to be with a nice man, even if only for a little while.

Brad hadn't danced in a long time. A very long time.

He was surprised the steps came back so easily. But then, he and Rachel had liked to dance. She had been a good dancer. Tall, with the build of a ballerina, she had been almost eye level with him when they danced. Sam was smaller, the top of her head barely brushing his mouth. And she was soft. She smelled good, too, and instinctively he tightened his hold.

Brad grinned ruefully as he considered the situation. If someone had told him a few hours ago that he'd end the evening on the dance floor with Sam Reynolds, Laura's flamboyant, uninhibited and—he hated to think it, but the term came unbidden—hot-to-trot friend, he would have stared at them in surprise. But then, he'd been surprised by a number of things about Sam tonight. He'd seen a vulnerable, insecure side of the woman in his arms that he had a feeling even Laura had never seen, and he'd had to revise his image of her. He didn't know exactly who Sam really was, but he suddenly suspected that she wasn't quite what she seemed to be to the world.

When the music ended, he stepped back and glanced down. Her green eyes looked soft and appealing and suddenly bereft, and he was surprised by the sudden rush of tenderness that swept over him. He took her hand once more, cradling it between his. "Thank you, Sam. I enjoyed the dance."

"So did I," she said, her voice unusually husky and tinged with regret now that it was over. It had felt good in this man's arms. Protected, somehow, and safe.

"Is someone taking you home?"

"Yes. Laura's brother, John."

"Then I guess I'll say—"

"Sam, I've been looking for you! Brad, are you still here? I thought you left half an hour ago," Laura's surprised voice interrupted them.

Brad transferred his gaze to Laura and grinned. "I got sidetracked."

"Well, don't sleep through your own sermon tomorrow," Laura warned with a laugh before turning her attention to Sam. "I wanted to say goodbye, and I was afraid I'd miss you. Nick's getting anxious to leave."

"*Anxious* isn't exactly the word I'd use, and leaving isn't the reason for it...but it'll do," Nick said with a chuckle as he came up behind Laura and wrapped his arms around her waist. When he pulled her back against him, she blushed becomingly.

Sam laughed. "Laura, the man has been patient beyond belief. Why don't you put him out of his misery?"

Laura's face went an even deeper shade of pink. "Will you two stop? There's a minister present."

Nick looked at Brad, and the two men smiled at each other. "I think Brad understands," Nick assured her, and then he leaned down and nuzzled her neck. "But just so I don't look too...anxious...how about one more dance?" he murmured huskily.

Laura turned to look up at him, her eyes shining. "I'd like that," she said softly. With an effort, she tore her gaze away from Nick and stepped toward Sam, drawing her friend into a warm embrace. "Thank you," she whispered, knowing that Sam would understand the wealth of meaning in those simple words.

Sam hugged her tightly, blinking rapidly to keep the tears at bay. She would not cry, she told herself fiercely. Not now. Not in front of everyone. The cool, composed, wisecracking Sam Reynolds wouldn't cry, she reminded herself. It would ruin her reputation.

With a superhuman effort, she steadied her emotions and stepped back. "Have a wonderful honeymoon, you two. And try to get at least a little sleep," she added, forcing her lips to turn up into a smile.

"Now *that* I can't guarantee," Nick replied with a grin, taking Laura's hand and urging her gently toward the dance floor. "Come on, Mrs. Sinclair. Let's have that dance so we can get started on the honeymoon."

Sam watched them move naturally into each other's

arms, as if they belonged there, and she sighed. "They look so right together, don't they?" she remarked wistfully.

"Yes, they do," Brad agreed, aware that Sam's emotions were once more on precarious ground. Again he was surprised at the contradiction between the woman across from him and his preconceived image of her.

Suddenly Sam frowned and turned to him. "Laura said you were planning to leave earlier. I must be the one to blame for keeping you here. I'm sorry."

"Don't be," he assured her. "As a rule I do try to get home at a reasonable hour on Saturday nights so I'm coherent for the early service. But after hearing about you all these years I'm glad we finally had the chance to get better acquainted."

"I've heard about you, too. But...can I tell you something?" she said impulsively. "You're not what I expected. Even though Laura said you were nice, my only experience with preachers is the fire and brimstone variety. Sort of intimidating and 'holier than thou,' you know?"

Brad smiled. "I think so. I've met a few of those myself. But hopefully they're a vanishing breed. And as long as we're playing true confessions, I'll admit that you're not what I expected, either. So we're even."

Sam looked at him thoughtfully. He didn't elaborate, and she was tempted to ask what he had expected. But she could imagine. For years she'd cultivated the image of a swinger. She purposely let Laura believe that she shared more than her time with the many men she dated. So it was reasonable to assume that while Laura may have talked to her minister in a positive light about their friendship, somewhere along the way the "swinger" image had been conveyed as well. For the first time, and for reasons she didn't quite understand, it bothered her that someone thought she wasn't exactly the girl-next-door type.

Brad, watching her face, accurately assessed her train of thought and decided to make a hasty exit before the blunt, outspoken Sam that Laura admired resurfaced and asked the question he knew was on her mind—and which he wasn't prepared to answer. He reached for her hand and cradled it between his. "Good night, Sam. And thank you for the dances. I enjoyed them."

Sam swallowed, her emotions once more close to the surface. "Thanks. I did, too." She tried to think of a typical "Sam" remark, something witty and lighthearted, but her gift for repartee seemed to desert her when she was around this man.

"Take care, okay?" he said, his warm, insightful brown eyes locked on hers.

"Sure."

He let go of her hand then, and Sam immediately missed the warmth of his caring touch. With one more smile, he turned and disappeared into the crowd.

Sam watched him leave. Now she understood why Laura always spoke so highly of her minister and why she turned to him in times of trouble for comfort and guidance. He had a gift for making a person feel that everything was going to be all right, that he really cared. Too bad Sam hadn't known someone like him seventeen years ago, she thought with a sigh. Maybe things would have turned out differently. Maybe…but it was too late for maybes, she reminded herself sharply. At thirty-five, seventeen years was almost a whole lifetime ago. She couldn't change what had happened. It was too late for amends, for regrets, for…a lot of things.

She looked at Nick and Laura on the dance floor, and once more she found herself envying her best friend's happiness. Which was wrong. Because Laura deserved a happy ending. Sam didn't. It was as simple as that. And as final.

Chapter Two

Sam deposited two bags of groceries on the breakfast room table with a thud, pushed her damp hair out of her eyes and shrugged off her dripping raincoat. Too bad the April showers had decided to arrive a few days early, she thought ruefully, although the gloomy weather suited her mood. She shivered and moved the thermostat up, hoping the heat would kick in quickly and take the chill out of her condo. It felt more like February than the end of March, she concluded in disgust as she fished in one of the bags for the mail she'd picked up on her way in.

As she flipped disinterestedly through the stack, a colorful postcard with a picture of a white sand beach and blue skies, framed by brilliantly colored flowers, caught her eye. She paused with a smile. Laura. Eagerly she flipped it over and scanned the contents, coming to the obvious conclusion: Nick and Laura's Hawaiian honeymoon was a resounding success.

Sam propped the card on the windowsill and gazed out at the gray, sodden landscape, her smile fading. She could use a little tropical sun herself about now, she thought wistfully. The idea of spending the afternoon stretched out on a beach, caressed by warm solar rays, instead of traipsing from one house to another with a hard-to-please client, was very appealing. And also totally unrealistic, she reminded herself. Not that she couldn't afford a trip to Hawaii. That was within her reach. Sharing it with a new husband who had pledged to love her for the rest of her life was not.

Wearily Sam put the kettle on the stove, hoping a soothing cup of tea would improve her mood. Ever since the wedding, she'd been on an emotional roller coaster, up one minute, down the next. But mostly down. It wasn't like her. Even a few of her colleagues had noticed her uncharacteristic melancholy, asking her if she was feeling okay. She had to get a grip, she told herself sternly. It wasn't the end of the world. She had been alone before the wedding. She was alone now. Nothing had changed in her life. Her situation was exactly the same as before.

And that, she realized with a sudden pang, was precisely the problem. That, and the fact that it would *never* change. Laura had found her happy ending. She had a wonderful husband and, unless Sam missed her guess, the newlyweds would start working very soon on the family they both wanted.

The sudden whistling of the kettle momentarily interrupted her reverie, and she absently selected an herbal tea bag and filled a mug with water. Distractedly she stared out the window, mindlessly dunking the tea bag, her thoughts far removed from the mundane action. Laura would be surprised at Sam's melancholy, she knew. Around her best friend, Sam was perennially upbeat and optimistic about finding a husband. She always told Laura that the right men for them were out there somewhere. And Laura had found hers. But Sam had always known that her own happy ending was an impossible dream. Her optimism had been for Laura's sake, not her own.

She sat down at the table and propped her chin in her hand. Sam knew she could get married. She was attractive enough, had a good personality, was reasonably intelligent. And there were plenty of available guys. Not too many like Nick, true, but she could find someone. There were probably a lot of men who could overlook the painful past that still haunted her.

The trouble was, *she* couldn't overlook it. She'd carried the guilt with her for years, would always carry it, because there was no way to right the wrong. All she could do was atone for it by denying herself the kind of happiness Laura had found. And by her weekly volunteer work at the counseling center.

Sam knew that most people would think her self-imposed punishment too severe. That what had happened hadn't been her fault. That she needed to get over the tragic event and move on with her life. And sometimes, when the nights got especially long and lonely, she almost began to believe that herself. Time had a way of softening the horror.

But then the nightmare would return with vivid intensity, bringing back the harsh reality of what she'd done, and she would wake up shaking, the sights and sounds so real that it always took her a moment to realize that it was, in fact, only a dream. Yet what it represented was real enough. She had *lived* that nightmare. It wasn't just a figment of her imagination. And for days afterward she would feel haunted. Because she knew that what had happened that fateful night *was* her fault.

Sam rose slowly and walked back to the stove to refill her cup. As she lifted the brass teapot, it suddenly reminded her of Aladdin's magic lamp, and she paused. She didn't allow herself many forays into fantasy. That was a waste of time. But just for a moment she broke her rule. If she had one wish, she thought wistfully as she gazed at the teapot, it would be to erase that night from her life. But it was too late, and no amount of wishing could change that.

Suddenly Sam felt a tear trailing down her cheek and

realized that she was crying—again. It had been happening with alarming frequency since the wedding, and it had to stop, she told herself firmly, heading for the bathroom to get a tissue.

The sudden ringing of the phone startled her as she passed, and she stopped in midstride, reaching for it automatically. "Hello," she sniffed.

There was a moment's hesitation. "Sam?"

"Speaking."

"This is Brad Matthews."

Brad Matthews...the minister? "You mean Reverend Matthews?" she asked cautiously, swiping at her eyes.

"The same. Although I thought we'd gotten past that to 'Brad.'"

"Oh. Right. I was just...surprised."

It was obvious to Brad that Sam was either crying or had been recently, and he hesitated. "Listen, is this a bad time? I could call back."

"No. It's fine. Really." For some reason she felt better listening to his voice. It helped even more than the hot tea.

"Are you sure? You sound...well...is everything all right?"

"Everything's fine," she lied, touched by the concern in his voice, struggling to get her emotions under control. Good grief, every time she had any contact with this man she was crying! He must think she was a nutcase! She searched for some plausible excuse for her emotional state, and her gaze fell on Laura's note. "I just got a postcard from Laura, and like I told you at the wedding...I'm a sap for happy endings."

Her explanation didn't ring quite true, but Brad let it pass. "So are they having a good time?"

"It sounds like it."

"Well, I guess we won't know for sure until they get back. If they look sleep deprived, we can assume they enjoyed themselves," he said with a smile.

Sam's eyes widened. "Isn't that a rather...racy...

remark for a minister?'' she asked in surprise.

"Why?''

"Well…I don't know. It just seems like maybe sex would be a taboo topic for a preacher.''

He chuckled. "Oh, you might be surprised at some of the subjects ministers tackle these days. Besides, Laura and Nick are married, and sex is a natural and good part of marriage. No reason not to hope they're enjoying it.''

Sam found herself smiling. "I must say, Reverend, you continue to surprise me.''

"Pleasantly, I hope.''

"Definitely.''

"Well, then here's another surprise. I'm actually calling for professional reasons.''

Sam frowned. "Professional reasons?'' she repeated, puzzled.

"Yes. Believe it or not, I'm in the market for a house, and I know from Laura that you sell real estate. So I thought maybe you could offer me some advice.''

"Well, sure, I'd be glad to. But I thought houses were usually provided for ministers.''

"That was true in the old days. But things are changing. The parsonage I live in is more or less falling down around me, and the congregation just doesn't want to sink any more money into it. Besides, we need to expand our parking lot. So…*voilà*…the parsonage is coming down. I've known about it for a couple of months, and I still have ten months before I have to move, but I figured I'd better start looking.''

Sam reached for a pad and pen and sat down at the kitchen table. "Okay, why don't you tell me what you have in mind, and I'll take a few notes.''

"Now?'' Brad hadn't expected to actually do anything today, just sort of get the wheels in motion. But Sam had other ideas.

"Why not? That way I can line up a few things for you to look at and get a better idea of what you're after. Ten months may seem like a long time, but it's really not when you're buying a house.''

Brad couldn't argue with Sam's expertise, so he did his best, with her prompting, to describe his ''ideal'' house. Within minutes she had the information she needed to line up some prospects.

''How about if we get together Wednesday to look at a few houses?'' she suggested. ''Would nine o'clock work for you?''

Brad flipped through his calendar, not at all sure how things had moved this quickly. He wasn't quite ready to let go of the parsonage. It was too filled with memories of his happy years with Rachel. But the day had to come sooner or later, and it looked like it was going to be sooner, if Sam was in charge. Which she seemed to be, he thought with amusement. ''That would be fine.''

''Great. I'll call to confirm on Tuesday night and let you know how many houses I've come up with. But don't get your hopes up,'' she warned. ''This first trip will be more fact finding than anything else. It takes one hunting trip before I get a good feel for a client's tastes.''

''I'm in no great rush.''

''Good. You can't imagine how many people expect to walk into their dream house first time out. I can't promise that, but we'll find it eventually.''

''I'm sure we will.''

Sam heard a hint of laughter in his voice and frowned. ''What's so funny?'' she demanded.

''Not a thing,'' he assured her, but she could still hear amusement in his tone. ''It's just that you don't waste any time, do you?''

''Oh.'' The light dawned. ''I came on a little strong, huh? Sorry about that,'' she apologized. ''I sort of get carried away when I have a prospective client. In my business we really live by that old saying, 'He who hesitates is lost.' Or, in this case, she.''

''Well, I'm impressed.''

"Don't be impressed until you see the results," she warned again, but this time there was a smile in *her* voice.

"I have a feeling my house search is in good hands. So I'll talk to you Tuesday?"

"You can count on it, Reverend. Goodbye."

Sam replaced the receiver and glanced out the window. The day was just as gray and rainy as ever, but for some reason she felt a whole lot better. It was illogical, of course. But for once she didn't try to analyze her emotions. She just enjoyed the sudden sense of well-being that her conversation with the preacher had produced.

Brad slowly hung up the phone and leaned back thoughtfully in his desk chair, swiveling to stare out at the soggy landscape. For the first time he'd gotten a glimpse of the Sam Laura had described all these years. Professionally, it was clear that she had her act together. She knew her stuff, had initiative—and then some, he thought with a smile—and seemed very efficient. She was confident, articulate, knowledgeable and clearly a go-getter. No wonder she was so successful at her job. He had no doubt that she would be a great help to him in his house search, and he was glad he'd contacted her.

But Brad was honest enough to admit that while he'd justified the call on the basis of needing her professional services, there had been more to it than that. For some reason she'd been on his mind ever since he'd found her in tears at the wedding reception. And while she'd quickly pulled herself together on the phone just now, it was obvious that she had been in tears just prior to his call, as well.

Brad frowned. Sam seemed like such a troubled soul, alone and adrift, almost as if she'd just lost her best friend. Which, in some ways, was true, he realized. Laura's first loyalty was now to Nick, as it should be. He was sure Laura and Sam would remain staunch friends, but it would be different. Sam's days of dragging a protesting Laura to singles events to spice up her nonexistent social life were over.

Brad smiled at that picture, shaking his head. He couldn't even imagine Laura in the singles scene. The fact that Sam had managed to get her to go spoke eloquently of the woman's considerable persuasive powers and the strength of their friendship.

Brad stood up and strolled over to the window, his hands in his pockets. Sam and Laura's friendship was still an enigma to him. From what he'd gathered during his conversations with Laura, the two women were as different as night and day. Laura's deep faith had provided a firm foundation for her, during her rocky years. Despite her hardships, she'd never wavered in her beliefs, and she led an exemplary Christian life. She had sound morals, a gentle and sensitive nature, and lived simply.

Sam, on the other hand, was apparently just the opposite—fashion conscious, outgoing, flamboyant, blunt, assertive and definitely not the "religious" type. At least that was the impression he'd formed based on Laura's comments. What had drawn the two women together initially he had no clue. But something had clicked, and they'd become the best of friends. Even though Laura admitted that they didn't necessarily share the same values, she admired Sam's strength and self-confidence and spoke with affection of her sharp wit and frank manner.

Until their phone conversation, however, Brad had seen little evidence of those qualities in Sam. Rather than the confident, outspoken, unsentimental, no-nonsense businesswoman he'd expected, he'd found a lost soul. For some reason Laura's wedding seemed to have thrown her off balance. She said it was because she was a sap for happy endings. He was convinced it was more than that.

But what? And, even more relevant, why should he care? Sure, as a minister his job often involved dealing with troubled souls. So he could say he had called her for professional reasons—*his* profession—wanting to help.

And there was some truth to that. But it wasn't the whole truth, and he knew it. The simple fact was that for the first time since Rachel's death, Brad found himself actually noticing an attractive woman. And, even more surprising, Sam brought out a protective instinct in him that had long lain dormant—the last thing he had expected. Laura always described Sam as self-sufficient, able to take care of herself. But she didn't strike Brad that way. Not even close. She seemed like someone desperately in need of just being held.

Which was silly, of course. Based on what Laura said, Sam led a *very* active social life that probably included a whole lot more than just being held. So then why did she seem so lonely? And if she led such an active social life, and really wanted to get married, as Laura said, why was she still single?

Brad raked his fingers through his hair in frustration. He ought to be working on his sermon for tomorrow, not worrying about one very attractive—if troubled—redhead. He walked back to his desk and sat down in front of the word processor, determined to finish his sermon. And even though he eventually found the words, he also found himself spending an inordinate amount of time staring at the screen and looking forward to his next encounter with Sam Reynolds.

The rain had stopped by Wednesday, but it was still unseasonably cold for April, and by the time Sam and Brad inspected the three houses she'd lined up she was chilled to the bone. She shivered as she slid behind the wheel of her car and reached over to unlock the passenger door, and when Brad climbed in beside her a moment later, he was rubbing his hands together.

"I don't know about you, but I'm freezing. How about a cup of coffee before we call it a day?" he suggested.

Sam nodded as she put the car in gear. "Great idea. Can

you believe this is April? I think somebody upstairs turned the calendar *back* a month instead of forward.''

Brad chuckled. ''It sure seems that way.''

''Besides, this will give us a chance to talk about the houses a little more,'' she said over her shoulder as she pulled out of the driveway. ''Have you ever been to Michele's?''

''No.''

''It's a little European tearoom not far from here. Great pastries!'' She glanced at her watch. ''In fact, it's almost noon. Would you like to grab a quick lunch while we're there?''

''Sure.''

Within minutes they were being shown to a cozy booth, and as Sam started to shrug out of her coat, Brad moved behind her and smoothly lifted it off her shoulders.

She turned her head at the courtesy and smiled. ''Thanks. You're quite a gentleman, Reverend.''

Brad gave her an exasperated look as he placed her coat on a nearby hook. ''Are we still hung up on that 'Reverend' bit? What's wrong with 'Brad'?''

Sam watched him slip off his leather bomber jacket. He was dressed casually today, in a cotton shirt with sleeves rolled up to the elbows and a pair of fitted, well-worn jeans that highlighted his athletic physique. He certainly looked different when he wasn't in clerical garb, Sam mused. Not at all like a minister. More like an ad for aftershave—one that featured a rugged outdoorsman or athlete. *Handsome* didn't even do him justice, she realized. Sam glanced around the room. Judging by the discreet looks being directed his way from women at nearby tables, she wasn't alone in her appreciation. However, he seemed totally oblivious to the admiring glances as he slid into the booth across from her and smiled.

''Well?''

Sam reined in her wayward thoughts and stared at him. ''Well what?''

"What's wrong with 'Brad'?" he prompted.

"Oh." She reached for her napkin and looked down on the pretense of adjusting it on her lap, embarrassed at the inappropriate direction of her thoughts. Although he didn't look it today, the man *was* a minister, for heaven's sake—and definitely out of her league, even if she was in the market for romance. Which she wasn't, she reminded herself sharply. "Sorry. I guess I just think of you as a minister, that's all. I'm so used to hearing Laura refer to you that way. And at the wedding you were *dressed* like a minister. But you do look…different…out of uniform."

He grinned. "Well, I'm off duty today. So I can dress like a real person."

She smiled at his down-to-earth sense of humor. "I noticed."

"Actually, I think I underdressed," he admitted a bit sheepishly. "You look great. I sort of feel like a poor relation."

Sam dismissed his comment with a wave. "I'm *on* duty, remember. This is *my* 'uniform.' Always look professional with clients, that's my motto. It helps build confidence." Nevertheless, his compliment left her with a warm glow. The black skirt and green jacquard silk blouse, embellished with a long gold and pearl necklace and a matching bracelet, was her favorite outfit, and for some reason she was pleased he'd noticed it.

Brad propped his chin in his hand and smiled. "Oh, you already have my confidence. After that third degree on the phone, I was convinced you knew your stuff."

She smiled ruefully. "I can come on a little strong, I guess. Laura should have warned you. Anyway, as for what you're wearing, you look fine. To be honest, it makes me forget you're a minister."

"Well, I won't complain if that makes it easier for you to call me Brad."

"It might." She didn't tell him that his attire today not

only made her forget he was a minister, but sent her thoughts in a physical rather than spiritual direction.

He grinned engagingly. "Well, we can hope."

The waitress arrived, and after they placed their order Sam pulled out her notebook. "Why don't we finish up the business stuff before the food arrives? That way, I won't have to eat and take notes at the same time."

Brad was agreeable, and by the time their food was served they'd moved on to other topics.

"So how long have you been in the real estate business, Sam?" Brad asked as he buttered a roll.

"About fifteen years. It's the only thing I've ever done."

"You seem to be very successful."

She shrugged. "I do okay. And I enjoy it. That's the important thing. Plus, I get to meet lots of interesting people. I imagine you could say the same about your work."

"Actually, in many ways we're in the same business," he remarked.

Sam tilted her head quizzically. "How do you figure?"

He shrugged. "Well, you devote yourself to helping people find *earthly* homes. I spend my time helping them find their *eternal* home," he said matter-of-factly.

Sam smiled. "Has anyone ever told you that you have a way with words, Rever— Brad?" she corrected herself, and was rewarded with a warm smile. "I enjoyed your talk at the wedding, too."

"Thanks. You know, that was the hardest part for me about becoming a minister."

"What?"

"Having to get up in front of people and speak. I do better one-on-one. It's pretty intimidating to stand up there every week and see all those faces looking at you expectantly for words of wisdom."

"You could have fooled me. You seemed totally at ease at the wedding."

"Well, it's nice to know that at least I *look* calm. But

I'm really kind of a stay-in-the-background kind of guy. I was pretty shy growing up.''

"Yeah, I know what you mean. So was I."

Brad looked at her with a skeptical smile. "Now *that* I find hard to believe."

Sam grinned wryly. "Most people would, I guess," she admitted. "*Shy* isn't exactly the word my friends use to describe me. But believe it or not, it's true. Or used to be," she said, correcting herself. "I was overweight as a child, and you know how kids can be. I was the butt of a lot of jokes, which made me even more self-conscious. But I finally figured out that the way to be accepted was to be sort of outrageous and funny. So I became the class clown, and I ended up being pretty popular. The only thing was, when I got to be about sixteen I realized that even though the guys thought I was a lot of fun, they never asked me out. So in my senior year I decided to lose weight, and by the time I graduated I was in pretty good shape. My weight's never varied more than a few pounds in all these years." Suddenly Sam frowned and looked down. "You know, I've never told that to anyone. Not even Laura," she said slowly.

"Why not?"

She shrugged. "I don't know. It's just part of a different life, I guess. And even though I'm glad I lost all that weight, it's sort of what led to my disastrous encounter with matrimony, so I don't think about it very often."

"I did get the impression at the wedding that your experience with marriage wasn't the best," he admitted.

Sam gave a mirthless laugh. "You could say that."

"Can I ask why, or would you rather not talk about it?"

Sam looked down and creased her napkin. There was something about this man's understanding manner that inspired confidences. Which probably came in handy in his job, she supposed. His job, she thought with a frown, the words echoing in her mind. Was this conversation part of his job? she wondered suddenly. Was his interest professional—as a minister lending a willing ear to someone who needed to talk—or personal? It shouldn't matter, but for some reason it did. And she needed to know. "Do you have your collar on now, figuratively speaking?" she asked, striving for a light tone.

Brad's gaze was direct and warm. "No. I'm not being a minister right now. I'm just trying to be a friend."

Sam stared at him, and her heart felt lighter. It was also beating just a little too fast. "Why do you want to be my friend?" she asked, finding it surprisingly difficult to keep her voice steady.

Because you seem to need one, he thought. But his spoken words were different. "Why not? A person can never have too many friends."

Sam stared at him a moment longer, still a little taken aback by the suggestion. "I think ours would be an odd friendship, Brad," she said slowly at last. "We're…really different…in a lot of ways."

"So are you and Laura," he pointed out. "And you two are the best of friends."

"Yeah, I know." He had a point. And it might be nice to have a male friend. It would be a welcome change of pace from the guys she usually met, who were out for a good time—and whatever else she was willing to offer. "Well, I guess it wouldn't hurt to give it a try."

"Good," he said with a smile. "So do you want to tell me what happened with your marriage? Or am I being too nosy?"

"No. But there really isn't much to tell. Randy played bass guitar in a rock band that came to town the summer after I graduated. He noticed me, and not having a lot of dating experience, I was flattered by the attention. We ended up falling in love, and he asked me to marry him. My parents were very strict fundamentalist Christians, and they were appalled that I was even *interested* in someone in show business, let alone that I would consider marrying him. But we got married anyway, and that caused a rift with my parents that never really healed.''

She paused and looked down at her plate, tracing the edge with a red-polished nail. ''They're both dead now,'' she continued more softly. ''I was a late-in-life only child, and I think they expected great things of me. The day Randy and I eloped and got married at the courthouse in a civil ceremony was sort of the last straw.'' She took a deep breath and looked up at Brad. ''To make a long story short, we were only married about five months when he just walked out one day, leaving me five hundred dollars and a note saying he wasn't ready to settle down and that getting married had been a mistake. So I got on a bus and came to St. Louis, which I'd visited once and liked, and started over. Now you have my life story.''

Brad looked at her silently for a moment. She'd said the words matter-of-factly, but he knew there was a wealth of pain and disillusionment, as well as courage, behind them. ''I'm sorry, Sam,'' he said finally, and the compassion in his brown eyes made her throat tighten.

She tried to laugh. ''Yeah, so am I. But Randy was right about one thing. Getting married was a mistake.'' Unfortunately, it hadn't been the only one, she thought sadly.

''What ever happened to him?'' Brad asked.

Sam toyed with her water glass. ''I never saw him again. But about six years after he left me I ran into one of the guys from the band. They were in town for a gig, and it was just one of those chance encounters. Anyway, he told me that Randy had died of a drug overdose a couple of years before.''

Again there was a moment of silence before Brad spoke. ''I'm sorry you had to go through all that, Sam,'' he said quietly at last.

She shrugged. ''Well, it's history now.'' She glanced down, and with a start she realized that he was holding her hand. She stared down at their entwined fingers, unable to recall when they'd joined hands, knowing only that it felt good. Too good. Suddenly self-conscious, she gently eased her hand out of his grasp, but she missed the connection immediately.

Brad took a sip of coffee, and Sam used the moment to compose herself. She was surprised that recounting the story had upset her. It was ancient history, and she rarely thought about the failed relationship anymore. Sometimes she could hardly even remember what Randy looked like. But there was one part of the story that she couldn't forget, and she'd very deliberately left it out. She was too ashamed. Besides, she'd already told Brad far more than she'd intended.

"Can I ask you something else?" he said slowly.

She looked at him hesitantly. There was something in his voice that put her on alert. "Sure. I guess so."

"Well, you're a very attractive woman, Sam," he said frankly. "And you have a great personality. From what Laura says, you lead a very…active…social life."

Sam's lips quirked wryly. "Is that how she described it?"

Brad felt his neck redden. "Well, not exactly. But that was the general idea."

"I do…go out a lot, Brad," she admitted cautiously.

"So your bad experience with Randy didn't turn you off men in general?"

She looked surprised. "Good grief, no! He was just a bad apple. That's what I used to tell Laura. We just happened to marry two losers. But there are lots of nice guys out there."

"So then how come you've never remarried?"

Sam stared at him. She should have seen that question coming. She'd set herself up for it, and now she had to find a way to avoid answering it. Because she couldn't tell him the truth. "I guess I'm just too picky," she said at last, forcing her lips up into a smile.

Brad looked at her with his perceptive eyes, and she knew he didn't buy that explanation. But before he had a chance to pursue the subject, she changed the focus of the conversation. "So tell me about your marriage, Brad. I have a feeling your story is much nicer."

He smiled. Sam had clearly revealed as much about herself as she intended to—for today, at least—and he respected that. He was actually surprised she'd been so open. And turnabout was fair play. So he took her cue.

"Yes, it is. Rachel and I had a wonderful marriage."

"How did you two meet?"

"Well, as I told you, I was pretty much a quiet, stay-in-the-background kind of guy. I didn't date much during high school, and hardly at all when I was in the seminary. Then, when I got my church, I was too busy. It was a plum call, but there were also high expectations, so I didn't have much time to rustle up dates. Rachel was an organist at another church nearby, and when our organist was on vacation she filled in. That's how we met, and it just seemed like a good match right from the start. We had so much in common. We liked the same things, we both had a strong faith, we laughed at the same jokes—you know, that kind of thing. We both loved kids, too, and we planned to have a big family."

Brad's eyes clouded, and he glanced down, stirring his coffee. "We only had four years together, but they were good years," he said quietly. "Rachel helped me see the world in a whole new way. For instance, one of her most enduring legacies to me was an appreciation for classical music." He smiled, his eyes distant and tender, and Sam knew that he was lost in remembrance. "Her uncle always gave us season tickets to the symphony. We couldn't afford it on our salaries, so that was a real luxury. We enjoyed it so much." Suddenly his smile faded and he cleared his throat. "I haven't been back since she died," he said softly. "I've missed it. I've missed everything I did with Rachel. She filled my life with music in many ways," he finished simply.

Sam gazed at him, deeply touched by what had obviously been a devoted relationship and an enduring love. Impulsively she reached over and placed her hand on top of his. "It sounds like she was a wonderful woman," she said, her voice catching.

Brad looked at her, and though he smiled, Sam saw the pain in his eyes. "Yes. She was."

"What happened to her?" Sam asked gently.

"A ruptured brain aneurysm. No warning. She was here one minute, gone the next."

"Oh, Brad, how awful!" Sam exclaimed in a shocked whisper.

"It was a very hard time for me," he admitted. "For a long time I was bitter, and I was angry at God. I even took a leave from the ministry for six months. But I eventually came to terms with Rachel's death. Ultimately I had to learn to live what I'd always preached—that sometimes we have to accept God's will even if we don't understand it."

Sam shook her head. "You're a better person than me, then. I don't know if I could ever accept something like that."

"That's where faith helps."

"Well, mine obviously isn't as strong as yours."

"So you do still believe at least?"

She shrugged. She hadn't thought about it in a long time. "Yes, I suppose so," she said slowly. "I guess some of my Christian upbringing stuck. Deep inside I still believe the basics. I'm just not into the external trappings. No offense intended."

"None taken," he assured her easily. "After all, everyone is at a different place on the faith journey."

"Well, I think maybe I've taken a few too many detours."

He smiled. "So I assume you haven't been to church for a while?"

"Except for Laura's wedding, I haven't been in a church in eighteen years. I don't think I'm church material."

"Why not?"

She toyed with her water glass. "Like I said, I think I've taken a few too many detours."

"Sam, churches aren't for saints. They're for sinners. Perfect people wouldn't need churches. If everyone in my congregation was perfect, I'd be out of a job. I like to think of a church as a kind of spiritual travel bureau that provides people with the maps they need to stay on course."

Now it was Sam's turn to smile. "That's a nice analogy."

"Only if it's convincing."

"You do have a point," she acknowledged. "But we got off the subject. You were telling me about your marriage."

Brad's face sobered. "There's really no more to tell. Rachel's been gone for six years now, and I still think of her every day. It's hard to let go of someone who's become so much a part of you."

"But don't you ever get lonely?" Sam asked.

"Only lately. For some reason I've suddenly started to notice the empty place in my life," he said, surprising himself by his admission.

"Loneliness is the pits," Sam agreed.

Brad looked at her in surprise. "Don't tell me *you're* lonely. I thought—" He stopped abruptly, embarrassed by his indiscretion, and his neck took on a ruddy color.

Sam smiled ruefully. "You thought I had plenty of male friends who were more than willing to warm my lonely bed on a cold night?" she said bluntly.

Brad's face flushed and he started to speak, but Sam held up her hand. "It's okay. I have no one to blame but myself for creating that image. It's what most people think, I suppose. Even Laura. But can I tell you something? Reports of my promiscuity have, to borrow a phrase from Mark Twain, been greatly exaggerated. I do go out a lot. We have a few drinks, dance a little, maybe go to dinner or a show, and then...well, I'm not saying that I haven't been…physically close…to some of the men I dated, but I know when to pull back. And that's long before we get to the bedroom door,'' she said frankly.

Brad stared at the woman across from him, taken aback by her blunt honesty. But he was also curious. ''Why are you telling me this?'' he asked.

She frowned. ''I don't know,'' she admitted slowly, as surprised as he was by the confession. ''I usually try to create a 'swinging single' image, and now I've just blown it.''

''But why do you want people to think you live that kind of life-style?'' he asked, puzzled.

Sam looked down, still frowning, and stirred her coffee. She'd never really analyzed it before. ''I guess maybe because I don't want anyone to know I'm lonely,'' she said slowly. ''I hate it when people feel sorry for me. It must be pride or something.''

''But you told me the truth,'' he pointed out.

''Yeah, I did,'' she conceded. ''And that was probably a mistake. Listen, do me a favor, will you?''

''What.''

''Don't spread it around. I wouldn't want to ruin my reputation.''

Brad chuckled. ''Okay. I promise. But Sam…can I tell you something? I don't think it was a mistake. I'm glad you told me.''

She looked at him, and the warmth and sincerity in his brown eyes filled her with a strange sense of optimism and hope. Those were feelings she hadn't experienced for a long time, and impulsively she leaned forward and smiled.

''Can I tell *you* something?''

''Sure.''

''So am I.''

Chapter Three

"Sam, there's a Don Williams on 7335. Do you want to pick up?"

Sam looked over at Kelly, seated at the next desk, and nodded distractedly. Don Williams was a corporate customer who sent a lot of relocations her way, and she couldn't afford to put him off, even if she was knee-deep in details on an especially tricky contract.

Sam propped the receiver on her shoulder so she could continue working on the contract while she spoke, and punched the appropriate button. "Hi, Don."

"Hi, Sam. How's it going?"

"Business is good. But it could always be better. Have you got a hot prospect for me?"

He laughed. "Never let it be said that Sam Reynolds beats around the bush. Sorry. Not this time."

"It doesn't hurt to ask, you know," she said with a smile. "So what can I do for you today?"

"Well, I have two corporate tickets to the symphony for tomorrow night that my wife and I aren't going to be able to use, and I wondered if you'd be interested in them."

"The symphony?" she repeated, her mind clicking into

gear. Might be fun. She hadn't been in a long time, and Powell Hall was such a beautiful place. But who in the world could she ask? Laura would enjoy it, but she was still on her honeymoon. Besides, she had Nick now, and Sam suspected her free time would be otherwise occupied for the immediate future. Sam mentally ran through her "black book," which she had pared down considerably since Laura's engagement, but came up blank. The few men she currently dated were more into sports than Schubert.

She opened her mouth to refuse, and then suddenly it hit her. Brad liked the symphony. She could ask him. It had been over a week since their house-hunting expedition and lunch, and this would give her a good excuse to call him. He'd been on her mind a lot these past few days. She liked being with him, and after all, he was the one who had suggested that they be friends. So a call wouldn't be out of line. Would it?

"Sam? Are you still there?"

"Yes. Sorry. I was trying to think who I could ask. Actually, I have a friend who might really enjoy that. So yes, thanks, I'd love them."

"Great! I'll have them sent over by courier later today. Have fun."

Sam hung up the phone thoughtfully. Brad might not even be available on such short notice. But she wouldn't know until she asked, she thought resolutely. Sam flipped through her client address book, took a deep breath and dialed his number.

Brad reached for the phone to call Sam, then dropped his hand. It was the third time he'd gone through this routine while his neglected paperwork stared at him accusingly. This is ridiculous, he told himself in frustration. It was only a phone call. What was so hard about that? After all, *he* was the one who had suggested to Sam that they be friends.

He rose restlessly and walked over to the bookcase, pausing in front of Rachel's picture. And there he found his answer. He felt guilty. For the first time since his wife's death he was actually thinking about another woman. Okay, so it was just a friendship thing. In fact, he was the one who had set those parameters. Because, despite Sam's revelation that she wasn't quite as loose and free as he'd assumed, they were still very different. Too different for anything serious to develop. But this was nevertheless a first, safe step back into the social world.

Brad reached over and picked up Rachel's picture. He knew she wouldn't want him to be alone. And yet he felt somehow disloyal even thinking about another woman. As if in doing so he was negating the beauty of the relationship they'd shared. Which was foolish. He knew that intellectually. But how could he convince his heart that it was okay to move on?

And how could he let go? He had so many wonderful memories of his time with Rachel. Those memories had helped keep his loneliness at bay during the six difficult years since her death. The thought of letting go of them was frightening. Because maybe there wouldn't be anything to take their place. And he had a depressing feeling that as difficult as it was to face loss, emotional emptiness would be even worse. But if he clung to those memories, to the past, he knew he was denying himself a future with someone new. As long as his heart was focused on memories, there would be no room for anything—or anyone—else.

Brad sighed and replaced the picture, leaving one hand resting on it lightly. There were no easy answers. Certainly none that he could come up with on his own. So he did what he often did in such situations—he closed his eyes and turned to the One he relied on for guidance.

Lord, he prayed silently, I need to find the courage to move on with my life. Help me to overcome the fear of risking a new relationship, to understand with my heart as well as my mind that without risk there is no growth. I don't know what the future holds, but I do know that I'd like an earthly partner to share it with, if that's Your will. I'm trying to take a first step by opening the door to friendship with Sam. She seems so in need of a friend, and I need to relearn how to relate to a woman socially. I think a friendship would benefit us both. But I can't seem to let go of the past and move on. Please help me.

Brad opened his eyes and once more looked into Rachel's face. I love you, he said in the silence of his heart. I always will. But I can't live on memories anymore. What you and I had was special and unique and will always be ours. A new love won't diminish what we shared. It, too, will be unique, just as ours was. No one can ever take your place, but I think there's room in my life for someone else. And I need to find out.

Brad let his hand gently fall away from the picture, taking a deep breath as he did so. He felt better. And he also knew what he was going to do. He was going to call Sam.

With a determined look on his face, Brad strode toward the desk and reached for the phone—just as it started to ring. With a startled exclamation, he jerked his hand back, his heart jumping to his throat. Talk about strange timing, he thought, shaking his head and smiling ruefully. But it was even more strange when he recognized the voice on the other end.

"Sam?" he asked cautiously after the woman said his name questioningly.

"Yeah. Are you okay? You sound kind of...funny." Sam was a little thrown by the odd tone in his voice. She wouldn't exactly call it welcoming. Or pleased.

"You're never going to believe this," he said incredulously. "I was just reaching for the phone to call you!"

"You're kidding!"

Brad sat down in his desk chair and shook his head. "No. It's the truth. Talk about weird timing!"

That explained his strange tone, Sam thought with relief.

At least it wasn't because he was sorry she'd called. "That's happened to me a few times," she said. "It is pretty weird. But I don't have any news on the house, if that's what you were calling about. I think I have a really good idea of what you want, and until I find the right one I don't want to waste your time."

"I appreciate that." No sense trying to explain the real reason for his call—especially since he wasn't sure of it himself. All he knew was that he wanted to hear her voice. But he couldn't very well say that. Better to let her think it was business. "So why were you calling, then?" he asked.

"Oh." Suddenly she felt uncertain, and she stared unseeingly at the contract on her desk, her fingers playing nervously with the phone cord. She took a deep breath, trying to steady the staccato rhythm of her heart. "Well, a client of mine has tickets for the symphony tomorrow night, and he's not going to be able to use them. He offered them to me, and I was wondering if…well, I know it's short notice and all…but if you're not busy, I thought…I thought maybe you might like to go." She finished in a rush, then drew a shaky breath, unconsciously holding it while she waited for his response.

Brad's eyes widened in surprise. Sam was asking him out! Okay, so it was only because she had free tickets and she knew he liked the symphony. Still, she could have asked someone else. But the symphony… He frowned. He hadn't been there since the last time he'd gone to a concert with Rachel. It wouldn't be easy to go back.

Brad hesitated uncertainly, knowing that if he accepted the invitation he would be bittersweetly reminded of the happy hours he'd spent there with Rachel. But what about his resolve to let go of the past and move on? he asked himself. This was his chance to implement that resolution. Only it was a lot harder to do than he expected.

As the silence lengthened, Sam felt her face flush. She'd obviously put him on the spot. When he'd suggested friendship, he clearly hadn't intended it to include something like this, she realized with disappointment. It had been a long shot anyway, she supposed. A minister wasn't likely to want to hang around with someone like her, not considering the "swinging" image she'd created all these years. He was too discreet and too kind to say that, of course, so she needed to get him off the hook.

"Look, I guess maybe this wasn't such a good idea," she said, striving for a light tone. "I know you're busy, and I guess I just took that friendship idea too literally. So just forget—"

"Whoa!" Brad interrupted, realizing she'd jumped to the wrong conclusion about his hesitation. "Did I say I wasn't interested?" His gaze fell on the calendar on his desk. "I'm just looking at my schedule for tomorrow. And if the offer is still open, I'd love to go."

"You would?" Sam said in surprise.

"Sure. I only hesitated because I haven't been there since the last concert I attended with Rachel. But it's time I went back."

"Well, that's great!" Sam suddenly felt more lighthearted. "The concert starts at seven, so I guess we could meet about—"

"Why don't you let me pick you up?" he asked.

"You don't need to do that," she assured him quickly, although she was touched by the offer.

"Maybe not. But you supplied the tickets. It seems only fair that I supply the ride."

"Well, if you're sure…"

"Absolutely. I've got a four-thirty appointment, so would six be okay?"

"Sure."

"Great. I'll look forward to it. And Sam…thanks for asking."

The husky tone in his voice sent a shaft of warmth through her, and she found herself smiling. "It's my pleasure," she replied. "I'm glad you can go."

"Me, too. See you tomorrow, then."

Brad slowly replaced the receiver. Talk about a turn of events! The last thing he had expected was a social invitation from Sam. Despite her revelation that she led a much more sedate social life than her image would suggest, Brad was sure she could have found someone more exciting to spend an evening with than him. He'd been honest with her about himself—he was a quiet, stay-in-the-background kind of guy, more interested in one-on-one relationships than crowd scenes or loud parties. Even if she wasn't quite the party girl he'd assumed prior to their lunch, she was still out of his league socially. And yet she'd picked him. Why?

Brad didn't have the answer. Maybe she just needed a friend, and he'd made himself available. But whatever the reason, he was pleased. Going out socially with a woman was a giant step forward for him. Okay, the symphony might be hard. But for some strange reason he had a feeling that with Sam by his side, it would be a whole lot easier.

It was funny, really, he thought as he pulled the stack of paperwork toward him. Initially he had been drawn to her because she seemed to need a friend—only to discover that he needed one just as badly. She had been good for him, prodding him to do things that he'd put off far too long already. Brad smiled to himself and shook his head. God really did work in mysterious ways.

Sam stared at her reflection in the full-length mirror and frowned. Maybe she was too dressed up. Maybe this outfit was too sexy. Maybe she should tone down her makeup. Maybe…

Sam cut the last "maybe" off in midthought. This was ridiculous, she admonished herself brusquely. It made absolutely no difference what she wore tonight. Brad's interest in her was purely as a friend. He'd said so himself. He probably wouldn't even notice what she wore. Which was fine, she told herself. Even if he was interested in her romantically, things would never work out. Their backgrounds were too different. And if he ever found out about—Sam cut that thought off, too. All of this speculation was a waste of time, she told herself harshly. Romance and happy endings weren't in the cards for her. She'd have to settle for friendship. And that was better than nothing, she consoled herself.

Sam tugged one last time at the hem of her black skirt, but there was no disguising the short length. She always dressed in the latest fashion, but suddenly she wished she had something in her wardrobe that was a more demure, classic length. Oh, well, maybe the dark hose would help hide the fact that so much leg was exposed, she thought hopefully. At least her short-sleeved jewel-neckline satin blouse was modest, and the short strand of pearls added an elegant touch against the shimmery forest green fabric.

Sam ran a comb through her shoulder-length hair, thankful that it was a good hair day. The ends were waving under nicely on her shoulders, and her bangs had fluffed out just right. Okay, so her makeup was a little dramatic. But that was her, and if Brad didn't like it, well—

The ringing of the doorbell interrupted her second-guessing, and Sam's heart suddenly kicked into double time. For goodness sake, she admonished herself, get a grip! This is not a real date. Brad is just a friend. That's all. Just a friend.

The funny thing was that when she opened the door she could have sworn that the quick yet thorough appraisal he gave her was much more than just "friendly" in nature. But she told herself she was reading far too much into a simple glance.

When his eyes returned to hers he smiled, and Sam's breath caught in her throat at the warmth in his gaze. "You look great," he said quietly, his voice shaded with a husky timbre that surprised them both. He'd been caught off guard by his own reaction to her discreet but alluring outfit, his gaze lingering just a moment too long on what the fashionably short skirt revealed—a pair of fabulous legs that just didn't quit. He'd have to be dead not to notice, he thought, trying to justify the surprising direction of his thoughts.

"Thanks." She tried to smile, but she suddenly felt shaky as her eyes took in his appearance. Tonight Brad did not look *anything* like a minister, she thought. His dove gray suit, starched white shirt and striking maroon and blue tie were more suited to a man of the world than a man of the cloth. If at lunch he'd made her think of an aftershave ad, tonight he looked like a successful executive or entrepreneur. The very faint brush of silver at his temples added a distinguished touch to his appearance and magnified his appeal. For just a moment she wondered what it would feel like to be held against his solid chest, to feel his gentle touch against her cheek, to— Disconcerted by the inappropriate direction of her thoughts, Sam abruptly took a step back and motioned him inside.

"Come on in. I'm ready. I just need to get my sweater," she said breathlessly.

Brad strolled inside and looked around with interest. The open room featured white walls and light gray modular furniture that could be easily moved into new configurations. Coffee and end tables were glass and chrome, and a fireplace was framed by a black screen. Throw pillows in magenta and cobalt blue added striking touches of color.

"Nice," Brad said as his gaze traveled around the room. "It makes me feel like I've stepped onto the pages of a decorating magazine."

Sam shrugged. "It's functional. And it suits my lifestyle. But I wouldn't exactly call it homey."

"It doesn't seem like 'homey' was what you were after," Brad said thoughtfully.

"You're right. It wasn't," she admitted slowly, surprised by his insight, realizing that she'd never consciously analyzed her decorating choices before. It was more as if she'd created a stage setting, a backdrop, for her as a single, socializing, professional woman, she thought, letting her own gaze circle the modernistic, picture-perfect room. In fact, it was almost as if no one actually lived here, she realized. And it certainly didn't reflect her real personality. Sam liked modern things, true. She wouldn't want Nick and Laura's old Victorian house, though she could appreciate its charm and realized it suited them. No, if she had a real home it would be contemporary, but she would intersperse the modern with the homey. A warm, hand-loomed throw on the sofa. A lovingly-stitched needlepoint pillow next to the fireplace. A brandy decanter on the mantel, with a pair of glasses for late-night toasts. A child's drawing framed and hung proudly on the wall....

Sam felt her eyes mist over at the last image. That was something she was never destined to have, she knew. She'd had her chance once, and she'd thrown it away. Better to live in this relatively sterile environment, where she could more easily pretend that those things were unimportant to her, she thought resolutely.

Sam suddenly realized that Brad was watching her with those insightful brown eyes of his, and she turned away and reached for her sweater. "So, are we ready?" she asked with forced brightness.

He seemed about to say something, but apparently he thought better of it and instead silently followed her to the door.

By the time they were seated in his car, Sam had regained her composure, and they chatted about inconsequential things during the drive into the city. As they entered the opulent lobby of Powell Hall, Sam looked around appreciatively, overwhelmed as always by the elaborate crystal and gilt decor, red carpet and sweeping grand staircase. "I always forget how gorgeous this place is," she remarked.

When Brad didn't respond, she turned to look at him.

He was frowning slightly, and his eyes seemed troubled. Sam assumed he was thinking about his last visit here, with Rachel, and she reached over to touch his arm.

"Brad?" It took a moment, but at last he looked down at her. "I'm sorry. I know this isn't easy for you," she said gently.

He sighed. "I'm the one who's sorry. I don't want to put a damper on our evening. It was just a jolt, coming through the door. I'm okay now."

"Are you sure?" she asked worriedly. "We don't have to stay."

"I'm fine, Sam. Really," he assured her. Then he smiled and reached for her hand. "But just stay close. That will help."

"Sure." A tingle ran through Sam as Brad's fingers closed over hers, engulfing them in a firm grip that gave her a comforting sense of protection and security. Okay, so he was only holding her hand to give him courage to see this evening through. But that didn't mean she couldn't enjoy it. She could even pretend for a little while that he was *really* holding her hand. What could it hurt?

When they reached their seats, Brad helped Sam off with her sweater, then reached for her hand again as the music started. A couple of times during the concert he absently rubbed his thumb across the back of her knuckles, and Sam felt her pulse rate quicken each time. She knew that he probably wasn't even consciously aware of the gesture, which made her reaction absurd. But she didn't seem to be able to control it.

When the last notes of the final piece died away, Sam turned to Brad and smiled. "Well, you made it," she said.

He returned the smile. "Yeah. Thanks to you."

"What do you mean?"

He lifted her hand, which he still held, and stroked his thumb across the back of it—consciously this time, she knew. "This helped a lot."

Sam flushed. "I didn't do anything," she protested, her heart rate once again quickening.

"Letting me hold your hand helped more than you know," he told her with quiet sincerity. "Sometimes a simple human touch goes a long way in giving people courage, in letting them know they're not alone."

Sam stared at him. She had faced her greatest crisis alone, so she knew what he meant. A simple caring touch, a choice offered in compassion, would have made a world of difference to her once. It could have changed her whole life, in fact. But there'd been no one there for her.

Her throat constricted and she squeezed Brad's hand. "You're not alone," she said softly, her voice uneven. Then she tried to smile, forcing a lighter note into her tone. "After all, what are friends for?"

Brad gazed at her speculatively. "You know, Sam, I think—" He stopped, and Sam looked at him curiously.

"You think what?" she prompted.

Brad cleared his throat. He'd been about to say that at the moment friendship was the furthest thing from his mind. It was true that at the beginning of the evening he'd sought her hand for courage. But she had nice hands— soft, with long, tapering fingers—and by the end he held on to it because it simply felt good. But that remark would surprise her. Good grief, the realization surprised him! And he sensed that now was not the time to reveal emotions he himself didn't understand. He glanced down toward their entwined hands with a frown, debating how to answer her question.

Sam followed the direction of his gaze, which seemed to be resting in the vicinity of her hemline, and removed her hand from his to tug self-consciously at her skirt. "You think my skirt's too short, don't you?" she said, embarrassed, misinterpreting the direction of his thoughts. "I suppose I'm not the type of woman a minister wants to be seen with. Listen, I understand. The friendship offer was probably made in haste, and—"

"Sam." Brad cut her off.

She stared at him, her eyes wide, taken aback by the touch of anger in his voice.

Brad frowned, aware that he sounded angry. And he was. At himself. For some reason she'd felt disapproval in his gaze. Which had been the last thing on his mind as he'd gazed at their entwined hands.

"I'm sorry," she said contritely. "I didn't—"

"Sam," he repeated, more gently this time, reaching for her hand again. "I was *not* going to comment on your skirt."

"No?" She looked uncertain, and Brad wanted to pull her into his arms and just hold her. The impulse took him off guard. What was the matter with him all of a sudden? he wondered. He wasn't a man usually given to such inappropriate thoughts. So, using a self-restraint that required a surprising amount of effort, he kept his distance. But he also kept a firm grip on her hand.

"No," he repeated firmly. "I'll admit I noticed your skirt," he said frankly, deciding honesty was the best policy. "Or rather, what your skirt reveals—a pair of absolutely fabulous legs. I doubt whether any man still breathing could overlook them. And I hope you don't think that's some sort of insulting sexist remark. My intent is to flatter, not criticize or demean."

"Really?" she asked, wanting to believe his words but finding it difficult.

"Really," he assured her. "I may be a minister, but I'm also a man. And I'm proud to be seen with you—because of who you are, as well as how you look."

Sam stared at him. She couldn't doubt the sincerity in his eyes. "Then what were you going to say before?" she asked with a frown.

Brad's mind went into warp drive. "I think we should stop on the way home and get something to eat," he said with sudden inspiration. "My appointment ran late, and I haven't had dinner. Are you hungry?"

"As a matter of fact, yes," she said, surprised to find that she was suddenly ravenous.

"Good. I know just the spot."

Twenty minutes later they were seated in a small café not far from Sam's condo. Classical music played softly in the background, and the atmosphere was cozy and intimate.

"This is charming, Brad!" Sam said, glancing around approvingly. "I never even knew it was here."

"I wasn't sure you'd like it," he admitted. "It's pretty quiet."

"Well, I've had my fill of crowded, noisy, smoky bars, thank you," she said wryly. "This is perfect."

During the light meal, they discussed the concert, and when the waitress came to offer dessert, Brad looked at Sam inquiringly. "Are you in the mood to indulge?"

"Why not?" she said, wanting to prolong the evening. It had been a long time since she'd enjoyed herself so much in a man's company, and she hated it to end.

"Well, I can highly recommend tonight's special dessert," the waitress said. "Apple cobbler. It's a new recipe the chef's just trying out, and it's a winner."

"Sounds good to me," Sam said with a smile.

"How about you, sir?" the woman asked, turning to Brad.

He hesitated, and Sam looked at him curiously. He was frowning, but when he realized she was watching him, his face cleared and he seconded the order.

"Don't you like apple cobbler?" Sam asked curiously after the waitress departed.

"Yes...I do," he replied. "It's just that, well, Rachel made a wonderful apple cobbler. She was a great cook. It took me back for a minute, that's all."

"Oh." Sam looked down and stirred her coffee. Was there anything his wife couldn't do, she thought in despair? No wonder he still loved her. She sounded perfect.

Brad heard the woebegone tone in Sam's voice, even if

she was unaware of it, and chided himself. If he was going to start dating again, he'd better *stop* singing the praises of Rachel in front of other women. No woman was likely to become interested in a man who was always talking about what a wonderful woman his late wife had been. A change of topic seemed to be in order, he thought, searching for some neutral, common ground.

"So...I understand Laura and Nick will be back this weekend," he remarked.

Sam looked up at him and forced herself to smile. What did she care how wonderful Rachel was? It wasn't like she and Brad's late wife were in competition for his affections or anything. Even if he *was* looking for a new romance, she was definitely not in the running. She'd better get that idea into her head once and for all.

"Yeah. I can't wait to hear all about it. Laura and I are going to have lunch next week," she replied.

"You and she seem to be very close."

"We are," Sam confirmed.

"What brought you two together in the first place?"

Sam shrugged. "I don't really know. We were both taking night classes at the junior college, and I used to run into her in the ladies' room. Not a very auspicious beginning," she said with a wry smile. "Anyway, she seemed kind of forlorn. There was this...haunted...look around her eyes. I found out later that her life was pretty awful at that point, so I guess she needed a friend, and I was available. I'm sure if she hadn't been so desperate she would have been a little more choosy," she said in a self-deprecating tone. "But something clicked, anyway, and we've been through a lot together since then."

Brad shook his head. "Don't sell yourself short, Sam. Laura's an excellent judge of character. She obviously recognized a good person when she saw one."

Sam stared at him, taken aback by the misplaced compliment. Then she lowered her eyes. "Thanks. But save your praise for someone who deserves it," she said quietly.

Brad frowned. "What's that supposed to mean?"

Sam shrugged and took a sip of her coffee. If he knew the truth about her, he wouldn't have to ask. But he didn't know, and she planned to keep it that way. "I'm not such a great person," she said lightly.

Brad's frown remained in place. "I don't think Laura would agree."

"Maybe not." But then, Laura didn't know her friend's secret, either. Sam felt her throat constrict, and before she lost control she decided it was time to change the subject. "Speaking of good people, tell me how you decided to become a minister. I've never known one before."

Brad noted that Sam's eyes were suspiciously bright and realized that he'd touched a nerve with his remark. A very sensitive nerve, it seemed. She honestly didn't think she was a good person, he realized in surprise. But what on earth could account for her low self-image? Based on what he'd learned during their encounters, the real Sam was totally different from the image she'd conveyed. Different in a good way, according to Brad's Christian code of ethics. So why did she seem to feel somehow unworthy? He wanted answers, but one look at Sam's face told him that she wasn't going to provide them tonight. Reluctantly, he let it go and turned his attention to her question.

"I guess I've always known this is what I was meant to do," he said slowly, his expression thoughtful. "I grew up in a house where Christian values were not only taught, but lived. And unlike you, I knew a couple of ministers who were about as far from the 'fire and brimstone' variety as you could get. They were really great people, down-to-earth and humble, and they seemed to find great satisfaction in their work. After all, as one of them used to tell me, what could be more worthwhile than spreading the good news of Christianity? I had to agree. Besides, I've always been drawn to helping those in trouble, and being a minister allows me to spend my life doing that."

"But isn't it hard, getting involved in people's problems? I mean, I'm sure it's great when you're able to help, but what about when you're not?'' She dealt with that issue every week at the counseling center. Maybe Brad could offer her some coping tips.

Brad sighed. ''I haven't quite figured out how to handle that yet,'' he admitted. ''I take things pretty personally, and it's hard for me to separate other people's problems from my own. Rachel used to worry about that, in fact. She said I needed to learn how to walk away sometimes, for my own mental health. But I've never quite gotten the hang of it.''

Sam rested her elbow on the table and propped her chin in her hand. Dealing once a week with women in trouble was hard enough. He did that kind of work every day. ''It all sounds pretty heavy. Don't you ever take time for fun?''

''Oh, sure. Mostly thanks to Rachel. Before she came into my life, I was a pretty serious guy.''

''And you're not now?'' Sam teased, her lips quirking up.

He smiled ruefully. ''Touché. Okay, I'm still serious. I think it goes with the territory. But I have learned to give myself a break from work now and then. Not much in the past few years, but maybe I'm making a new start tonight. Going to the symphony was a big step for me.''

Sam looked at him speculatively. She liked this man. He was nice, sensitive, attractive, a great conversationalist, had a good sense of humor. He was the kind of man, under different circumstances, that she would pursue. But given the present circumstances, getting involved with Brad Matthews was not an option.

Yet it didn't seem right that he should be alone—and lonely. Maybe she could help on that score. She knew some nice, single women she could introduce him to. After all, Brad had gone out of his way to be nice to her, offering her the hand of friendship when she'd desperately needed it. She should try to repay him in some way.

At the same time, she realized that the thought of him going out with another woman was extremely unappealing. But that was just being selfish, she berated herself. She should put his best interests first. And if that meant setting him up with some nice women, so be it.

"Brad, I think what you need to do is start dating again," she said bluntly, before she could change her mind.

Brad almost choked on the coffee he was swallowing, and by the time he was able to speak, they'd attracted the attention of half the patrons in the café.

"Are you all right?" she asked with concern when he finally stopped coughing.

Brad dabbed at his lips with the napkin and stared at her. "May I ask where that remark came from?"

Sam shrugged. "I don't know. You just seem lonely. I know some nice single women you might enjoy meeting." She leaned closer and touched his hand. "I know you loved Rachel, Brad," she said softly. "But she's gone. You can't live on memories. Maybe I can help get you into circulation again."

Brad was speechless. Sam had voiced the thoughts that had been running through his head ever since the wedding. But they were just thoughts at this point. He had no immediate plans to move on them. Seeing Sam on a "friendship" basis was about all he was ready for at the moment.

"Look, Sam, I appreciate your concern," he acknowledged. "But I'm just not at that point yet. And, to be honest, I'm really rusty on the finer points of dating. Rachel was the only woman I ever seriously went out with, and that was a long time ago."

Sam frowned. "When you say 'seriously,' what do you mean exactly?"

He shrugged. "Honestly? I never got past a good-night kiss with any other woman."

"And you haven't gone out with anyone since Rachel died?"

"No."

Sam digested that information—and its implications. It was hard to believe that there was a man Brad's age alive in today's world who hadn't slept around to some extent before marriage and who would remain celibate for six long years after his wife's death. Certainly none of the men she knew. But here was one sitting right across from her, and she was impressed—and deeply moved. "I understand your reluctance," she said slowly. "It would be kind of scary to date again after such a long time. But you have to start sooner or later."

"I was sort of thinking along the lines of 'later,'" he admitted.

"Why?"

Brad shifted uncomfortably in his chair. Sam's reputation for directness was one thing Laura had *not* exaggerated. "Sam, I'm not even sure I remember how to talk to a woman—as a woman," he said frankly.

"Oh, that's silly," she replied, dismissing his comment with a wave. "You seem perfectly at ease with me."

"Yeah, I know," he admitted. "I guess maybe that's because we set the ground rules right up front—friendship. There are different pressures when you're actually dating."

Sam felt a sudden heaviness in her heart. He had just confirmed what she already knew—friendship was their destiny. But for some reason, when he put it into words, a little bit of the glow left her heart. With an effort she fought down the sudden melancholy that swept over her.

"That's true," she admitted, striving to keep her voice light. "But I think we can get around that. I know a woman who might be just your type. Sort of quiet, refined, likes music and books. She hasn't dated much, either, so she'll probably be just as nervous as you are. You'll be even on that score. Why don't you let me give her a call and see if she's interested?"

Brad shook his head. "I don't know," he said doubtfully.

"What do you have to lose with one date?" Sam argued.

Brad didn't have an answer to that. He'd told himself it was time to allow for the possibility of romance again. Sam was willing to help him. Why was he hesitating? He couldn't think of an excuse, so finally, with a sigh, he capitulated.

"You win. I can't think of any reason not to meet this woman," he said.

Sam felt her stomach sink to her toes, but she smiled. "Good. I'll give her a call tomorrow. By the way, her name's Stephanie Morris, and she's a librarian. Now why do you have that funny look on your face?" Sam asked suspiciously, when his lips turned up into a crooked smile.

"What funny look?" he asked innocently.

"You know what I mean," she asserted accusingly. "That look…like you're secretly laughing at something."

"I'm not laughing," he said with a smile, shaking his head. "I'm just amazed. First you get me out house hunting before I've really decided to do anything concrete about finding a new place, and now you're lining up dates for me—sooner, as you put it, rather than later. I'm just wondering what I'm going to get pulled into next."

Sam smiled. "You never know with Sam Reynolds," she warned. "Just ask Laura."

"I might. But you have to promise me one thing, Sam," he said, suddenly serious.

"What?"

"No singles bars."

Sam laughed, realizing that he was teasing her. "Don't worry. I wouldn't even think about it. I just can't picture you in one of those places."

"Well, I couldn't picture Laura there, either, and you managed to get her to a few."

Sam chuckled. "Yeah, but kicking and screaming. Besides, it didn't do any good. Although I must admit that the night we ran into Nick seemed to be a turning point in their relationship,'' she said thoughtfully.

"Sam," Brad warned, not liking the speculative look he saw in her eyes.

Her smile of response seemed somehow shadowed with sadness. "Don't worry, Brad. You're safe with me," she said quietly.

It was only later, after he dropped her off at her condo with a simple good-night and a warmly clasped hand, that he took time to analyze why her suggestion about arranging a date for him left him cold. He should feel something, he thought. Anticipation. Nervousness. Excitement. But he felt nothing. He just wasn't interested.

It was odd, really. It wasn't as if he was immune to women anymore. He'd noticed Sam's fabulous legs tonight. And he noticed the way her eyes could sparkle one minute and then suddenly cloud over with sadness the next. He noticed the way her striking red hair framed her heart-shaped face with vibrant color. He sensed her deep loneliness, which triggered an unexpected protective response in him—and something more, he admitted. Ever since he'd met her, there'd been occasions when he wanted to reach over and touch her for reasons that were not altruistic. His motivation had been purely physical, not spiritual.

So given his reaction to Sam, who was only a friend, he was relatively certain that the right woman, someone like Rachel, could trigger a strong emotional response in him. He was also relatively certain that he was ready to allow someone new into his life.

Then why did he feel absolutely nothing about this date Sam was arranging? He should be looking forward to it. She sounded like a nice woman. They might have a lot in common. It could be the beginning of a whole new chapter in his life. He should be enthusiastic and optimistic. He *would* be enthusiastic and optimistic, he told himself resolutely. He would go to sleep imagining what Stephanie Morris looked like, he thought determinedly.

Funny thing was, try as he might to conjure up her image, every picture he created as he drifted off to sleep featured a woman with startling green eyes and striking red hair.

Chapter Four

Sam dashed into the café, muttering an unflattering comment about the weather as she paused to catch her breath. April was supposed to bring showers, not monsoons, she thought irritably. She'd been dodging raindrops all morning with two different clients, both of whom lingered far longer than expected at every house, and then she'd run into a major traffic jam. All of which meant she was twenty minutes late for her lunch with Laura.

Sam brushed her hair back from her face and sighed as she peered at her reflection in a small mirror just inside the door. She not only *felt* frazzled, she *looked* frazzled. For someone who was always meticulous about her appearance, it was a distressing realization. But then, she'd had a lot of distressing realizations lately, she thought wryly. This one was low on the scale of importance compared to the others.

Sam ineffectually ran her fingers through her hair and then gave up, acknowledging that it was a lost cause. With a sigh, she turned, scanning the room rapidly. It took her only a moment to spot Laura, seated at a quiet corner table, sipping a cup of tea, looking absolutely placid and dreamy-eyed, a faint smile on her face. That's what a honeymoon did for you, Sam supposed wistfully.

She was almost to the table before Laura saw her and smiled a warm welcome. "Sam! Oh, it's so good to see you!"

Sam slid into the seat across from Laura and grinned. "Well, better late than never. Listen, kiddo, I'm sorry. You wouldn't believe the morning I had. Two difficult clients, a traffic jam—"

"Sam, it's all right," Laura said. "I didn't mind waiting. But you look stressed out. Do you want some tea? Or would you prefer something stronger?" she asked with a smile.

"I'm on duty. Tea will have to do," Sam said resignedly. "I'll have whatever kind you're drinking—it seems to have a relaxing effect."

Laura grinned. "Well, I think my state of mind has more to do with three weeks in Hawaii," she admitted.

Sam studied her friend's face. The fine lines of tension that had always been around her eyes were gone, and the faint, parallel etchings on her brow had all but disappeared. "I have to say I don't think I've ever seen you look this...mellow."

Laura smiled. "I *feel* mellow. I don't know, Sam...ever since the wedding it's like a missing piece of my life has dropped into place. I feel...well...more alive, I guess. Nick is so wonderful..." Her voice caught, and she smiled ruefully. "I guess I still can't believe I really have him."

"Believe it, honey," Sam said. "And count your blessings."

"I do. Every single day," Laura said fervently.

"Okay, so enough of this mushy stuff," Sam declared. "Let's have some of the fun details. Tell me everything you did...other than the obvious," she said with an irreverent grin and a wink that brought a blush to Laura's cheeks.

Sam found herself smiling frequently at Laura's enthusiastic retelling of her dream honeymoon. Her face was animated and alive, and Sam's throat tightened at the soft, tender look that came into her eyes whenever she mentioned Nick's name. Clearly he was everything he seemed to be, and for that Sam was grateful. Laura deserved a caring, richly faceted relationship after her traumatic first marriage and the subsequent years of guilt and loneliness. It had taken Nick, with his patience, understanding and tenderness, to help her overcome her fear of commitment and find the courage to take a second chance on love. It was a classic story of triumph over tragedy, and Sam was truly happy for them both.

"And so it was really hard to come back," Laura concluded as they finished their dessert. "Hawaii is truly a tropical paradise, and I felt like I was in a dream. I don't think anyone ever had such a perfect honeymoon," she said with a sigh.

Sam grinned. "Well, based on everything you said, I think you're probably right. Do you know that you're actually glowing? And you look like you gained a few pounds, thank heavens."

"I did," Laura confirmed. "It was the first real vacation I've ever had. I mean, all we did was walk on the beach, eat fantastic meals, sleep and…well, you know," she said, a blush once more staining her cheeks becomingly.

Sam laughed. "Yeah, I know. And if Nick had anything to say about it, I have a feeling you did a lot of that 'you know' stuff."

Laura's blush deepened. "Well, after all, he waited patiently for a long time."

"I know. The man is a saint, if you ask me," Sam said with a grin.

"I won't argue with you there," Laura agreed. "But you know something, Sam?" she said earnestly. "I think we both feel like it was worth waiting for. The waiting made it even more special."

"Well, that's all that matters, then." Sam grinned. "I'll

have to tell Brad that his theory about judging how much fun you had by how sleep deprived you looked was wrong."

"Brad?" Laura tried to recall which one of Sam's wide circle of male friends he was, but she came up blank.

"Yeah. Brad Matthews."

Laura frowned. Brad Matthews. She didn't recall Sam ever mentioning anyone by that name before. She tried to keep Sam's many admirers straight, but this one eluded her. "Do I know him?" she asked.

"Of course. Brad Matthews," Sam repeated. When Laura still looked confused, she laughed. "Your minister," Sam explained.

Laura stared at her uncomprehendingly. "Brad...my minister?" she repeated.

"Yeah. How about that?" Sam said, striving for a flippant tone. She supposed she shouldn't be surprised that Laura was shocked at the incongruous pairing. It was pretty bizarre, after all. Talk about two different kinds of people!

Laura still looked confused. "Now wait a minute. When did Brad say this? At the wedding?"

"No. On the phone after the wedding. He called me."

"Brad called you?" Laura knew she was beginning to sound like a parrot, but she was having a hard time linking her minister and her best friend in any way whatsoever.

"Uh-huh. They're going to tear the parsonage down, so he needs to find a house. He thought I could help," Sam explained.

"Oh!" That made a little more sense. Laura had told Brad that Sam sold real estate, and they *had* met at the wedding.

"He's a nice man," Sam ventured, keeping her tone light. "I'm surprised you and he never...clicked, you know what I mean?"

"Brad and me?" Laura said in surprise. "Oh, Sam, I grew up with Brad. He was more like a brother. And when he became a minister, I just started thinking of him in that role. I never even considered anything romantic. Anyway, he was married until six years ago, and at that point the last thing on my mind was romance. Besides, he was really in love with his wife.''

"Rachel. Yeah, I know," Sam said, playing with her teacup. "It sounds like she was a wonderful person."

Laura studied her friend curiously. She seemed...*vulnerable* was the word that came to mind, although Laura had a hard time associating that characteristic with the self-confident, in-control Sam she'd always known. Yet it seemed to fit today. Why? And how did she know about Brad's wife? "Did Brad tell you about Rachel?" Sam asked curiously.

Sam shrugged. "It just sort of came up during our phone conversation, and then again at lunch."

Laura set her cup down carefully and folded her hands. "Now let me get this straight," she said slowly. "You and Brad had lunch?"

"Yeah. It was no big deal," Sam said lightly. "I took him out to look at a few houses, and we stopped for a bite to eat afterward."

"Okay. But how on earth did you get him to talk about Rachel? He never talks about her."

"He doesn't?"

"No. I've always gotten the impression that it was too painful for him. Her death was such a tragedy."

Sam frowned. "Yeah, he told me. It must have been awful for him." She took a deep breath. "I don't know why he talked about her to me," she admitted. "But he seems lonely. And sometimes people have to talk about things before they can let them go. Anyway, I think he's ready to consider romance again. Why else would he have agreed to the blind date I suggested after the symphony? Okay, so I pushed it a little, but—"

"Sam." Laura cut her off, starring at her friend uncomprehendingly. "Wait a minute. You went to the symphony with Brad? And he's going on a blind date?"

"Yeah." Sam shifted uncomfortably. "Listen, maybe he doesn't want anyone to know. You won't spread it around, will you?"

"No. Of course not. But...all of this happened in the three weeks I was gone?"

"Uh-huh."

Laura shook her head. "I don't believe it. How did this symphony thing come up?"

Sam shrugged. "I got some free tickets, and at lunch that day Brad mentioned that he and Rachel used to enjoy going. So I figured he might like it. After all, he was the one who suggested that maybe we could be friends, and offering the ticket seemed like a friendly thing to do. Besides, he's a really nice guy, Laura."

"Oh, I know. Absolutely. You couldn't find many guys nicer than Brad." Laura eyed her friend speculatively. Sam actually looked flushed—an unusual condition for her. Laura had never seen her ruffled or embarrassed by anything. "It's just that..." Her voice trailed off.

Sam grinned sheepishly. "You don't have to say it. Let me. Why in heaven's name—pardon the ecclesiastical pun—would someone like Brad be interested in having a friend like me? I asked him the same thing. He just said a person can't have too many friends, and then pointed out that you and I are really different, and we're friends. I couldn't fault his logic. Anyway, I like being with him. He's really solid, you know? And he's kind and empathetic and intelligent. Plus, he has a good sense of humor."

Laura took a sip of water. "He's not bad looking, either," she said innocently.

"Not bad looking?" Sam replied with a snort. "Honey, he's a hunk. Okay, if it's in bad taste to say that about a minister, I'm sorry. But let's give credit where it's due. He *is* a hunk."

"Yeah, I guess he is," Laura agreed, trying not to smile.

"Not that I'm interested in him in that way, you understand. Can you imagine that? Swinging single Sam and straight-arrow minister Brad. Not a good fit. Besides, I'm not really in the market for romance at the moment," she said with a careless lift of one shoulder.

"You're not?" Laura said in surprise. "I thought you were always looking for Mr. Right."

"Not anymore, kiddo. I've called a moratorium on the search. I'm just glad you found your Prince Charming."

"But why aren't you looking?" Laura persisted with a frown. For as long as Laura had known her, Sam had claimed to be on the hunt for a husband.

Sam waved the question aside. "It's a long story, hon. Too long to go into today." They were moving onto dangerous ground, which meant she needed to distract Laura. And the next topic was sure to do the trick, she thought wryly. "Besides, I have a favor to ask."

"Sure," Laura replied, still pondering Sam's last remark. What was the long story? she wondered.

"Now don't fall off your chair, kiddo, but I was wondering if I could go with you sometime to one of your Bible study classes," Sam said lightly.

Laura's eyes grew wide and she stared at her friend, speechless. It was about the reaction Sam expected. She'd felt sort of the same way when the idea occurred to her out of the blue, right after the lunch with Brad, which had given her a new "take" on religion. If a man like Brad had chosen to make it his life's work, and if someone of Laura's fragile sensitivity had found strength enough in her faith to carry her through the traumatic years of her marriage, then maybe it was worth checking out, Sam figured. She'd been off balance ever since the wedding, feeling lost and more alone than she had in years. She needed direction and support, and maybe she could find it in her long-neglected faith. It wouldn't hurt to try, and Laura was her entrée. *If* she ever got over her shock.

Sam smiled and reached over to teasingly snap her fingers in front of her friend's face. "Hello? Is anybody home?"

Laura blinked and made an attempt to regain her wits. Sam was always full of surprises, but today she'd outdone herself. "You want to go with me to Bible study class?" she repeated slowly, wanting to verify that she'd correctly heard Sam's request.

"Yep. I figured I'd give it a shot."

"Well, sure. Of course," Laura said, recovering quickly. She'd invited Sam a few times through the years, but without success. She had a feeling a certain minister was responsible for this change of heart. "We meet on Thursday from seven-thirty to nine."

"And this is a group of people from all over the area, right? Not just Brad's congregation."

"Right."

"And it's not at Brad's church?"

"No."

"Good. Listen, don't say anything about this to anyone, okay? It's jut a trial thing, really, and I'd rather keep it quiet."

"What about Brad? You're going to tell him, aren't you?"

"No. Not yet, anyway. You won't say anything, will you?"

"Not if you don't want me to," Laura promised.

"Good. Who knows? I might only last one session," Sam joked. Then, before Laura could probe any further, she glanced at her watch. "Oh, good grief! Have we been here two hours? I've got to meet a client in thirty minutes way out west. You may still be a lady of leisure for a few more days, but some of us aren't so lucky." Sam slung her purse over her shoulder and reached across the table to squeeze Laura's hand. "I'm really glad you had such a great time, Laura. You deserve it. Give Nick my best, okay? And let's talk soon."

"Oh, absolutely," Laura said. Real soon, if she had anything to say about it. There were an awful lot of holes in Sam's story that needed to be filled in. "I'll call you in a couple of days with details about the class."

"Thanks. You take care now." Sam said as she stood up.

"You, too," Laura replied.

Laura watched her friend walk toward the door, her self-confident saunter and swinging red hair the same as always. But there was something different about Sam. Something very different. Could it be that… Laura shook her head. Brad and Sam? No, it wasn't possible. Or was it? She'd have to run it by Nick and see what he thought. But Laura already knew what *she* thought. There was romance in the air.

"You've got to be kidding!" Nick looked up from the complex architectural rendering on his computer screen and stared at Laura.

"No! It's the truth!" Laura said excitedly, still out of breath from her dash up the stairs to Nick's second-floor home office in their sprawling Victorian.

"But Sam and Brad? That's ridiculous!"

"Why?"

"Oh, come on, Laura. Can you imagine two people any more different?"

"That's what Sam said," Laura replied impatiently. "But I'm telling you, when she talks about him she gets this look in her eyes…" Laura's voice trailed off dreamily.

Nick smiled indulgently. "What look?"

"You know. That look, like he's special."

"Oh, *that* look," he said, his eyes twinkling.

"Nick, will you be serious!"

"How can I be? Sam and Brad?" He shook his head doubtfully. "Laura, sweetheart, you know I have great respect for your instincts. But I think you're jumping to the wrong conclusions in this case. This all started out as a business arrangement, remember? He called her to help him find a house. Period.''

"Yeah, but then they had lunch, and they went to the symphony."

Nick shrugged. "Well, you know Sam. She can be pretty forceful. Brad probably just didn't want to hurt her feelings."

Laura frowned, somewhat deflated. "Well, he is going out on that blind date Sam's fixing him up with," she admitted. "But that doesn't mean he isn't interested in Sam, too," she declared stubbornly.

Nick stared at her. "Sam convinced Brad to go out on a blind date?" he asked incredulously.

"Yeah."

Nick chuckled and shook his head. "That woman is amazing." Then he sat forward and propped his elbows on the desk. "Look, Laura, I really like Sam. She's a great gal. But you might be stretching it just a little to think that she and Brad would get together."

"Well, opposites can attract," Laura pointed out. "And you know, the Lord often works in mysterious way."

"Yeah, but it would take Agatha Christie to figure this one out," he said with a grin.

"Oh, Nick," Laura said, coming around the desk and settling herself on his lap. "I just want Sam to be as blissfully happy as I am. Maybe I can sort of help things along and…"

"Laura." Nick's voice held a warning note. "We are not going to play matchmaker."

"Why not? Sam tried to fix me up plenty of times. I still remember those awful events for singles she used to drag me to," she said with a shudder. "I think turnabout is only fair play."

"I don't know," Nick said doubtfully.

Laura smiled and leaned down to nibble on his ear. "What don't you know?"

He drew in a sharp breath as a flash of heat ricocheted

through him. "Are you by any chance trying to distract me?" he asked.

"Mmm-hmm. Is it working?" she murmured.

"You might say that," he replied huskily, his hands beginning to touch her in ways that sent a delicious shiver up her spine.

"Do you want me to stop?" she offered, pressing even closer against him.

"Stop?" He chuckled deep in his throat. "Sweetheart, you may not know it, but this is just the appetizer," he said, bending to claim her lips.

By the time the kiss ended, both of them felt breathless, and Nick slid his arm under Laura's knees and stood up. She nestled contentedly into his shoulder, her arms around his neck as he headed for the door, Sam and Brad forgotten—for the moment.

"Mmm," she murmured throatily. "I can't wait for dessert."

Sam's throat constricted as she gazed at the confused and frightened eighteen-year-old girl seated across from her, so alone and in need of love and understanding. Impulsively she reached for her hand, and the girl's icy fingers clutched hers convulsively.

"You've told me what everyone else thinks, Jamie," Sam said gently. "But what do *you* want to do?"

The girl chewed on her bottom lip, and tears suddenly flooded her eyes. "I—I don't know," she admitted helplessly. "My mom and dad and John and all my friends are sure it will ruin my life if I have the baby, but it feels so...so wrong to just...get rid of it."

Sam nodded understandingly, "I know what you mean. You'd like to believe there's not really a life at stake, because then your decision would be easy. But your heart is telling you there is."

"Yeah. That's exactly right," the girl affirmed, clearly

grateful and relieved that someone at last seemed to understand how she felt.

"Let me ask you something, Jamie," Sam said slowly, choosing her words carefully. "Has anyone suggested that it might ruin your life if you *don't* have the baby? If you 'get rid of it' as you said."

The girl looked surprised. "No."

"You might want to give that some thought," Sam suggested, her voice still gentle. "Ask yourself how you'll feel in a few years when you see a little child that would be the same age as your baby. That's a hard thing to face, Jamie."

"But I'm not ready to be a mother! Especially a single mother!" the girl cried, her voice agitated and once more desperate. "John doesn't want any part of it, and Mom and Dad are against it. I'd be totally on my own."

"We can offer you a lot of support here," Sam said encouragingly. "We can help with medical expenses, and I'm available to talk any time you need me. As for being a single mother, that's your choice, of course. And we'll help you in every way we can if you decide to take on that responsibility. But we have a list of dozens of couples, who, for whatever reason, can't have their own children. They'd welcome your baby with open arms and give him or her all the love they've stored up in their hearts. We've checked them out thoroughly, and they're all fine people, so you can be sure your baby would have a wonderful home."

Jamie dabbed at her eyes. "I just feel so confused," she said, her voice breaking.

"That's understandable," Sam empathized, her heart going out to the distressed young woman. "It's a big decision, and it's hard to make a rational choice when you don't have much support from family and friends. But remember, Jamie—you do have a choice."

There was silence for a moment, and then the girl

sighed. "I guess I'll just have to think about it some more," she concluded.

"That's a good idea. In the meantime, I'm here if you need me." Sam reached for a notepad and scrawled two numbers. "The top number is the counseling center," she told Jamie as she tore off the sheet and handed it to her. "The bottom one is my home phone. You can call me anytime, day or night, if you want to talk. Okay?"

The girl took the piece of paper and tucked it into the pocket of her jeans. "Okay. And thanks for listening tonight. It helped a lot."

"I'm glad. In fact, why don't we set up another appointment for next week? I can give you more details on our program and answer any questions you might think of between now and then."

"Okay."

After they chose a mutually agreeable time, Sam walked with her to the door. "Take care, Jamie," she said, letting her hand rest lightly on the girl's shoulder. "And call me in a couple of days, okay? Just to talk. Will you do that?"

"Yeah. Thanks."

Sam watched the rail-thin girl disappear down the hall, then closed the door. She walked slowly back through the counseling center to the director's office, a frown of concern etched on her face.

Carolyn looked up when Sam paused on the threshold. "How did it go?"

Sam shook her head and sighed. "I don't know. She's obviously trying to do the right thing, but it's equally obvious she's not getting any support at home. I'm just not sure I got through to her."

Carolyn set her glasses on her desk and gave her hardest-working volunteer a sympathetic look. "You did everything you could, Sam. That's all we can ask."

Sam looked at the motherly, gray-haired woman in frustration, then stuck her hands into the pockets of her slacks.

"I just don't think it was enough this time. I don't have good feelings about this one."

Carolyn tapped her pen on the edge of the desk and studied the younger woman. "Sometimes I worry as much about you as the girls who come in here, Sam," she told her soberly. "You take this so much to heart. I know it tears you up inside whenever you fail. And yet you keep coming back. I admire that kind of dedication."

Sam waved the praise aside impatiently. "Don't admire me, Carolyn. You know better." The director of the counseling center was the only person who knew even a piece of the tragic incident in Sam's past.

"Sam, whatever drives you to come here week after week and put yourself through an emotional wringer is your business. The motivation doesn't negate the good work you do. Thanks to you, a lot of children are here today—happy, healthy and enjoying the gift of life."

Sam felt tears prick her eyelids, and she blinked to keep them at bay. "But a lot of them aren't, Carolyn," she said dejectedly. "And it's those children who haunt me."

"Listen, Sam, I know it's an imposition, and I'm really sorry to put you on the spot like this, but it would save my life if you'd fill in."

Sam frowned, trying to get Jamie out of her mind and focus on her friend's request. Normally she wouldn't hesitate to help Laura out, but it might be awkward. Since Brad had unenthusiastically reported to her on his date, they hadn't spoken. Doing a seminar at his church under those circumstances...well, it probably wasn't such a good idea. Even though he hadn't sounded terribly upset on the phone, he'd made it clear in their brief conversation that he didn't intend to go on any more blind dates.

"Sam?" Laura prompted.

"Yeah, I'm still here. Listen, does Brad know about this?"

"What?"

"Me filling in."

"No. But these seminars are my responsibility and he doesn't usually get involved other than approving the topics."

"Explain to me again what this is exactly," Sam said, trying to buy some more time while she thought this through.

"Sure," Laura said patiently. "Brad believes that the church should offer assistance to people in all facets of living, not just spiritual. So about a year ago he got a committee together to plan some practical seminars for people in different phases of their lives. We decided to try it once a month for six months and see what kind of response we got. So far we've had seminars on how to choose child care, what to look for in nursing homes, planning for retirement and coping with loss. This month's topic is how to buy a home, and it's designed for young couples just starting out. About thirty people are signed up. You might even pick up some new clients," Laura pointed out.

"And it's this Saturday?"

"Uh-huh. One to three." Laura held her breath. It was sheer providence that their scheduled presenter, a member of the congregation, had to go out of town unexpectedly. And Laura intended to take advantage of it.

Sam frowned. She was available. And it really did sound like Laura was in a bind. Besides, Brad might not even be around. And Laura was right. Sam might pick up some new clients.

"Okay, kiddo. I'll be there," she said.

Laura let out her breath and smiled. "Great! And thanks a bunch, Sam."

"No problem. See you Saturday."

Laura hung up the phone, a satisfied smile on her face. Mission accomplished. Or at least phase one.

Sam didn't even notice when Brad slipped into a chair

in the back of the room during her presentation. And she didn't see him during the lively question and answer session that followed, either. It wasn't until afterward, as she tried to collect her materials amid a barrage of one-on-one questions, that she realized he was the person handing her a cup of coffee. She paused midsentence as their eyes connected.

"I'll talk to you when you're finished," he said quietly, with a smile.

She nodded and forced her attention back to the eager young couples who were still plying her with questions.

When at last the final, lingering attendees departed, Laura stepped forward and gave her a hug. "You were a hit," she declared. "Great job! Why am I not surprised? See," she said, turning triumphantly to Brad as he joined them, "didn't I tell you she'd be great?"

Sam looked at Brad, and his warm smile played havoc with her metabolism.

"Yes. But I never doubted it. I know from personal experience that she's one sharp businesswoman." And she truly had been in top form today, he thought. Animated, wisecracking, high energy—she'd not only passed on important information, she'd kept her audience entertained in the process. "And the presentation was great. I wish my sermons were that dynamic," he said with a grin.

Sam felt a flush creep up her neck at his compliment and turned away on the pretense of putting some papers in her briefcase. "I just hope it was useful," she said.

"I know it was," Laura assured her. "Listen, Sam, I hate to run, but Nick and I have dinner plans tonight. Do you mind if I take off?"

"No, not at all. If I had someone like Nick waiting for me at home, you can bet *I* wouldn't be hanging around a church basement with a girlfriend," she said, turning to Laura with a grin.

Laura laughed. "I'll call you next week."

"Okay. Have fun tonight."

"Thanks. Brad, will you lock up?"

"Sure."

"Great. See you two later."

As Laura disappeared out the door, Brad turned back to Sam, and his smile seemed to grow even warmer. Or was it just her imagination, she wondered?

"You really were good, you know," he said.

She shrugged. "I'm glad I could fill in." She paused and took a deep breath, deciding she might as well clear the air about the date thing right up front. It had been on her mind ever since their one brief phone call following the less-than-successful event. "Look, Brad, I'm really sorry the date didn't work out. I understand if you're upset and felt I'd been too pushy, and I—"

"Who said anything about being upset?" he interrupted with a frown.

"Well, you didn't sound too happy on the phone afterward, and I haven't heard from you since, so I just assumed—"

"Sam." He took her hand, and a sweet shiver ran through her at his touch. He had wonderful hands—gentle, but strong and sure. "Can we sit down for a minute, or do you have to rush off?"

"No. I have some time," she said, her voice suddenly hoarse. Must be from all that talking for the past couple of hours, she thought.

Still holding her hand, he led her to the first row of chairs and drew her down beside him. "First of all, I am not upset about the date," he said, angling himself toward her. "Stephanie is a very nice woman, and we had a lot in common. You made a good match. But...I don't know. If you've talked to her, she may have told you the same thing. There just wasn't any...spark."

He was right. At least, half-right. Stephanie liked Brad—a lot. But she sensed his lack of romantic interest.

"Maybe it's too soon, like you said," Sam suggested,

employing the same theory she had used to console Stephanie.

Brad shook his head. "No. That's not it." He stood up and walked a few steps away, jamming his hands into the pockets of his slacks. "I should have felt something. I don't know why I didn't. She was very nice, and it was a pleasant, relaxing evening. Almost too relaxing, if that makes any sense. She was just too quiet. I guess I like people who are a little more…lively. I don't know," he repeated with a frustrated sigh, raking his fingers through his hair. "But for whatever reason, we just didn't click."

"Well, we can try again."

"No," he said quickly. At her surprised look, he amended his response. "I mean, not right away, anyway."

"Are you sure?"

"Yeah."

Sam shrugged. "Okay. If that's the way you want it." For some reason Sam wasn't inclined to push him this time. In fact, she was almost relieved that things hadn't worked out with Stephanie. Which was wrong, of course. But she couldn't help how she felt.

"I do appreciate your efforts, Sam."

"Hey, no problem. What are friends for? I'm just glad you're not mad. When I didn't hear from you, I got a little worried."

Brad sat down next to her again and closed his eyes, rubbing his forehead with the tips of his fingers. "I apologize for that. The week after that date was hectic, and for the last week I've had my father here visiting."

"Does he still live in Jersey?" Through the years Sam had heard a great deal about Laura's—and Brad's—hometown in southern Missouri.

"Yeah. My mom died about six months ago, and Dad's just never been able to regroup."

"I'm sorry," Sam said softly, reaching out to touch his hand.

"Thanks. It was hard on all of us. But I have my work,

and Rebecca, my sister, has her restaurant in St. Genevieve, so life went on for us. But for Dad—well, Mom
was always his main interest in life. They had a great marriage. Talk about two peas in a pod…'' He sighed. ''Anyway, he just kind of lost interest in everything when she
died. Even his gardens, which were always his pride and
joy. He hasn't even touched them this year. Rebecca and
I have been really worried about him. She gets down there
as often as she can. But since she opened the restaurant
about a year and a half ago she hardly has a minute to call
her own. I finally convinced Dad to come up here for a
week, thinking maybe I could lift his spirits a little. But I
can't say I've had much luck,'' he admitted with a sigh.
Then his eyes grew thoughtful. ''Say, I don't suppose
there's any chance you're free tonight and would consider
having dinner with a stodgy minister and his lonely old
dad, would you?''

Sam stared at him, taken aback by the unexpected invitation. ''Well, I don't know…'' she said slowly, her
voice trailing off.

Brad gave her a sheepish grin. ''Look, never mind. It
was a dumb idea. I'm sure you already have plans. And
even if you don't, there are lots more exciting things you
could do—like clean out your closets or vacuum the furniture.''

Sam smiled. ''As a matter of fact, Brad, I don't have
plans tonight. And I'd love to have dinner with you and
your dad. But he may not like having a third party there,
especially if he's feeling down.''

''Well, I think it would be good for him to meet someone like you,'' Brad said. ''You're really great with people, and *I* always feel better around you. You have a knack
for making me smile and feel lighthearted. Maybe you can
do the same for Dad.''

Sam had a feeling Brad didn't even realize that he'd just
paid her a terrific compliment. Which was okay. *She* realized it, and that was the important thing. It was one of

those lovely moments she intended to file away in her heart.

"I can certainly give it a try," she said with a warm smile.

"Great!" Brad glanced at his watch. "Let's see. It's already four…how about if we pick you up at six?"

"Are you sure you don't want me to just meet you somewhere?"

"I'd rather pick you up, if that's okay."

"But it's not a date or anything."

"Yeah, I know. Not too many guys would bring their fathers along on a date. I do remember that much," he said with a grin. Then he grew more serious. "But with the world what it is today, I'd just feel better seeing you to the door afterward."

"Well, sure, that would be great, if you don't mind."

"It's my pleasure," he said with a smile that warmed her right down to her toes.

"Is this going to be casual?" she asked.

"I think my dad would be more comfortable, if that's all right with you."

"Sure. I'll just run home and change." She stood up and Brad followed suit, his gaze sweeping over her in a quick but appreciative appraisal.

"Too bad," he said. "I like that outfit."

Sam was surprised—and ruffled—by the compliment. She looked down and adjusted a button on her fitted short-sleeved tunic jacket, then smoothed down her short skirt. She'd debated whether to wear low, comfortable shoes or dressier two-inch heels, and she was suddenly glad she'd chosen the latter, which emphasized the shapely line of her legs.

"Are you wearing that?" she asked, nodding toward his khakis, blue shirt and lightweight off-white cotton sweater.

"Yeah. I was planning to."

"Then this is a little too dressy," she said.

"I could change," he offered.

She grinned, tilting her head to look up at him. "Do you like this outfit that much?"

He smiled. "Uh-huh."

"I'll wear it again sometime, then," she promised.

"It's a deal. But Sam…"

She looked at him curiously when he paused. "Yes?"

"I hope this doesn't sound too forward, but…maybe you could wear one of those short skirts? They look really great on you."

Sam stared at him in surprise, and a warm tingle raced along her spine. "Are you sure a minister should be asking a woman to wear a short skirt?" she chided teasingly, trying to keep her voice light…and steady.

"No," he promptly admitted. "But they suit you. And besides, sometimes when I'm with you I forget all about being a minister."

She smiled. "You know what?"

"What?"

"Sometimes I forget, too."

He looked thoughtful. "Maybe that's good."

"Why do you say that?"

"Well, I know your past experience with ministers hasn't been great. Maybe we get along so well because you do forget. So it might be a good thing."

"Maybe," she said slowly. Then she frowned. She was letting herself get too carried away here. It would be in both of their best interests for her to *remember* his profession so she was reminded of the impossibility of anything ever developing between them. She reached for her briefcase and turned to go, suddenly subdued. "Then again, maybe not," she said enigmatically. "See you in a little while, Brad."

Brad watched her leave, puzzled by her last remark. Had he been too forward, after all? He probably shouldn't have mentioned the skirt, he thought. In retrospect, it seemed out of line—and out of character. Maybe she'd gotten the impression that he wanted to change the status of their relationship from friendship to…something else. And maybe he did, he realized suddenly with surprise.

Brad frowned at that unexpected insight. Where on earth had that idea come from? Of course he was only interested in friendship. Sam wasn't his type. Okay, maybe he found her physically attractive. No, he corrected himself. There were no "maybes" about it. He *definitely* found her physically attractive. He'd had hormones kick in around Sam that had lain dormant for six long years. But physical attraction wasn't nearly enough to sustain a permanent relationship. And that was all they had, really. Or at least all *he* had. He had no idea whether Sam felt any attraction for him.

But what if she did? he suddenly wondered. An unbidden surge of adrenaline swept over him at the thought, but he quickly squelched it. Unfortunately it would never work between them. They were too different. Not that he didn't enjoy being with Sam. He enjoyed it a lot. She was lively, and that was something he hadn't had much of in his life. She was also attractive, intelligent, articulate, had a good sense of humor and was clearly a good person in many ways.

But even though her current social life was apparently much quieter than he'd imagined, he suspected that comparing the history of their romantic escapades would be like comparing Pollyanna to Madame Du Barry. His choices regarding intimacy had been grounded in a deep faith; hers…he didn't know her motivations, but her rules had clearly been much more liberal than his.

Even beyond differing philosophies on intimacy, though, it would be very difficult for him to become involved with someone who didn't share his basic Christian values, beliefs and life-style. Not to mention his strong faith. And Sam didn't seem to, apart from a few remnants that had survived from her Christian upbringing. While he had no doubt that she was highly principled and ethical—admirable qualities, to be sure—those attributes alone didn't make one a Christian.

No, Sam and he weren't right for each other. There were too many obstacles in the way of a romantic relationship. And yet…he felt drawn to her. He couldn't deny that. But what was he supposed to do about it?

Brad stood up in frustration and turned off the lights, then locked the door. Slowly he made his way upstairs, pausing at the church door. With a quick glance at his watch, he detoured inside and sat down in the last pew, bowing his head and closing his eyes.

Lord, I asked You to help me find the courage to put the past to rest and open myself to a new relationship, he prayed silently. *With Your help, I'm making progress. But now I have a new dilemma. Sam. I certainly never intended to feel anything more for her than friendship. And I don't want to now. But I forgot that the heart doesn't often listen to logic. I really like her, Lord. And I think it could grow to more than that. But we're so different… Could this possibly work? She says her reputation has been exaggerated, and I believe her. There is a sadness in her eyes, an honesty when she talks about it, that I cannot doubt. I believe that she's a very special lady who hasn't seen enough kindness or caring in her life. And I'd like to show her both. But I'm not sure how to proceed—or even if I should—beyond a friendship basis. Please, Lord, help me to discern Your will.*

But no matter what happens between the two of us, Lord, help Sam overcome her disillusionment about her faith and find her way home to You again. Because I believe that is the only way she'll find the lasting peace she seems to so desperately need.

Chapter Five

"I hope you won't be sorry," Brad said with a frown as he guided Sam toward his car, his hand at the small of her back. "Dad wasn't overly enthusiastic about having to carry on a conversation all during dinner with someone he's never met. He's gotten quieter and quieter these past few months. I'm afraid this could be uncomfortable."

Sam grinned. "Don't worry, Brad. I like a challenge," she assured him.

His features relaxed. "Thanks for being a good sport. And for agreeing to have dinner with us tonight."

"I think it will be fun," she said optimistically.

"I hope you still feel that way in a couple of hours," he replied dubiously.

They stopped beside the car, and a slight, thin man with fine gray hair climbed out of the back seat. Sam saw the resemblance immediately. Although Brad was a good four inches taller than his father, they had the same brown eyes and slightly angular nose. But while Brad's stance was typically relaxed, his father held himself somewhat stiffly, as if he felt awkward and would rather be somewhere else.

"Dad, this is Sam Reynolds," Brad said, his hand still at the small of her back. "Sam, this is my father, Henry."

Sam smiled and held out her hand. "It's very nice to meet you, Mr. Matthews. And thanks for letting me join you tonight for dinner. It's not often that a woman gets a chance to go out with *two* handsome men."

Her comment elicited only the smallest of smiles from Brad's father as he took her hand. "How do you do, Miss Reynolds. I'm very happy to meet you," he said politely.

"Thank you. And please call me Sam."

"Well, shall we go?" Brad asked, opening Sam's door. He gave her an I-told-you-so look as she slid into the seat, but she just winked and smiled confidently.

Brad's father remained quiet, answering her questions politely but in as few words as possible, during the drive to the restaurant. She tried to draw him out as they perused the menu, with little success. So once they had ordered she decided it was time to unveil her secret weapon.

"So, Mr. Matthews, Brad tells me you're a gardener," she said conversationally.

"Used to be," he replied, fiddling with his napkin.

"What do you grow?" she asked, ignoring the past tense.

"Roses. Perennials."

"What's your favorite rose variety?"

"Tea roses."

"Hmm. Me, too. Do you have any Double Delights?"

For the first time he looked directly at her, his eyebrows raised in surprise. "A couple."

"Best scent of any rose I've ever grown," Sam declared, helping herself to a roll from the basket.

He tilted his head and peered at her intently. "You grow roses?" he asked.

"Uh-huh. And perennials, too. I have a little garden at the back of my condo. But I have a feeling yours is a lot bigger."

Brad's father shrugged. "It's a fair size, I guess. Thirty-two tea roses, and a couple of nice-sized perennial beds."

"Thirty-two roses!" Sam repeated incredulously. "Gosh, I only have eight. And just a little strip of perennials. How long have you been at this?"

"All my life. I've always liked flowers. Lot of people don't bother with roses, though. Say they're too much trouble."

Sam gave an unladylike snort. "Hmm. Spray them once a week, feed them once a month, cover them up for the winter—how hard is that?"

"That's what I think," Henry nodded in vigorous agreement. "They're no trouble at all, considering they bloom all summer. What kind of spray do you use?"

As Sam and his father launched into a lively discussion about the merits of one kind of spray versus another, Brad just sat back and watched the exchange in awed amazement. He would never have tagged Sam, with her sophisticated clothes and perfectly polished nails, as a gardener. He was beginning to realize just what a multidimensional and surprising woman she was. With Sam, it was becoming clear that he'd better learn to expect the unexpected.

Such as this dinner. Brad would have laid odds that it would be a disaster, despite Sam's outgoing nature and optimism. But, amazingly, she had done what no else had been able to—she'd drawn his father into an animated conversation and brought the sparkle and interest back to his eyes. She even got him to laugh. And as far as Brad was concerned, that was a miracle.

By the time they arrived back at her condo after an extended dinner, Sam and his father were on a first-name basis.

"Now, Henry, you aren't going to neglect those poor roses anymore, are you?" Sam asked, as Brad's father climbed out of the car to say good-night.

"Nope. Think I'll tackle'em first thing when I get home tomorrow," he said purposefully. "And you won't forget to send me some of those perennial hollyhock seeds, will you?'' he asked eagerly. "Sounds like a mighty pretty plant, and can't say as I've ever seen 'em down in Jersey.''

"I won't forget. I'll put them in the mail next week,'' Sam promised. She held out her hand, and this time Henry shook it vigorously.

"It's been a pleasure, Sam. And you're welcome anytime to come down and see my gardens. Course, give me a little time to get them in shape,'' he said. "Maybe Brad'll bring you down some weekend,'' he suggested.

"Well, he's a busy man,'' Sam replied quickly, avoiding Brad's eyes. "But I'll be sure to stop by if I get down that way.'' Before Brad could say anything, she hurried on. "Now you take care, okay, Henry? And try that spray I told you about. It really does work wonders in this Missouri humidity. I haven't had a touch of black spot since I started using it.''

"I sure will. And...thanks for having dinner with us, Sam. I had a good time,'' he added almost shyly.

"Me, too,'' she assured him with a warm smile.

"I'll just walk Sam to the door, Dad,'' Brad said.

"No hurry. You two take your time,'' he replied.

As they made their way toward her condo, Brad was silent, and Sam wondered if he felt awkward about his dad's suggestion. Maybe she should bring it up, say she didn't expect—

"Sam!'' Her elderly next-door neighbor opened her door halfway and peered out.

"Hello, Mrs. Johnson,'' Sam said.

"I'm sorry to bother you, Sam, especially since you have a gentleman friend with you, but I've been watching for you. Did you have a chance to pick up those things for me?''

"Of course. I'll bring them over in just a couple of minutes,'' she said.

"That would be fine, dear. You go ahead and say goodnight to your young man first.''

Sam's face flushed again, and she turned to Brad helplessly. "Sorry about that," she apologized.

"What?"

"That 'your young man' business. And I'm afraid your father has the wrong impression about our relationship, too."

Instead of commenting on her remark, he nodded at her neighbor's door as they passed. "What was that all about?"

"Oh. That's Mrs. Johnson. She's eighty-five, would you believe it? Anyway, her kids want to put her in a nursing home, but she's hanging on to her independence for dear life. Literally, I think. And she's perfectly able to look after herself with just a little bit of help. Like she needs someone to do her grocery shopping every week and pick up a prescription now and then. It's no big deal to me, and if it helps her stay independent, I'm glad to do it," Sam said with a shrug as they stopped in front of her door.

"That's a very nice thing to do," Brad said, touched by her thoughtfulness.

She shrugged again. "Who knows, maybe someone will do the same for me someday when I'm old and all alone," she said with a crooked smile, fishing for her key.

When she found it, Brad reached over and took it from her hand, and she looked up at him in surprise. He closed his fingers around it and leaned against the door frame with one shoulder, crossing his arms in front of his chest. "What makes you think you'll be all alone?" he asked quietly.

Sam lifted one shoulder and averted her face slightly. "I don't know," she said evasively. When he didn't respond, she looked up at him. He was watching her with an odd expression that made her heart stop, then race on. "Brad, your dad is waiting," she said, suddenly breathless as she tried to control the panic that swept over her.

"He said to take our time," Brad reminded her.

"Yes, but there's no reason to keep him waiting."

"Maybe there is," he said quietly.

Sam looked at him uncertainly, her heart thumping painfully in her chest. "What do you mean?" she asked, a strange catch in her voice.

He paused, as if choosing his words carefully. "Sam, I want to thank you for what you did for Dad tonight," he said slowly.

She dismissed his thanks with a shake of her head. "It was no effort. He's a nice man."

"Where did you learn so much about flowers?"

"I've always liked them."

"Do you really have a garden?"

She looked surprised. "Of course."

"You never told me."

She frowned. "I guess it just never came up."

"It seems like I learn something new about you every day," he said. "You're a pretty terrific lady, do you know that? And by the way, I like your skirt." He let his gaze flicker briefly down to the short hemline.

Sam blushed. His voice had a warm, intimate tone that set off alarm bells and made her nerve endings tingle. And she still hadn't figured out that look in his eyes. If she didn't know better, she'd think he wanted to kiss her. But of course that was ridiculous.

"Well, thanks," she said, her voice still uneven. "Um, Brad, you really ought to get back to your dad."

He frowned. "Yeah, I guess so." He paused and took a deep breath. "Sam, I—"

"Brad." This time the panic in her voice was evident. "It's getting late."

He remained unmoving for a moment, studying her face with his perceptive eyes. Finally, with a sigh, he straightened up. "Yeah, I know." Before she realized his intent, he quickly leaned down and gently kissed her forehead. Then he put her key in the lock and pushed open the door. "I'll call you soon, Sam," he said quietly.

She stared at him, her heart banging against her rib cage, her breathing shallow. "Okay," she whispered.

Brad lifted his hand, as if to touch her, then dropped it and turned away, striding quickly down the walk.

Sam closed the door and sagged against the frame, not trusting her shaky legs to support her. Things were starting to get out of hand here.

When Brad had first suggested friendship, she'd been touched—and pleased. But she'd really never expected it to go beyond that. Oh, sure, he was an attractive man. He was fun to be with, intelligent, sensitive. He had all the qualities she most admired in a man. Husband material for sure. But she'd known from the beginning that there was no possibility of that. They were too different. And even if those differences could be worked out, he would never be able to accept what she'd done. Even *she* couldn't accept it. Which was why she'd long ago ruled out marriage. And now was not the time to start changing the rules.

But then again, she hadn't expected to actually fall in love.

Sam let her eyelids fall, and hot tears welled up behind them as she acknowledged intellectually what her heart already knew—she loved Brad. How could she have let this happen? she cried silently. She should have seen it coming. And she supposed she had. She'd just chosen to ignore it. Because she wanted to be with him, and she figured she could handle the inevitable emotional upheaval. But she wasn't so sure anymore.

And how did he feel? she wondered, as she began assembling the groceries for Mrs. Johnson. He seemed to like her. Sometimes she thought she even detected stronger feelings than that in his eyes. Like tonight. But maybe gratitude was the explanation for tonight. After all, even though he *had* kissed her, it had felt more brotherly than romantic.

And she should be glad that's all it had been, she reminded herself sharply. Because if he showed any deeper interest, she'd have to stop seeing him. Immediately. Otherwise she would be misleading him, building up false expectations, and that would be wrong. In the end he would be hurt, and the last thing in the world she wanted to do was hurt Brad.

Yet how could she walk away, if that became necessary? she wondered desperately. The thought of never seeing him again was almost too painful to consider. But how long could she hide her real feelings? Tonight she had wanted him to kiss her. Really kiss her. She had almost lost control, reached out to him. And that out-of-control sensation frightened her. Given the depth of her feelings, she ought to stop this thing before it was too late.

Except that she had a feeling it already was.

"Seems like a nice girl."

Brad looked over at his father as he backed the car out of the parking spot. He thought about telling him that "girl" wasn't the politically correct term, but he doubted it would do any good, so he refrained. "She is," he replied shortly.

"Known her long?"

"Since Laura's wedding. She was the maid of honor."

"Let's see, that's been…what? Two months ago?"

"Just about."

"Hmm."

Brad gave his father a warning look. "Don't get any ideas, Dad."

"Ideas about what?" his father asked innocently.

"Ideas about Sam and me," Brad said.

"Well, she's a nice girl," he persisted.

"Yes," Brad agreed. "She's a very nice *woman*. But there are a lot of nice women in the world."

"None that you've noticed in recent years, far as I can tell," his father countered promptly.

"You're right," Brad admitted. "I haven't been looking. And I'm still not. Sam and I are just friends."

"Humph" was his father's only response.

Brad looked over at him in exasperation. "Now what's that supposed to mean?"

"Son, I may be old, but my sight is just fine. I watched you tonight, and when you look at Sam I don't see 'friendship' in your eyes."

Brad frowned. He obviously hadn't given his father's powers of perception enough credit. He himself was only now coming to grips with his feelings for Sam, still struggling to understand their implications, and his father had summed it up in one accurate, pithy sentence.

"So?" his father persisted.

"So what?" Brad asked.

His father sighed heavily. "So what are you going to do about it?" he asked impatiently.

"Dad, it's too soon to be even thinking about that," he protested.

Henry snorted. "Baloney. I only knew your mother two weeks when I decided she was the one for me. Took her a little bit longer," he admitted. "But she came around. We were married six months later. So it's not too soon."

Brad shook his head. "I'm not ready for anything that serious."

"Why not?" Henry demanded. And then his voice gentled. "It's been six years, son. And you're still a young man. You could still have that family you always wanted," he said, reaching over to touch Brad's shoulder. "Rachel was a wonderful woman, but she's gone and she wouldn't want you to be alone. You know that."

Brad sighed. "Yeah, I know. But it's hard to let go."

Henry looked down and fiddled with his seat belt. "That's for sure."

Brad glanced over at him. Some of the life had left his father's eyes, and he berated himself for dampening the spark that Sam had so successfully fanned back into life.

"So you think I should pursue this, then?" he asked,

more to refocus his father's thoughts than to prolong the conversation about Sam.

Henry looked up. "Course I do. Wouldn't have brought it up if I hadn't."

"I take it you like Sam."

"What's not to like? She's got spirit, that girl. Did you see the way her eyes shine when she talks about gardening? Does a person good to be around that kind of enthusiasm."

"I know. I always feel good around Sam."

"Well, there you go. Can't believe somebody hasn't grabbed her up by now," Henry said, shaking his head.

"She was married once, Dad. Years ago."

His father's head swiveled toward his son. "She was?"

"Yes. When she was eighteen she married a musician. He just walked out on her one day after only a few months. It sounds like he left her high and dry, to use a cliché. She never saw him again. He died a few years later of a drug overdose."

His father had a few choice words for Sam's former husband before he turned his attention back to Brad. "Well, I bet the right man could get her to take the plunge again."

"Maybe," Brad admitted. "But Sam and I are different in a lot of ways, Dad. Too different to get seriously involved."

His father folded his arms across his chest. "Well, I don't see it. Seems to me like you two get along just fine. And it would do you good to be around somebody spunky like Sam. She'd sure keep life interesting."

Brad chuckled. "I can't argue with you on that."

"You think about it, son," Henry said. "Because those kind don't come along too often. It'd be a real shame to let Sam slip away without ever givin' it a try. I think you'd always regret it."

Later, as Brad prepared for bed, he recalled his father's words. He had a feeling that the older man was right about regrets. And also about his son's interest. Because what Brad had felt tonight for Sam as he said good-night had definitely *not* been friendship. He'd wanted to kiss her. She had looked so appealing, so sexy, so...wonderful, he thought.

And he kept discovering new facets to her personality. She had been absolutely fantastic with his father tonight, drawing him out with her easygoing manner and surprising knowledge of gardening. He had actually seen the spark in his father's eyes rekindle. For that alone he would be eternally grateful to her. And then he'd discovered the assistance she gave her elderly neighbor. Few people would put themselves out like that on an ongoing basis. It was the Golden Rule in action. Then there was her volunteer work on Tuesday nights. He'd never discovered just what that involved, only that she was dedicated to it, but he was beginning to realize that this was the way Sam operated. She did good things but never called attention to them. Whether Sam knew it or not, and whether she went to church or not, she was living the principles of the Christian faith.

Yes, Sam was quite a woman. And yes, he was attracted to her. But he'd promised her friendship, nothing more, and he had a feeling tonight that she'd sensed he had something else in mind. Something that she either hadn't considered before, so she'd been surprised, or considered and rejected. Why else would she have suddenly seemed so nervous and uncomfortable?

Brad hoped that the explanation for her reaction was surprise rather than rejection. Because he decided to follow his father's advice. If he didn't at least give this thing a chance, he'd grow old regretting it, wondering what might have been. And he didn't want to look back in twenty years and say, "What if?"

But how would Sam react to the notion of romance? They'd never actually gone out on a real date. She might even laugh at the suggestion. Then again, she might be willing to give it a try. What did he have to lose by testing the waters? He'd give her a call tomorrow and do just that.

It was Wednesday before Brad actually connected with Sam in person. Until then they communicated by voice mail, which was very handy for some things and very unsatisfactory for others—like asking a woman out on a first date. It wasn't something you left a message about.

Brad had thought the whole thing through and decided that a safe first "date" would be the annual church picnic. It would be a date, but not a "romantic" type date, which was probably a good way to start. *If* Sam was willing. And *if* he ever had a chance to ask her, he thought in exasperation. As her phone rang for the third time he sighed, certain that the answering machine was going to kick in any second. But just then a slightly breathless Sam answered.

"Sam? It's Brad."

"Brad! Finally! A live voice!" Sam sank down into a kitchen chair and pulled off her gloves.

"You sound out of breath."

"Yeah. I was working in my garden between appointments and I forgot to take the portable phone out with me. Oh, if you talk to your dad, tell him I mailed those hollyhock seeds."

"I will. He had a great time Saturday night, by the way."

"I'm glad. I enjoyed his company. He's a very nice man."

"Yeah, he is. So how's everything else going?"

Sam's eyebrows rose in surprise. Brad never called to just chat. He always had a purpose. And she had a feeling he did today, too, but for some reason he was taking the long way around to it. Which was all right with her. It felt good just to hear his voice.

"Oh, busy as always. I've got to go to Chicago next week for a few days, and trying to get everything squared away before I leave is always a hassle."

"You're going out of town?" he asked in surprise.

"Uh-huh. The company is having a regional seminar that I have to attend. It's a pain, but they do this every once in a while. It's only from Sunday night through Thursday."

"Then you'll just be getting back when I'm leaving."

"Where are you going?" Now it was her turn to be surprised.

"Jersey. When mom died Rebecca and I decided to go down together for a few days over the Memorial Day holiday, thinking we'd have some family time with Dad and try to lift his spirits. But thanks to a certain redhead, the trip probably isn't even necessary," he said, and the teasing warmth in his voice made her smile. "Dad's busy as a beaver with his garden, and he's going to meet his buddies again for cards. Frankly, I'd probably cancel except that Rebecca needs a vacation desperately, and if I don't go she probably won't, either."

"Well, I guess I won't see you for a while, then. But I hope you have a good time."

Did he detect a note of disappointment in her voice, he wondered? Or was it only wishful thinking? In any case, he'd have his answer soon enough, because she'd given him a perfect opening for the invitation.

"I guess not. We'll have to make up for lost time when we both get back. In fact, arranging a get-together was one of the reasons I called." He paused long enough to take a deep breath, feeling like a schoolboy about to set up his very first date. "We always have a church picnic the first weekend in June, and I was wondering if you'd like to go. One of the couples in our congregation has a farm about forty-five minutes from St. Louis, and we use it every year for the picnic. It's just a down-home kind of thing, but you might have fun."

Sam stared unseeingly at the refrigerator. Was Brad asking her out on a date? Or did he just think, as a friend, that she might enjoy meeting some of the people in his congregation? She didn't have a clue. Should she ask, she wondered? Part of her wanted to know and part of her didn't. If it wasn't a date, she could continue seeing Brad as a friend without worrying about misleading him. If it was a date, she would need to proceed with extreme caution. Maybe even consider ending their relationship. No, she decided, she didn't want to know. But she *did* want to go.

When Sam didn't respond immediately, Brad forced himself to laugh. "Is the thought of going to a church picnic that shocking? I promise this is not a revival meeting in disguise. There will be no sermon and no hymn singing. It's purely social."

Sam smiled. "I wasn't worried about that. Yes, I'd like to go. It sounds like fun."

"That's great!" he replied, feeling a strange, euphoric elation. "I'll call you when I get back to arrange the details. In the meantime, have a safe trip."

"You, too. And thanks for asking, Brad."

"My pleasure," he said warmly. "See you in a couple of weeks."

"So…are you going to tell me about Sam?" Rebecca asked as they sat on the back porch of their childhood home eating ice cream cones.

Brad had been waiting for this question. He'd seen his sister's speculative look when they arrived earlier in the day and his father immediately asked about Sam. Brad took a leisurely bite of his ice cream before turning to Rebecca.

"What about Sam?" he asked innocently.

Rebecca rolled her large, hazel eyes. "What about Sam?" she mimicked. "Give me a break, big brother. You know exactly what I mean. What's the scoop?"

"You're eating it," he teased, pointing to her double-dip ice cream cone.

She rolled her eyes again. "Spare me the bad puns. I

hope you do better than that in your sermons,'' she said with a grin. ''But don't try to change the subject. Who's Sam?''

''She's my real estate agent,'' Brad replied.

''Oh.'' Rebecca's face fell momentarily, but then she glanced at him suspiciously. ''Then why does Dad know her?''

Brad chuckled. ''You know her, too.''

Rebecca frowned. ''I do?''

''Uh-huh. You met her at Laura's wedding. She was the maid of honor.''

''Oh, yeah! The redhead,'' she said thoughtfully. ''I remember. She seemed really nice. Kind of perky and upbeat.''

''Yep,'' he confirmed, crunching into the cone.

''Brad Matthews, are you going to tell me anything? Or do I have to give Dad the third degree?'' she said in exasperation.

Brad chuckled again. He and Rebecca had a good rapport, an easy give and take, and he always enjoyed teasing her—within limits. But he also knew when to stop. She had a sensitive nature that made her vulnerable to hurt, and he was always mindful of that. ''Okay, what do you want to know?'' he capitulated.

Her longish russet-colored hair, usually secured in a French twist, swung freely tonight as she turned toward him eagerly. When it was loose like this she looked so youthful that it was hard for him to believe she was already thirty-two. ''Everything,'' she said simply.

''Everything is a big order,'' he replied with a smile.

''Okay.'' She frowned in concentration, the evening shadows highlighting the delicate bone structure of her face. ''Why does Dad seem to know her so well?''

''She had dinner with us when he was in town. In fact, she's responsible for that miracle.'' He nodded toward Henry, who was energetically weeding the perennial bed. ''She and Dad had a lively discussion about gardening, and the next thing I knew they were sending seeds back and forth in the mail.'' He shook his head and smiled tenderly, his eyes growing soft. ''She is one amazing woman.''

Rebecca studied his face, her own eyes widening in surprise. ''Why Brad Matthews—I don't believe this!'' she said softly. ''You're in love!''

He turned to stare at her, his smile evaporating. ''I wouldn't go that far,'' he protested.

Rebecca grinned smugly. ''I would. It's written all over your face. Maybe you haven't admitted it yet, but your heart knows the truth. I can see it in your eyes. And I'm happy for you,'' she added softly.

Brad continued to stare at her. He liked Sam. A lot. And he was definitely attracted to her. That's why he wanted to pursue a romantic relationship, see where it led. But he didn't think he was actually in love. At least not yet.

''Don't jump to any conclusions, Rebecca,'' he warned. ''I only met her two months ago.''

She shrugged. ''It doesn't take long if it's the right person.''

''Now how would you know?'' he teased.

Rebecca's hand paused imperceptibly as she raised the ice cream cone to her mouth, then moved on. It was a nuance, but Brad saw it and realized he'd spoken too rashly. She'd always been sensitive about the lack of romance in her life.

''Becka…I'm sorry,'' he said contritely, reverting to her childhood nickname.

She shrugged, but there was a stiffness in her shoulders that hadn't been there before. ''It's okay. You're right. I'm certainly no authority on the subject.''

Brad frowned. He didn't understand why his sister remained unmarried. Even as a child she loved romantic stories, dreamed of having her own home someday, talked of the children she would lovingly raise. But at some point she simply stopped mentioning those things. She rarely dated, as far as he knew, instead devoting all her time to her business. It had never made sense to him.

"Becka." He reached over and touched her arm, but she averted her gaze, and he saw her swallow convulsively. "Becka," he repeated more gently. He was treading on off-limits territory, and he knew it. But he worried about her, and there was rarely an opening like this to discuss the subject. "You have so much love to give," he said carefully. "You should have a husband and kids to share it with. Is there some reason you don't? Would you like to talk about it?"

She glanced down, and there was a long moment of silence. When at last she looked up at him she was smiling, but he saw the glimmer of unshed tears in her eyes. "Thanks for the offer, big brother. I can see why you're such a good minister. But I'm fine. Please don't worry about me. I have a good life."

Brad let it drop. She wasn't going to tell him anything, and that was her choice. But she was such a loving, giving, caring person that it seemed wrong for her to live a solitary life. Despite the challenges and demands of her business, which kept her extremely busy, she had to be lonely. And loneliness, as he well knew, was a heavy cross to bear.

"Well, I'm here if you ever need a sympathetic ear," he said.

She nodded. "I know. And thanks. But we were talking about *your* love life, remember?" She touched his arm gently. "I hope this works out for you, Brad. Rachel was a wonderful woman, but maybe it's time to let go. I'd hate to think of you spending the rest of your life alone. You could still have that family you always wanted, you know? You'd make a great father."

"That may be jumping the gun just a little," he cautioned her. "But I have to admit a family would be really nice," he added with a wistful smile. "It's one of those dreams I gave up when Rachel died. But maybe there's hope after all."

Rebecca squeezed his arm. "I'll keep you in my prayers." She smiled, and for a moment in the growing darkness their eyes connected, further solidifying the brother-sister bond that seemed to grow stronger with the passing years. Then Rebecca dropped her hand and crumpled her napkin, turning to look toward her father. "Well, do you think we should drag Dad in before the mosquitoes finish him off?" she said with a laugh, lightening the mood.

Brad grinned. "Yeah. I don't know how he can see in the dark, anyway."

It wasn't until much later, as he lay in the familiar bed of his childhood, that Brad had a chance to think back on his conversation with Rebecca. Her instincts were probably correct, he suspected. His relationship with Sam seemed to be heading in a serious direction. He wouldn't call it love yet, but the possibility was certainly there. And that left him with a deep feeling of hope and happiness.

At the same time he was troubled by his sister's loneliness. She would deny it, of course, but he knew it was true. And he also knew instinctively that a solitary existence was not the life the Lord had intended for her. She had *chosen* it, he suspected—for reasons she didn't want to share.

As he drifted to sleep, he took a moment to send a request to the Lord. Help Rebecca to find a man deserving of her love, he prayed. And help her overcome whatever it is that holds her back from sharing that love.

When the morning of the picnic finally dawned, Sam felt as if a lifetime had passed since she'd seen Brad. This was their longest separation since Laura's wedding, and she had missed him more than she expected. His mere presence brought a spark to her life, and without him the days seemed dull and lifeless.

Even talking to Laura a couple of times a week at Bible class—which Sam was actually enjoying—or on the phone didn't help much. Besides, when Laura found out that Brad had asked her to the picnic, she began firing questions that Sam either couldn't answer or wouldn't consider. So their conversations were brief and unsatisfactory. Sam would have liked to talk with Laura about her feelings—she desperately needed to talk to somebody!—but she couldn't very well say she had a dilemma without saying why. And she wasn't about to share that secret with anyone.

Sam eyed herself critically in the full-length mirror in her bedroom. Her khaki shorts, which Laura had assured her were perfectly appropriate, were of a modest length, and the short-sleeved madras cotton blouse cinched in with a hemp belt flattered her figure without being flashy. Her hair was sedately French braided and she'd used only a little makeup. She looked very respectable for a church picnic, she thought with a satisfied nod. Now it was just a matter of waiting for Brad to arrive. Except the waiting wasn't easy.

By the time the doorbell rang twenty minutes later, Sam was a bundle of nerves. She still hadn't resolved the "date" issue—was it or wasn't it?—but it sure *felt* like a date. Except that she was never this nervous before an ordinary date. And it only got worse when she opened the door and Brad smiled at her.

"Hi, Sam."

She swallowed. She'd seen Brad in many types of attire, but today was the most casual so far. He had on those well-broken-in and oh-so-nice-fitting jeans he'd worn for their house hunting expedition, and a light blue golf shirt hugged his broad chest. The sleeves called attention to his impressive biceps, convincing her that he must visit a gym on a regular basis. A vee of brown hair was visible at his neck, and her eyes got stuck there just a moment too long as she completed what she hoped had been a discreet perusal.

But not discreet enough, she realized, when her eyes returned to his and he was grinning.

"So...do I pass?"

She blushed, but pretended to misunderstand his meaning. "I'm just glad you dressed down. I was afraid maybe my outfit was too casual."

He gave her a thorough, lazy appraisal that didn't even pretend to be discreet, and her breath caught in her throat. "I'd say you look perfect," he declared huskily, his deep brown eyes smiling into hers. Then he propped one shoulder against the door frame, crossed his arms and gazed directly into her eyes. "I missed you, Sam," he said quietly.

Sam stared at him. He was acting...different...today. Undisguisedly interested. And not just in friendship, either, if she was reading his body language correctly. But she couldn't be sure with Brad. She had plenty of experience picking up signals from men, but Brad wasn't the type of man she typically dated. So maybe she was wrong.

"Um, thanks," she said, finding her voice at last. "Let me just grab my purse and we can get started." She turned away and reached for her shoulder bag on the hall table, willing her heart to behave and her lungs to keep working. Since she wasn't sure exactly what to make of his behavior, the best plan for today was to act the same as always, she decided. Ignore anything that indicated otherwise. Then later, when she was home and alone and more rational, she could analyze the situation logically and consider what to do next. But the first order of business was to get through this day without giving away her own feelings to this perceptive, virile man.

Fortunately for Sam's blood pressure, their conversation during the drive to the farm focused on "catching up." She described some of the houses she'd looked at—and rejected—for him, and he told her about his visit to Jersey. By the time they arrived she felt much more relaxed and in control.

Her first view of the crowd behind the barn, however, made her step falter slightly. Sam didn't mind crowds. She could schmooze and make small talk with the best of them. But this was a different kind of crowd. These were religious people, and this was a church picnic. What on earth would she find to say to them? And why did it seem that everyone was staring at her assessingly in the sudden hush that descended over the group at their appearance?

Brad's eyes narrowed imperceptibly at the group's reaction to their arrival. It had never occurred to him that Sam—as his date—would attract so much attention. But it should have. Most of these people were long-time members of the congregation. They had known and liked Rachel, watched in sympathy as he deeply mourned her loss and then spent the subsequent years alone and bereft. If he chose to bring a woman to a church event, they would correctly assume it was because she was someone special. As a result, she was bound to be scrutinized. Even Sam, with her outgoing personality and self-assurance, was bound to feel some unease in a setting that was both awkward and unnatural for her.

He took her arm reassuringly, and she looked up at him with an uncertain smile. "Time to run the gauntlet, I guess," she tried to joke, but he heard the underlying tension in her voice.

"It won't be that bad," he promised, praying his words were truthful. These were all good people. But they were human, too, and Sam might not fit their image of a suitable date for their minister. *Please, Lord, let them find it in their hearts today to practice Christian charity and make Sam feel welcome,* he silently implored.

Brad stayed close, acutely aware of her nervousness, his hand comfortingly—and possessively—exerting gentle pressure in the small of her back.

They made their way around the small groups clustered near the barn, and Sam tried to relax. She couldn't fault anyone's manners—they were all pleasant. But she sensed a reserve, a withholding of approval, as if they weren't yet sure whether to accept this intruder who had caught their minister's eye—and maybe his heart. Sam supposed she couldn't blame them. Compared to Brad's first wife, she was sure she fell short. Her spirits took a nosedive, and she suddenly wished that this picnic, which she had looked forward to so eagerly, was ending instead of just beginning.

As they made their way toward two older women, Brad leaned down. "So how are you doing?" he asked in a low voice.

Not so good, she thought. But she couldn't very well say that. "Okay," she replied. "They all seem nice."

The two women looked at her pleasantly when they approached, and Sam summoned up a smile.

"Rose, Margaret, I'd like you to meet Sam Reynolds. Sam, this is Margaret Warren and Rose Davies. Rose is our wonderful organist. Her playing always inspires me to sing," he said, giving Sam a conspiratorial wink over their heads. Sam stifled a smile at Rose's pained expression, remembering Brad's comment at Laura's wedding about his lack of singing ability.

"It's very nice to meet you both," Sam said.

"Well, we're certainly glad you could make it, my dear," said Rose. "Do you by any chance sing? We're always looking for good voices for the choir." She emphasized the word good, and Sam tried not to grin, relaxing for the first time.

"I'm afraid I'm not much in the voice department," Sam admitted. "I'm more the I - like - to - sing - in - the - shower - but - you'd - need - earplugs - if - I - sang - in - public type."

"Well, I'm sure you have many other talents," Rose declared, reaching over to pat her arm reassuringly. "And I always think it's good when we can recognize our own limitations. For example, if you really can't sing, then it's better to just not sing. Don't you think so, Reverend?"

Brad looked at her solemnly. "Oh, absolutely."

Sam choked back a laugh at the look of defeat on Rose's

face, coughing to camouflage her smile. "Let's get you some lemonade, Sam," Brad said solicitously, his eyes twinkling as he took her arm. "Excuse us, ladies."

As soon as they were out of earshot, Sam laughed and shook her head. "You're awful, do you know that?"

"Why?" Brad asked innocently as he poured her a cup of lemonade.

"As if you don't know," she accused.

Now it was Brad's turn to chuckle. "Poor Rose. I guess I do give her a hard time. I ought to just shut up and make her life easier, but I really do like to sing. I have toned it down, though. So I don't think she minds quite as much."

"Sam! Brad!"

They turned in unison to see Laura heading their way, waving two pieces of paper with identical numbers on them, a burlap sack draped over her arm. "Will you two help me out? I'm supposed to be organizing the games, but nobody seems to want to be the first to sign up. So I put you down for the three-legged race. Do you mind? I think once I have a couple of names down, it will break the ice."

Sam eyed her doubtfully. "The three-legged race?"

"Don't worry. It's a piece of cake," Laura assured her. "We're going to start in five minutes."

"Laura, I'm not the athletic type," Sam protested.

"But you don't have to be. It's a short race. Brad, talk her into it, will you, while I try to round up a few more people?" Laura implored over her shoulder as she dashed off to recruit two more victims.

Sam looked up at Brad, who seemed to be taking Laura's strong-arming in stride. "I don't know about this. What do you think?" she asked with trepidation.

He smiled and shrugged. "I'm game if you are."

Sam bit her lip. She'd heard of three-legged races, though she'd never seen one, and she assumed that there was some physical proximity involved. She had a sudden suspicion that Laura had set them up, but her friend had long since made herself scarce. Purposely, no doubt, Sam thought grimly.

"So what do you think?" Brad asked, pulling her back to the matter at hand.

She frowned. If Brad could make her heart go into triple time with just a look, what would it do to her metabolism to actually be physically touching him? But it was just a race, an impersonal thing, in front of his congregation. Nothing could possibly happen. In fact, it was a safe context in which to get close to him. Maybe she ought to enjoy it. The opportunity might never come again.

"All right," she capitulated. "But I wasn't kidding when I said I'm not the athletic type. If you want to win, I'd suggest you find another partner."

"I'll take my chances with you," Brad told her with a smile. "Turn around so I can pin your number on."

Sam did as instructed, but her fingers seemed to have a mind of their own when it was her turn to do the pinning. She'd never quite realized how broad his shoulders were, she thought, as she fumbled with the uncooperative piece of paper. And was it her imagination, or were the two of them once more drawing speculative glances from his congregation?

"Is it on?" he asked over his shoulder.

It was slightly crooked, but Sam didn't trust herself to touch him anymore when the urge to run her hands over his back was so strong, despite the watchful eyes she felt riveted on her back. "Yes."

"Okay, step in," he said, leaning down to hold the burlap bag open. "Try your left leg."

"What?" she asked blankly.

He looked up with a grin. "We each have to put one leg in the sack," he explained patiently.

She swallowed convulsively at the unbidden image that flashed across her mind. But judging by his matter-of-fact expression, Brad was oblivious to the double entendre.

With a determined effort she tried to stifle her overactive imagination as she silently followed his instructions.

He straightened up and put his leg in beside hers, and the next thing she knew he slipped his right arm around her waist and pulled her close, until they were touching along the entire length of their bodies, from ankle to shoulder. Sam drew in her breath sharply, vowing to seek revenge on her so-called friend Laura for making her endure this sweet agony.

"Can you hold on to this excess burlap?" Brad asked, apparently unaware of her distress and seemingly unmoved by their proximity. So much for her concern about his interest level, she thought wryly.

Sam reached down to take hold of the fabric, noting for the first time that his left hand was ringless. When had that happened, she wondered?

"Maybe we should practice a little," Brad said easily. "I know there's a trick to this. You have to be in sync, establish a rhythm, I think. You want to try it?" he asked.

She was still staring at his bare left hand, trying to comprehend the significance, and it took a moment for his words to penetrate her overloaded sensory circuits. "Sure. Why not?" she replied helplessly, not at all certain that her legs would cooperate.

He grinned and gave her a squeeze that sent a hot wave shooting through her entire body. "Okay. Let's give it a whirl."

As it turned out, just staying upright demanded her full and undivided attention, and hormones quickly gave way to hilarity as they stumbled around awkwardly, giggling like teenagers at their uneven gait. She even momentarily forgot about their audience.

"Hey, you two, no fair!" Laura called as she passed. "If you practice ahead of time you'll have an advantage."

"I don't think you have to worry," Brad assured her as they dissolved into laughter after another misstep.

His words proved prophetic. They made a good start

when the gun went off a couple of minutes later, but in the heat of the race Sam apparently pulled too hard on the edge of the canvas bag she was holding. The next thing she knew she lost her footing, and she clutched at Brad to regain her balance. Unfortunately, he was in no better shape, and suddenly they both pitched forward. As they fell Brad twisted toward Sam and yanked her against his chest, bringing her down on top of him to cushion her impact.

For a moment after they hit the ground, neither of them moved. Sam was sprawled over Brad's firm body, her head pressed to his shoulder, his arms around her protectively. It took her only a moment to decide that she was just shaken, not hurt. But the trembling of relief she felt quickly turned to another kind of trembling as her mind—and body—absorbed their intimate position. Her heart seemed to stop, then race on, and her breathing became erratic as a surge of longing swept over her. She didn't want to move. Not now. Not ever. It felt so good in his arms!

But they couldn't stay like this. Reason told her that, even while her heart directed her otherwise. What would people think? They had to get up before his congregation suffered a collective heart attack.

Except that Brad hadn't moved, she suddenly realized with a frown. Maybe he'd struck his head or something, she thought in panic. But at least he was still breathing. And she could hear the hard, uneven thudding of his heart against her ear.

Quickly she backed off, bracing her hands on either side of his head so she could look down at him.

It was immediately obvious that Brad wasn't unconscious. Not even close. In fact, the ardent light in his brown eyes made her realize that physical injury was the *last* thing on his mind.

"Are you hurt?" she whispered, her eyes locked on his. His arms molded her even more firmly against him and his hands stroked her back ever so slightly. "No. Are you?"

Mutely she shook her head, her breath catching in her throat as his hands moved to frame her face, his thumbs gently caressing her cheeks. Sam stared at him in shock at the blatant intimacy of his touch.

Only a few seconds passed during the entire mishap. And Sam knew they'd only fallen a short distance and spoken barely half a dozen words. But she also knew that in that brief interlude they'd traveled to a whole new world. Because one thing was now very clear. The original ground rules for their relationship might have been based on friendship. But the rules had just changed.

Chapter Six

"**H**ey, you two, are you okay?"

Sam was so mesmerized by the compelling intensity of Brad's eyes that it took a moment for Laura's concerned voice to register. But when it did, she also became aware once again of her suggestive sprawl on top of the hard planes of Brad's body. Her cheeks flamed in embarrassment, and she rolled sideways, frantically trying to untangle her leg from the burlap sack. When it was finally free, she scrambled to her feet, studiously avoiding Brad's eyes as he stood up beside her and brushed himself off.

"I'm fine," she said breathlessly. "Just a little shaken up."

"Brad?" Laura turned to him, and Sam ventured a glance in his direction. He flexed his shoulder gingerly, and she saw a flicker of pain cross his face, but his words didn't reflect that momentary flash of discomfort.

"A few minor bruises, I think. Nothing serious," he replied with an easy smile. He didn't seem at all embarrassed by their position of moments before, Sam noted in surprise.

Relief washed across Laura's features. "Thank goodness! Listen, you guys have been good sports, but why don't you find a cool spot and just be spectators for a while? I think you've had enough games for today.''

Brad's clear, direct eyes locked on Sam's and refused to let go. "Yeah. I'd say our games are over," he replied quietly.

Sam swallowed convulsively. The man obviously wasn't talking about three-legged races.

Laura looked from one to the other, a smug expression on her face, and decided that three was a crowd. "Well, I'll talk to you two later," she said, tossing the words over her shoulder as she turned to make a hasty exit.

When she faced forward again she ran squarely into Nick, who steadied her with two firm hands on her shoulders.

"Why do I have a feeling you're up to some matchmaking tricks?" he admonished her with mock sternness. Then his mouth quirked up into a smile and he leaned down, his lips close to her ear. "Your ploy was a little obvious," he said in an undertone.

She grinned impishly and shrugged. "It worked, didn't it?"

He laughed and draped an arm around her shoulders. "It sure looks that way," he agreed, glancing back at Sam and Brad, who were still staring at each other, transfixed. Then he shook his head. "I would never have believed it. Maybe I should go over and rescue Brad before it's too late," he said, making a halfhearted attempt to turn back.

Laura grabbed his arm. "Don't you dare!" she said, tugging him in the opposite direction. "Besides, it's too late, anyway," she added with a smug smile.

Sam was thinking the same thing as she stared at Brad, the flame in his eyes speaking more eloquently than words of his desires. She tried to disguise her own feelings, but she knew she was failing miserably. The attraction was almost palpable, and neither could deny it.

''Sam?'' Brad's voice was gentle, his gaze sharp and probing.

She licked her lips, which had suddenly gone dry, and his eyes released hers as they dropped to her mouth. Which did nothing at all to slow her metabolism. She wasn't ready to deal with this yet, she thought in desperation. At least not this level of intensity. She had to calm down, think rationally. And she sure wasn't going to be able to do that with Brad standing just inches away.

''I…I think I'll find the ladies' room,'' she stammered breathlessly. ''Will you excuse me for a couple of minutes?''

Before he could respond, she fled toward the house, grabbing her purse en route.

Brad watched her flight, realizing that was exactly what it was. For all her sophistication and experience with men, she was thrown by his overtures. Thrown, but not unreceptive, he reminded himself, recalling how his own desire had been mirrored in her eyes. But for some reason she was running scared.

He frowned as she disappeared into the house. Had he come on too strong, he wondered, revealing his feelings too soon and too intensely? But he was an honest man, and game playing wasn't his sport. He figured it was better to lay his cards on the table, be up-front. But Sam might be used to men who did play games. If so, his direct, open approach could have thrown her.

She was probably surprised, too. After all, he himself had only recently come to grips with the fact that despite their differences, a relationship was worth exploring. Maybe she hadn't come to that realization yet. The attraction was there, certainly; the air between them had practically sizzled in the moments following their fall. But rationally she might still be hung up on their differences.

His congregation certainly seemed to be, he mused, glancing around at the group. He'd sensed their reserve, and he was sure Sam had as well. She wasn't a stereotypical minister's date, that was clear. And maybe, given their obvious differences, he was wrong to think they could build a relationship. Maybe his life-style as a minister wouldn't suit Sam in the long run. Then again, maybe it would. And despite the vibes he was picking up from his congregation, his heart told him that he should pursue this attraction, see where it led. Sam didn't seem as certain as he was about that, but he felt confident that once they talked things through, he could convince her to give it a try.

Yes, a nice long talk was exactly what they needed, he thought, speculatively eyeing the door where Sam had disappeared. Folding his arms across his chest, he leaned against a convenient tree, determined to wait her out. He wasn't sure he agreed with Rebecca about being in love. But now that she'd voiced that observation, he was giving it a lot of thought. Maybe he wasn't in love yet. But he knew with certainty that there was a good possibility he could be.

Once Sam reached the privacy of the bathroom, she closed the door and sagged against it. Things were moving *way* too fast. She'd suspected that Brad might consider this a real date. What she hadn't suspected was the depth of his attraction. Okay, so maybe she'd had a *few* clues, she admitted. Like the night he took her home after dinner with his father, when she'd thought he wanted to kiss her. She'd attributed the look in his eyes then to gratitude. Talk about a wrong call! Considering all the men she'd dated she should be an expert at picking up signals. So why had she been so far off the mark with Brad?

The answer was obvious, of course—she cared too much, and she didn't *want* to pick up his signals. Because she'd known all along that if his feelings ever deepened beyond friendship, she'd have to end their relationship. To do otherwise would be misleading and grossly unfair to him.

Well, she couldn't ignore the signals anymore, she admitted resignedly. Brad had made it clear that he wanted more than friendship. And unfortunately that was all she could offer, even if her heart was willing to give more. Much more.

Sam drew a deep, shaky breath and leaned over to inspect her face in the mirror. She *looked* pretty much the same. A little pale, maybe, although her makeup disguised most of that. But she sure didn't *feel* the same. Earlier she had been filled with a tingling sense of anticipation and happiness as she looked forward to a day in Brad's company. Now she was overwhelmed by sadness and a feeling of hopelessness as she realized that it was the last such day they would have together.

Her eyes filled with tears, but she brushed them away angrily. She had no one but herself to blame for this mess. If she'd had the courage to deal with her own deepening feelings sooner, she wouldn't be in this position now. She'd already waited too long, and it would only get worse if she let more time pass.

Sam smoothed back her hair and straightened her shoulders. She'd survived without Brad before, she told herself resolutely. She could again. The difference, of course, was that before she could only *imagine* what she was missing. Now she *knew*. Because she'd had a tantalizing taste of what it was like to be cared for by a decent, sensitive, sincere—and passionate—man.

The passionate part was what really threw her. Up until a few minutes ago, Sam had thought of Brad as a very disciplined, in-control person. But the glimpse of fire she'd just seen in his eyes told her there was a whole other, exciting facet to this man. And it was a facet she yearned to explore. In fact, the very thought of doing so sent shafts of desire ricocheting through her. But that was not in the cards. Brad was a fine man who deserved a woman equally fine and, unfortunately, she didn't qualify.

As if to reinforce her self-assessment, the voices of two passing women suddenly penetrated the door.

"...so surprised when they walked in."

"She's nothing like Rachel, is she?"

The other woman gave a humorless laugh. "That's putting it mildly! Whatever do you think he saw..."

The voices faded away.

Sam gritted her teeth and took a deep breath, ruthlessly blinking back her tears. She had to pull herself together, make it through this day. And later, when they got back to her condo, she'd find a way to tell Brad that she couldn't see him anymore. She didn't have a clue yet just how she was going to do that, or what she was going to say, but maybe something would come to her. In the meantime, the easiest way to survive the day was to make sure that she and Brad were never alone.

Much to Brad's consternation, Sam executed her plan quite successfully. He finally admitted defeat, watching her from a distance as she laughed and chatted with members of his congregation, seemingly lighthearted and happy. But he knew her well enough to realize that the real Sam was hiding behind a facade. Her eyes were a little too bright, her smile a little too forced. And she was avoiding him like the plague.

Clearly, he wasn't going to have an opportunity to talk with her at the picnic, he realized, watching her disappear into the barn several hundred feet away with Laura and a few other women to retrieve the food. But he consoled himself with the knowledge that he'd have her all to himself on the drive home. And they *were* going to talk then.

Brad's musings were interrupted by several members of his congregation, who wanted to discuss plans for an upcoming meeting, and he didn't turn back to the barn until a startled voice drew everyone's attention.

"Watch out everybody! A bee's nest just fell by the door!"

A murmur of alarm ran through the crowd, which

moved as one away from the barn, and Brad's eyes swept the throng, searching for Sam. Near the food table he spotted Laura and the other women who'd been with her, but there was no sign of Sam. And she was easy to find in a crowd, with her striking red hair. Was she still inside? And if so, had she heard the warning? he wondered in alarm. A sudden surge of adrenaline propelled him toward the door, just as she stepped out balancing a tray holding two cakes.

"Sam! Get back inside!" he yelled desperately, increasing his speed to a flat-out run.

She gave him a puzzled look and stopped. "What?" she called.

"Get back—" It was too late. She was directly on top of the swarm, and her puzzled tone suddenly changed to a startled cry of pain as the first few bees simultaneously pierced her tender flesh. She dropped the tray and glanced down, trying to wave the bees away. The sweet frosting on the ground diverted the attention of most of the swarm. But a few bees preferred Sam to the cake. She panicked and began to run, attempting to elude them.

Brad reached her in seconds, just as she began to stumble. He steadied her with one hand, waving away the remaining bees with the other. He felt a sharp sting or two on his hand, but was almost oblivious to the discomfort, aware only of Sam's gasps of fear and pain as she writhed in his grasp.

By the time the last bee was banished, Sam's complexion was as white as the coconut frosting on the cakes she had carried, and she was shaking badly. There was a sting just above her lip, another over her left eye, and both were already swelling ominously.

Linda Perkins, the owner of the farm, came up behind Brad, her face a mask of concern. "Let's get her inside," she said, worriedly. "Sandy's here and she can help."

Brad turned toward the physician, sending a "thank

you" heavenward that her hectic schedule had allowed her to attend today's picnic.

"I sent John for my bag in the car," she said crisply as she stepped forward, her eyes on Sam's face. "Sam, are you allergic to bee stings?" she asked.

Sam shook her head jerkily.

Sandy gave the other woman a quick but thorough look. "Brad, do you think you could carry her inside? She's got a lot of stings on her ankle, and she seems too shaky to walk."

Brad's jaw tightened, his own face almost as colorless as Sam's. "Yeah." He put one arm around her shoulders, the other under her knees, and lifted her in one smooth motion, cradling her in his arms. His gut wrenched as she clung to him and whimpered softly, her arms around his neck, her face buried in his chest. He could feel the tremors that ran through her body, and he lengthened his stride, desperate to relieve her misery as soon as possible.

Linda led them to the guest room, and Brad gently deposited Sam on the bed. Her pain-filled eyes stared up at him helplessly, and his gut clenched as he tenderly brushed some stray strands of hair off her face.

"Brad, she may need to undress so I can assess the damage," Sandy said. "You'd better wait outside."

He didn't want to leave her. Not when she looked so hurt and vulnerable. But she was in good hands. He couldn't add anything except moral support, and Laura, who had slipped in behind him, could provide that. He nodded curtly. "I'll be right outside if you need me."

Brad reluctantly left the room, gently closing the door behind him, then began to pace. He didn't even notice when Nick joined him until the other man laid a hand on his shoulder, causing him to flinch.

Nick frowned. "Are you okay?"

Brad glanced at Nick and shook his head dismissively. "I guess I bruised my shoulder when I fell. It's nothing. I'm more worried about Sam."

Just then the door opened, and as Laura slipped out both men turned to her questioningly.

Seeing the tense line of Brad's jaw, she reached out to touch his arm reassuringly. "She'll be okay," Laura said quickly. "She's got about a dozen stings, enough to be very uncomfortable but not enough to be dangerous."

Brad raked his fingers through his hair and expelled a long breath. "Thank God!"

"It looks like Sam wasn't the only victim," Laura noted with a frown, her eyes on his hand.

He glanced down. He had two welts on the back of one hand, but he only vaguely remembered the sharp stings. They were throbbing now, he realized. But compared to what Sam must be experiencing—he waved Laura's concern aside. "I'm fine. Listen, would you two go out and try to keep the party going? I know Sam would feel awful if this incident disrupted the picnic any more than it has already. I'd do it myself, but I'd rather stick close here."

"Sure," Nick said. "Come on, Laura."

"Maybe I should stay in case Sam…"

"Come on, Laura," Nick repeated more insistently. "Brad will be here if she needs anything," he added meaningfully.

"Oh. Right. Well, I'm sure you'll want to take Sam home after this, Brad, so just tell her I'll call tomorrow, will you?"

"Okay."

Brad watched them leave and then resumed his position outside the door. Another ten interminable minutes passed before Sandy appeared, and by then Brad was on the verge of going in, invited or not. He was in no mood for small talk when she appeared at the door.

"Well?" he said tensely, without preamble.

Sandy smiled. "Relax, Brad. She's okay. Uncomfortable, but okay."

Brad felt the tendons in his back and neck loosen

slightly, and the rigid line of his shoulders relaxed as he closed his eyes. "Can I take her home now?"

"Yes. She's not going to feel too hot, though. I've already told her what she needs to do, but I'm not sure she took it all in, so let me repeat it for you—aspirin every four hours as needed, put this on the stings," she handed him a bottle of lotion donated by Linda, "and keep an ice pack on the swelling on her ankle. She has multiple stings in very close proximity there, which is going to make walking difficult for a couple of days. After that, the swelling and redness will dissipate. In a week she'll hardly even know this happened."

"Can I go in now?" he asked.

"Sure. She's decent. And since I know I'm leaving her in good hands, I think I'll head outside and have some food before it's all gone," she said with a wink.

Brad waited until Sandy disappeared down the hall, then took a deep, steadying breath before he turned the knob and walked inside.

Sam was sitting on the edge of the bed, holding an ice pack, her pale face and the lines of strain around her eyes providing silent but eloquent evidence of her pain. She gave him a wan smile, and he crossed the room in three strides, dropping to one knee in front of her.

"I guess I look a mess, huh?" she said, a tremor in her voice.

He swallowed convulsively. "You look just fine to me," he replied sincerely, his own voice husky. Objectively speaking, however, her words were more accurate than his. The welts near her upper lip and above her eye were an angry red, but as he surveyed the rest of the damage, he realized her right hand and left ankle had taken the brunt of the attack. Two of her fingers were swollen, and her ankle was puffy and covered with crimson welts.

When his gaze traveled back to her face, he saw the glint of unshed tears in her eyes, and his throat constricted painfully. He wanted to pull her close, to hug away all of her hurt, but he knew that in this case physical proximity would probably exacerbate the pain. So he refrained, contenting himself by running a gentle finger down one cheek.

"Oh, honey, I'm so sorry," he said, his eyes anguished.

"It's not your fault," she replied, her voice still unsteady. "Listen, Brad, I know this is a big event for your church, and everyone expects you to attend. I can just rest here until you're ready to leave." At least the attack gave her an excuse to skip out on the rest of the event, she thought, trying to look on the bright side.

He stared at her. Did she really think he'd let her lie here and suffer while he was out socializing? "Sam, I'm taking you home right now," he said, in a tone that brooked no argument.

"But I don't want to ruin your day," she protested.

Brad shook his head in amazement. Despite her pain she was worried about ruining *his* day.

"You have *not* ruined my day," he said firmly. Before she could reply, he stood up and held out his hand. "Can you make it to the car, or do you want me to carry you?" he asked.

Sam tried to smile again, but the effort seemed to be too great, and she only managed a slight grimace. "The next thing we'll be dealing with is a back injury if you have to keep lugging me around. I think you did that once today already."

Sam had very little recollection of the recent disaster. She remembered coming out of the barn, and Brad's frantic waving. Then everything was shrouded in a cloud of sharp, stinging pain that had washed over her in wave after wave. She did have a vague memory, though, of being swept into Brad's arms, followed by a floating sensation as he carried her into the house.

"I don't mind doing it again," he told her with a smile.

"Thanks. But I think I can manage." She took his hand and he eased her up, noting the way she bit her lip to keep from crying out.

"Sam, I—"

"I'm okay, Brad," she said. "Just…give me a minute."

He watched her silently as she took several deep breaths, and the fact that she wouldn't meet his eyes convinced him that she was struggling to mask her pain before she looked at him. When at last their gazes met, it wasn't her eyes that gave her away, but the tight, narrow line of her mouth and her deeply knit brow.

"Okay. I'm ready."

Brad thought about protesting. She didn't have to put up a strong front for him. But at this point he didn't think she could handle an argument. He suspected it was requiring all of her energy and willpower just to remain upright. So he put his arm around her waist for support, and they slowly made their way out the front door, avoiding the crowd in the back. Sam leaned heavily on him the whole way, favoring her injured ankle.

By the time they reached the car and she carefully eased herself into the front seat, she was breathing heavily and the lines in her forehead were etched even deeper.

"Listen, Sam, maybe I should get Sandy again," Brad said worriedly.

"No. I'm all right."

Her answer didn't surprise him, but neither did it convince him. However, Sandy *had* assured him that her condition wasn't serious, just uncomfortable. He figured the best thing he could do was get her home as quickly as possible.

Sam didn't speak at all during the drive back into the city. Brad couldn't tell if she was asleep or just trying to conserve her strength. But in either case, he didn't bother her. He had some thinking to do, anyway. Because even though he'd intended this to be a "date," a turning point in their relationship, a lot more had happened than even he'd expected.

First, there was his intense, purely physical response when she'd fallen on top of him and he'd felt her soft, supple curves molded against his body. That physical response, more than the fall, was what had taken his breath away.

Then there was his emotional reaction to her distress. When he saw her engulfed in that swarm of bees... His stomach turned over and his jaw clenched at the memory. Her startled cries of pain would haunt him for a long time. The fear he experienced, his sheer terror at the threat to her physical safety, went far beyond simple empathy.

Even now, he felt as if his heart was being squeezed in a vise when he looked at her. She seemed so fragile and defenseless, and the fierce surge of protectiveness that had engulfed him when he'd carried her into the house earlier returned with renewed intensity. He desperately wanted to ease her hurt and simply take care of her.

It was that sense of desperation that made him realize how deeply his feelings ran. It surprised him, and it had clearly surprised Sam. Yet her feelings matched his, he knew. He'd seen the fire smoldering in her eyes when they'd stared at each other after they'd fallen, their faces only inches apart. But she was running scared.

Brad shook his head ruefully. The day had certainly not turned out the way he'd expected. If this was a first date, they were not off to an auspicious beginning. Between the tumble and the bee incident, *disaster* might be a better term than *date*. But he'd learned a lot about himself and Sam.

He glanced over at her again, wanting to talk this thing through, knowing she wasn't up to a heavy discussion today. But as soon as she was feeling more like herself, he intended to find out why she was so frightened of the idea of a romantic involvement. And then he intended to put those fears to rest. Because after today, he knew beyond a shadow of a doubt that their days of being ''just friends'' were over.

''Sam?'' he touched her shoulder gently, and her eyelids flickered open. ''We're home.''

Sam wasn't really asleep. She'd been drifting in a sort of self-induced trance as she tried to shut out the pain that seemed to radiate through her hand and ankle. She'd succeeded marginally, managing to reduce the pain to a dull throb, but the thought of moving was extremely unappealing. Unfortunately, however, she couldn't very well stay in the car.

"Okay," she mumbled.

"Stay put till I come around," Brad said.

Sam didn't argue. She'd stay here all night if he would let her. But a moment later her door swung open and he leaned down, his face a mask of concern.

"Do you feel any better?" he asked.

"Well, the stinging isn't quite so bad," she said. Thankfully, that had subsided somewhat.

"I think I can read between the lines on that answer," he said grimly. "And the offer of a lift—literally—is still open."

She managed a shaky smile. "Thanks. But what would the neighbors say?"

"Oh, I have a feeling Mrs. Johnson would approve. After all, she thinks I'm your young man." He tilted his head and gave her a crooked grin. "Come to think of it, maybe she needs her vision checked. *Young* is hardly an accurate description."

"It's all relative," Sam replied with a faint smile. "Remember, she's eighty-five."

"You have a point," he admitted. Brad knew Sam was attempting to psyche herself up for the walk to her condo, and he gave her the time she needed.

"Brad?"

"Mmm-hmm?"

"I'm sorry about today. This really messed up your plans."

She didn't know the half of it, he thought. But he'd make up for lost time later. "Don't worry, Sam. There will be other picnics."

She took a deep breath. "Okay, we might as well go in."

"How can I help?"

"If you could hold this," she said, handing him the ice pack, "and just let me lean on you when I get out, I think I'll be fine."

Sam bit her lip as she struggled out of the car, then leaned against the door for support. Brad moved beside her and slipped his arm around her waist, and they made their way slowly up the steps and down the walkway.

By the time they reached her front door, there was a thin film of perspiration on her upper lip. As she fumbled for her key, the look of exhaustion and strain on her features convinced Brad that she needed to lie down as soon as possible.

When Sam at last withdrew the key, Brad took it from her trembling fingers, fitted it into the lock and pushed the door open. Then he guided her inside and toward the couch, where he eased her gently onto the cushions. As she sank down, she expelled a shaky breath and closed her eyes, letting her head drop back wearily.

"I'll refill the ice pack," Brad said quietly.

He completed the task as quickly as possible and then sat down beside her, careful to jostle the cushions as little as possible. He reached for her uninjured hand and she opened her eyes, giving him a tired smile.

"I bet you're sorry you asked me to that picnic," she said ruefully.

"No. Just sorry about everything that happened." Well, not quite everything, he corrected himself silently. But certainly the bee incident.

She glanced at her watch and frowned. "I guess it's too late for you to go back, isn't it?"

Brad looked at her steadily. He'd already thought this through, and he was ready to argue the point if necessary. Maybe his congregation wouldn't approve. Maybe what he was about to suggest flew in the face of the propriety he always so carefully observed. But at the moment he cared more about Sam than propriety. Besides, abandoning her, alone and in pain, just seemed wrong. "Sam, I have no intention of leaving here until tomorrow," he informed her, his voice firm.

She stared at him. "What do you mean?"

Brad knew that Sam wasn't seriously ill or injured. But neither was she in any shape to function on her own. She could hardly walk. And he didn't intend for her to try, at least for tonight. "I'm staying until morning," he replied.

"But...why?" she asked in bewildered surprise.

"Because I want to. Because you're in no condition to be left alone." Because I care about you more than you're willing to acknowledge, he added silently.

"But...you can't," she said in panic, instinctively sensing danger. It would *not* be a good idea to have Brad in her condo all night. "I'll be fine," she assured him.

He'd expected a protest. He'd also decided that the subject was not open for discussion. "Look, Sam," he said, rubbing his thumb gently over the back of her hand. "Let's not make a big deal out of this, okay? I can't just walk out and leave you in pain to fend for yourself."

Sam's throat contracted convulsively at the tenderness in his voice. No man had ever cared for her this much before. She tried not to cry but she was powerless to stop her reaction.

Brad had expected resistance. Instead, he watched her face crumple, saw the tears fill her eyes and silently spill onto her cheeks, heard the muffled sob. Throwing aside his resolution to keep his distance until she was fully recovered, he pulled her into his arms and pressed her fiercely against his chest, stroking her back with one hand as his other gently caressed her nape.

"It's okay, Sam," he murmured, his lips in her hair. "Let it out. You deserve a good cry after the day you've had."

Sam clung to his shirt, her fists balling the fabric, as she struggled for control. She didn't want to cry. Crying never solved anything or made a hurt go away. But the combined emotional and physical trauma were no match for her shaky control. She couldn't stop the tears, so she simply tried to stifle the sobs as much as possible.

Brad just held her, rocking her gently in his arms and murmuring soothing words, his cheek against her hair, until her sobs subsided and she rested quietly against him.

Sam would have liked to stay right where she was indefinitely, drawing comfort from the strength and compassion of Brad's arms, but at last she drew a shaky breath and ventured a glance at him. "Sorry about that," she apologized with a tremulous, watery smile. "I don't usually cry."

"You had good reason," he replied, stroking her cheek gently with the back of his knuckles.

Sam's breath caught in her throat at his touch and at the tender caring in his unguarded eyes. She couldn't let him stay tonight, she told herself, much as she'd like to. It would only complicate things even more.

"Brad, about tonight…"

"Sam. Let it rest, okay? For me."

When he put it like that, how could she refuse him? she thought helplessly. Besides, she simply didn't have the strength to argue. She'd just have to deal with the consequences tomorrow, she thought, capitulating with a sigh. "I think there's some microwave stuff in the freezer. And there's some extra bedding in the closet in the office. If you need to—"

"Sam," he said, his voice gentle but firm. "Stop worrying. You don't have to play hostess. I'll be fine. I'm used to coping on my own. And I'm a master at microwave. In fact, why don't I fix us both something to eat?"

She shook her head wearily. "Thanks. But I think I'll pass. To be honest, all I want to do is lie down and try to sleep."

Brad didn't argue. Rest would probably be better for her

tonight than food, anyway. "Okay." He stood up and then reached for her, carefully drawing her to her feet. "Come on, let's get you to the bedroom," he said as he put his arm around her waist.

At any other time that comment would have set a thousand butterflies loose in her stomach and inspired all sorts of romantic fantasies. But the stings were beginning to throb with renewed intensity, and her sole priority was the oblivion of sleep, which would bring welcome relief from her misery.

Brad gave her bedroom a cursory glance as they entered. Like the living room, it featured ultramodern decor. So modern, in fact, that it was almost stark, he realized, the predominant color a cool blue. Not at all the sort of boudoir he'd imagined for Sam, he thought in surprise. This sterile, monotone room definitely did not seem designed to induce romance.

Sam's quiet sigh effectively refocused his attention on the woman beside him, and he reined in his wayward thoughts as he guided her to the bed. She sank down carefully, and he squatted in front of her, his concerned eyes searching her wan face.

"I'll get some water and aspirin, and I'll bring in the lotion that Linda sent," he said gently.

"Thanks."

When he returned, he found Sam struggling with her hair, hampered by two swollen fingers that rendered her right hand almost useless.

Brad deposited the collected items on the nightstand and sat down beside her. "Can I help?"

Sam sighed in frustration. "If I don't unbraid my hair before I go to sleep it will be too tangled to even get a comb through tomorrow," she said, her voice quavering. "But my fingers aren't working right."

"Then let me do it for you," he said, grasping her shoulders and gently angling her away from him. Brad eyed the tucked-under French braid with a frown. He had very little experience with women's hairstyles. Rachel had favored a short, simple cut, and he didn't have a clue where to begin with this complicated style.

"Okay, I give up," he said at last. "Where are the pins?"

"Down at the bottom," Sam replied, her voice muffled as she bent her head.

There was something endearing about Sam's trustingly submissive posture, and an unexpected surge of desire jolted through Brad as he looked at the vulnerable and enticing expanse of skin that was exposed at her nape. Although a sharply indrawn breath was the only auditory evidence of his acute physical reaction, Sam picked up on it.

"Brad?" Her voice was uncertain, and Brad forced himself to focus on the task at hand. Now was *not* the time to wonder how that patch of creamy skin would feel against his lips, he told himself sharply.

"Just trying to figure out where to start," he said, hoping his voice sounded more in control than he felt.

"I think I got one pin partly out," she volunteered, her voice still hesitant.

He scanned her hair and finally saw the pin in question. "You're right," he said, reaching over to gently extract it. Then he took a deep breath, trying to slow the pounding of his heart, and with unsteady fingers began to probe the soft hair at the base of her head for the elusive pins. Gradually he located them, carefully withdrawing them one by one until the bottom of the braid hung free.

"I think that's it," he said at last, hoping his voice didn't betray his elevated hormone level. The intimate nature of his task had set his heart pounding, and try as he might, he couldn't stop his imagination from creating a picture of what this scene might mean in another context.

Sam reached around with her good hand and made an unsuccessful attempt to loosen the braid, but Brad stilled her uncooperative fingers with his own.

"I started the job. I might as well finish it," he said, his voice oddly hoarse.

Sam hesitated momentarily. The feel of his hands in her hair was sending electric currents through her body, overriding the pain of the stings, and a tightly wound coil of tension began to pulsate deep within her. The intimate nature of the act wasn't lost on her, either, despite her injuries. It was sweet agony to sit passively and let this man run his fingers through her hair when what she really wanted to do was turn in his arms and taste his kisses. The struggle of trying to stifle that impulse was actually making her quiver.

Brad's hand was still covering hers at the back of her head, and he could feel her trembling. Or at least he *thought* it was her. He was so shaky himself at this point that he couldn't be sure.

"Sam?" he asked questioningly.

The best thing right now would be for him to leave the room, she thought frantically. But what about her hair? It would be impossible to handle tomorrow if she left it alone, and he'd gone this far. How much worse could it get? Drawing an unsteady breath, she removed her hand from under his and let it fall to her lap in silent acquiescence.

Brad didn't say anything, either. He no longer trusted his voice.

A muscle in his jaw twitched as he began to methodically unbraid her hair, trying desperately to keep his imagination and hormones in check. It had been a long time since he'd touched a woman like this, and he was stunned by the impact it was having on him physically.

When at last her hair was loose, he reached for the brush he'd seen earlier on her nightstand. "I'll get some of the tangles out for you," he said quietly, and before she could protest he began to gently run the brush through her hair.

Sam had never had a man brush her hair before, and the pure sensuousness of the gesture sent a shock wave down her spine, producing a surge of desire that radiated all the way to her toes.

It was also a first for Brad, and the effect on him was exactly the same. Sam had incredibly soft hair, and as it slipped through his hands it awakened nerve endings in his fingertips that he didn't even know existed. What would she do if he tossed the brush aside and ran his fingers through her hair instead? he wondered recklessly. If he pressed his lips to the silky strands, and turned her head to taste—

Brad's flight of fancy was abruptly halted when the brush dislodged a small object from Sam's hair. She glanced down as it fell on the bed beside her and, with a sudden shriek of terror, she shot to her feet and backed away, staring at it in horror.

Brad was so startled by Sam's reaction that it took him a moment to identify the cause—a bee. A very dead bee, actually. With one quick motion he scooped it up, crushed it inside a tissue and deposited it in the trash. In the next instant he was beside her, gathering her into his arms and pressing her face to his chest.

"Sam, it's okay. It's dead. It won't hurt you. Nothing's going to hurt you," he whispered, his breath warm on her forehead.

The rigid lines of her body suddenly went limp, and a sob caught in her throat as she sagged against him. "I think I'm go-going to have a bee pho-phobia for life," she gasped.

She was shaking again, and Brad gently but firmly guided her back to the bed, steadying her with one hand as he pulled back the covers before easing her down. She lay docilely as he applied lotion to her stings, swallowed the aspirin he handed her, and felt him press the ice bag gently against her ankle.

Sam watched him as he pulled up the sheet and sat down next to her, her wide eyes still slightly glazed. Brad took her good hand in his and studied her face as he laced his fingers through hers.

"I'll be close by, Sam," he said softly. "Will you call me if you need anything?"

She nodded mutely.

He hesitated, then slowly leaned down and gently, lingeringly, pressed his lips to her forehead. Her eyes seemed even wider when he straightened up, and he tenderly brushed some stray strands of hair back from her forehead.

"Remember that I'll be here for you," he said, his eyes compellingly locked on hers. Then he rose, and with one last glance back at her supine form, gently shut the door behind him.

For a long time Sam drifted in a place somewhere between sleep and pain-dulled reality, Brad's pledgelike words echoing through her mind. But even as she clung to them, suspecting a deeper, longer-term meaning, she knew they applied only for tonight. Because soon Brad, like his words, would be just a distant, treasured memory that was filed carefully and lovingly away in her heart.

Chapter Seven

The beeping of the microwave timer diverted Brad's gaze from his view of Sam's small but well-tended garden. He strode quickly across the room to turn it off before the high-pitched tone disturbed her. As he withdrew the container of fettuccini, his stomach reacted loudly to the savory aroma, and he glanced at his watch—8:00 p.m. No wonder he was so hungry. His last meal had been more than twelve hours ago, and that had consisted of a bagel and black coffee before his early service.

Brad downed the first several forkfuls quickly to appease his grumbling stomach, but then slowed his pace as a bone-deep weariness suddenly overcame him. It didn't seem possible that he and Sam had arrived at the picnic only five hours ago. It felt like a lifetime had passed since then. Sam had the right idea about sleep, he decided. They could both use a good night's rest.

He remembered her mentioning something about extra bedding in the office closet, so when he finished his meal he went exploring. He'd given the office only a quick glance earlier as he passed, but his first impression of a neat, businesslike setup was confirmed as he stepped inside and flipped on the light to reveal a no-nonsense, work-oriented room.

Brad found the extra pillows, blankets and sheets stacked in the large closet, as Sam had said, and he reached up to retrieve what he needed, only to halt in surprise when his shoulder twinged painfully. He frowned and lowered his arm quickly, flexing it gingerly before reaching up again, this time more carefully, to remove a pillow and blanket. A sore shoulder seemed to be *his* souvenir of their outing, he thought ruefully.

As Brad closed the closet door something on a lower shelf tumbled onto the floor. He opened the door again and bent to retrieve several videotapes, glancing at the titles as he replaced them. He quickly came to the obvious conclusion—for all her apparent sophistication, Sam was a romantic at heart. And she liked happy endings. The shelf was filled with classic romantic movies, including what appeared to be a complete collection of Cary Grant and Rock Hudson/Doris Day flicks. Brad smiled and shook his head as he closed the closet door. No question about it, Sam was full of surprises. And pleasant ones, at that.

Brad deposited the bedding on the couch in the living room and stretched wearily. A shower would sure feel great, he thought longingly. And under the circumstances, he doubted whether she would mind if he took one.

He rummaged around in the hall linen closet, emerging triumphantly a moment later with a towel. Then he stepped into the guest bath and quietly closed the door, glancing in the mirror as he passed the sink. The image reflected back at him, however, made him stop dead in his tracks. His hair was tousled, a five-o'clock—no, make that nine-o'clock—shadow was darkening his face and his shirt was streaked with dirt. Disreputable would be a kind way to describe his appearance. But at least the shower should help, he consoled himself.

Brad crossed his arms to pull off his shirt, pausing abruptly as his shoulder once again protested. Moving more slowly, he stripped off the shirt in one smooth but careful motion, then turned his back to the mirror and glanced over his shoulder to check out the damage.

Brad's eyes widened in surprise at the large, ugly black-and-blue mark that marred his skin. He'd known at the time that he'd taken the brunt of their fall—purposely—and it had hurt, but he hadn't had a clue about the severity of the bruising.

He supposed he should put some ice on it, he thought halfheartedly. But he was just too tired.

Brad took a longer shower than usual, angling his injured shoulder away from the warm, soothing spray, and by the time he finished and combed his wet hair, he felt much more human. Not to mention cleaner. Unfortunately, he couldn't say the same for his clothes, he thought, surveying them critically. He shook out his jeans, which helped a little, and pulled them back on, not bothering with the belt. But he quickly came to the conclusion that washing was the only thing that would improve his shirt. He'd noticed Sam's small washer and dryer earlier in the utility room next to the kitchen, and with one more distasteful glance at his shirt, headed in that direction.

While he waited for the wash cycle to finish, he made a makeshift bed on the living room couch and checked his voice mail at the parsonage. He also spent a few minutes in contemplative prayer, as had become his custom at the end of every day. He'd gotten into the habit after Rachel died, when that quiet time alone with the Lord had provided a special source of strength. But even in normal times he found the practice to be refreshing and renewing.

By the time Brad heard the washer shut off, he was beginning to fade. As he headed for the utility room and tossed his shirt into the dryer, he yawned hugely. Maybe he'd lie down and rest until it was done, he thought wearily, padding back to the couch to stretch out. Then he would follow Sam's lead and get some sleep.

But half an hour later, when the dryer signaled the end of its cycle, there was no one awake to hear it.

Sam emerged from sleep slowly, feeling groggy and out of sorts. She squinted at the window, where bright light was trying to penetrate the blinds, then turned to peer at the digital clock on her nightstand, which said 8:30 a.m.

Her brain felt muddled, and she frowned as she stared at the ceiling. What on earth was wrong with her? Could she be coming down with the flu or something? In June? That hardly seemed likely. She threw back the sheet, preparing to rise, only to discover to her amazement that she was fully dressed. What was going on here? But as Sam sat up and swung her legs to the floor, the sight of the angry red welts and swelling on her ankle brought her memory back in a flash. She shuddered as she recalled yesterday's nightmare.

She stood up carefully, grateful that the stinging sensation had finally disappeared. The swelling and redness might not look pretty, and the area around the stings was tender, but the worst of her discomfort seemed over, thank goodness.

Sam limped to the bathroom and leaned against the sink to peer cautiously into the mirror. The two stings on her face were more subdued today, though still quite apparent, and although she was naturally fair, her complexion was paler than usual. Yesterday was one day she never wanted to repeat! she thought ruefully. She just hoped the incident hadn't completely disrupted the picnic. She'd have to ask Brad about that. The poor man...

Brad! Her eyes widened and she straightened up abruptly. He'd said he was going to spend the night. Had he? She held her breath and listened, but her condo was silent.

Sam moved to the door of her room and paused to listen again. Still no sound. Gently she eased it open and peered down the hall. Nothing. Walking slowly and stiffly, her feet silent on the thick carpet, she passed the empty kitchen, hesitating on the threshold of the living room. He must be on the couch, she thought. But it faced away from her, toward the fireplace, so she couldn't tell for sure. Slowly, trying to still her suddenly rapid pulse, she moved closer and peeked over.

Brad was there, all right—lying on his stomach, one arm bent under his head, the other trailing to the floor. But it wasn't his position that caught her attention—it was his attire. Or lack thereof, she corrected herself.

He didn't have a shirt on. That registered immediately. Except for one shoulder partially hidden by a throw pillow, his broad back was totally bare. And totally masculine, she thought, her heart rate increasing dramatically. Her eyes traced its strong contours, down to the edge of the sheet which was draped over the lower half of his body, the edge of his jeans just visible.

He shifted slightly, dislodging the throw pillow, and Sam took a steadying breath. She forced her eyes back toward his shoulders, and that's when the next impression slammed home, taking her breath away for another reason.

Sam had seen bruises. But she'd never seen one like Brad's. It was almost totally black, with traces of purple at the edges, and it had to be four inches square. She knew he'd purposely taken the brunt of their fall, and she remembered seeing him wince as he flexed that shoulder yesterday when Laura asked if they were all right. She'd meant to ask him about it later, but events had taken several unexpected turns, and it had completely slipped her mind. But she couldn't forget about it now, not when that bruise was staring up at her in living color.

Sam frowned. It looked really bad. Bad enough to need medical attention, perhaps. Maybe she should suggest that he get his shoulder X-rayed. But she couldn't very well do that while he was sleeping. Should she go back to her bedroom and wait till he woke up? she debated silently.

Or rattle around the kitchen a little to alert him to her presence? Or maybe...

The decision was taken out of her hands when he suddenly sighed, turned over and opened his incredibly gorgeous sleep-hazed eyes to stare directly up at her.

For the briefest moment he seemed disoriented, but Sam didn't mind. She needed the time to recover from the powerful impact of his naked chest, with its T of curly dark brown hair, and to notice the day's growth of stubble on his chin that for some reason made her pulse flutter even more than it already was. She was used to seeing him impeccably groomed, and his magnetism was strong then, but in this ''natural'' state it was almost overwhelming.

Unfortunately Sam was still trying to absorb the assault on her senses when Brad's eyes cleared.

Her voice came out in a kind of squeak, and she cleared her throat and tried again. ''Good morning.''

He pulled the sheet off, swinging his jeans-clad legs to the floor and faced her, planting his hands on his hips.

''How are you feeling?'' he asked, his astute eyes not missing a thing as they raked over her.

''Better than yesterday.''

She did look better, he thought. She had more color, and the welts on her face weren't quite as red or swollen. ''How's your ankle?''

She glanced down. It was a good excuse to tear her eyes away from his chest. ''Well, I don't think I'll be entering any races in the near future. It's still pretty swollen, and the stings are tender. But compared to yesterday I really do feel a lot better.''

Relief flooded his face, and she saw the lines of tension visibly ease around his mouth and eyes. ''Thank God! And I mean that literally. You had a really rough day.''

''So did you.'' She nodded toward his shoulder. ''You've got an awful bruise,'' she said, her eyes reflecting her concern.

For the first time Brad seemed to realize that his shirt

was missing, and he glanced down with a frown. The last thing he remembered was putting it in the dryer. He gave Sam an apologetic smile. "Sorry about this," he said sheepishly, gesturing toward his torso as he moved toward the kitchen. "I washed my shirt last night and I must have fallen asleep before it finished drying."

"It's okay," she called after him. She heard him open the dryer, and a moment later he reappeared, tucking in his shirt as he padded barefoot back to her. "But what about your shoulder?" she persisted. "It looks bad. Maybe you should have it checked out."

He shrugged aside the suggestion. "It's just a bruise. Believe me, you got the worst of the deal yesterday. I think in the future we'd better include an 'attend at your own risk' disclaimer on the picnic announcement. The two of us look like the walking wounded."

Sam smiled. He looked great to her, but she couldn't very well say that without starting something that she wasn't up to dealing with just yet.

"How about some breakfast?" he said. "You didn't eat anything last night."

"Yeah, I am kind of hungry," she admitted. "I've got some eggs and cheese in the kitchen. We could have omelettes. And there's juice and English muffins."

"A veritable feast!" he declared with a grin.

"Let me just take a quick shower and change, and I'll fix something," she said.

"No hurry," Brad replied. "My morning is free."

Sam's eyes widened, and she covered her mouth with her hand. "But mine isn't! I'm supposed to meet a client at ten-thirty!"

Brad frowned. "I think you ought to take it easy today, Sam. Do you really feel up to traipsing around, showing property?"

As a matter of fact, she didn't. Her ankle was beginning to throb already and her right hand was still too swollen to be of much use. She sighed and glanced at her watch. "I guess I could try to cancel."

"Good idea. Go ahead and make your call and freshen up. I'll wait."

Sam was able to reschedule her appointment, and by the time she showered, washed and blow-dried her hair and applied a little makeup she was feeling almost human. As she slipped into a short-sleeved knit top and denim jumper she realized that despite her hunger, she would gladly settle for a muffin and juice for breakfast. Her energy level just wasn't up to par, and preparing even a simple meal seemed like far too much effort. But she owed Brad, after all his kindness. It wouldn't kill her to make a couple of omelettes.

However, it appeared that Brad had taken matters into his own hands. By the time she stepped into the hall tantalizing aromas were wafting from the kitchen, and she paused in the doorway to find him slipping a huge omelette onto a platter.

He glanced her way and smiled. "I figured we could split this," he said. "Go ahead and sit down. Coffee's ready, and I just took the muffins out of the toaster."

"But...but Brad, I would have made breakfast," she said, surprised and deeply touched by the thoughtful gesture.

"I know. But I didn't have anything else to do," he replied easily. "Come on. Let's eat before it gets cold."

He held out her chair, and Sam sat down carefully, giving him a crooked smile over her shoulder. "This is a first," she said.

"What?"

"Being waited on in my own kitchen."

He looked at her as he took his seat, his gaze direct and unwavering, and when he spoke his voice was quiet. "We've had a lot of firsts in the last twenty-four hours, haven't we, Sam?"

Her fork was halfway to her mouth, and her hand froze

for a brief second before continuing on its journey. It was a good thing they were eating eggs, which slid down easily, she thought, or she was sure the food would stick in her throat. As it was, she swallowed with difficulty and then stared at him, completely at a loss for words. She wasn't up to a heavy discussion this morning.

When she didn't speak, Brad took a slow sip of coffee, his eyes never leaving her face. "We have to talk, you know."

She tore her eyes away from his and looked down at her plate. Denying the obvious would be foolish. They did need to talk. Only the talk wasn't going to end the way Brad expected. And Sam just wasn't up to the emotional scene that was sure to occur when she told him she couldn't see him anymore.

She took a deep breath and toyed with her food. "I know. But—"

"But you're not up to it today." He completed the sentence for her, as if reading her mind, and she looked over at him gratefully.

"Right."

"I didn't think you would be. But I just wanted to make sure we both agreed that the topic of our relationship needs discussing. And the sooner the better."

"Yes."

"Good," he said with a satisfied nod. "Now go ahead and eat my culinary masterpiece before it gets cold," he added with a grin.

Sam smiled, relieved that he hadn't pressed the issue today, grateful for the reprieve.

Brad kept the conversation light during the rest of the meal and then insisted on cleaning up when they were finished, despite her protests.

"It's not a big deal, Sam. I've got another few minutes. Actually, I'd stay longer, but I have an appointment at one and I need to return some calls before that. And I have a church board meeting tonight. Can we get together tomorrow for lunch or dinner?''

Sam shook her head. "I'll be swamped, considering I'm taking today off. And I have my volunteer work in the evening.''

Brad frowned. "Wednesday morning I'm driving down to see Dad, and I had planned to spend the night. How about dinner Thursday?''

Sam shook her head again. "I'm taking a class on Thursday nights.''

Brad looked at her in surprise as he rinsed the last dish. "When did that start?''

"About a month ago.''

"Something work related?''

Sam shifted uncomfortably. She didn't want to tell Brad about the Bible class. He might think she was going to please him, and that wasn't the case at all. It was just that she'd become increasingly aware of the emptiness and despair in her life, along with a troubling spiritual vacuum. And though she'd originally gone to the class more out of desperation than with any great confidence that it would help, surprisingly enough she now looked forward to the Thursday-night study group. But her reawakening faith was still too new and fragile to discuss. "No. Just…personal interest.''

Brad turned away and squeezed the dishcloth, then carefully hung it over the sink. He recognized Sam's tone of voice. It meant Keep Out. So he did.

Sam looked at Brad's ramrod-straight back. He was probably hurt by her refusal to discuss a seemingly innocuous subject, she realized. But she wasn't trying to shut him out, and she needed to make him understand that. Suddenly an idea occurred to her. Why not invite him to dinner on Friday night? After all, she owed him big-time after everything he'd done for her in the past twenty-four hours. And maybe it would make up a little for her reticence just now.

"Brad, since we both have such busy schedules this week, why don't you come over Friday night for dinner?"

He turned in surprise. "Here?"

She grinned. "Yeah."

"You mean for a home-cooked meal?"

Actually, she planned to order dinners from a local gourmet shop. Cooking wasn't her forte. It always seemed too much bother just for herself. But she couldn't disappoint him, not when he had that look of hopeful anticipation on his face.

"Uh-huh."

"That would be great! But are you sure you want to go to all that trouble?"

"Why not?" she said recklessly. After all, how hard could it be? There were plenty of cookbooks out there. She even had a couple in a closet somewhere. She could read as well as the next person, and cooking was just a matter of following a recipe, after all. It wasn't rocket science.

"Do you think you'll feel up to it?" he asked, a frown of concern suddenly marring his brow.

"Well, the doctor said the swelling would go down pretty fast. And I feel a lot better already."

Brad poured himself another cup of coffee and sat back down at the table. "Dinner here will be nice," he said with a smile, the intimate warmth in his eyes soaking into her pores like sunshine.

Sam was saved from having to reply by the sudden ringing of the phone. She started to rise, but Brad restrained her with a hand on one shoulder and stood up to take it off the hook, passing it to her as he sat back down.

Sam gave him a smile of thanks as she greeted the caller. "Hello?"

"Sam? It's Laura."

"Hi."

"You sound better."

"Yeah, well, yesterday wasn't exactly my day."

"Are you okay?"

"Uh-huh. The stings are pretty red and swollen, but at least they don't hurt as much."

"Thank heavens! We were all so worried. And Brad was a wreck."

Sam looked over at the man in question, who smiled disarmingly, making her heart flip-flop. "Really?"

"Yeah. I thought he was going to have a heart attack or something while he was waiting for Sandy to come out and report on your condition."

"Hmm," was Sam's only response.

"So did he stay long when he took you home?" Laura asked, her studiously casual tone not fooling Sam. Laura was fishing for information, and Sam decided to have a little fun.

"Uh-huh."

There was silence, and when it became clear that Sam wasn't going to offer any more information, Laura tried another tack. "I'll probably give him a call later this morning and see how he is. Nick thinks he hurt his shoulder in the fall. We were all so worried about you that no one really paid attention to him."

"Do you want to talk to him now?" Sam asked innocently.

There was a long moment of stunned silence. But at last Laura found her voice. "You mean he's there?" she asked cautiously.

"Uh-huh. We just had breakfast."

By now Sam was grinning, and Brad raised his eyebrows questioningly. Sam just shook her head. She was enjoying this. Laura was too discreet to come right out and directly ask a personal question, but Sam knew she was dying of curiosity. So she waited her out.

"Well…that's nice," Laura said finally. "He must have come over really early."

"No. Actually, he never left. And Nick was right. His shoulder is badly bruised."

By now Brad was on to her game, and he leaned back with a smile and shook his head, sipping his coffee.

Sam knew Laura's brain was in overdrive, so before things got too out of hand, she stepped in. "He slept on the couch, Laura," she said deliberately.

"I'm sure he did," Laura replied quickly. "I mean, I've known Brad a long time, and he's a real gentleman. Besides, sleepovers aren't his style." She paused. "Listen, Sam, I wasn't trying to pry or anything, so…"

"Yes, you were," Sam interrupted with a chuckle. "And it's okay. I gave you the third degree plenty of times when you were dating Nick, remember? After all, what are friends for?"

Laura's soft laugh came over the line. "Yeah. I do remember. Well, take care of yourself. And tell Brad to do the same. Will I see you Thursday night?"

"I'll be there. And thanks for calling, Laura."

"Like you said, what are friends for? 'Bye."

Sam replaced the receiver, and Brad chuckled as he set his cup down on the table. "I think I got the gist of that conversation."

Sam flushed. "Sorry about that. I couldn't resist putting her on a little." Then she frowned in sudden concern. "Oh, Brad, I probably shouldn't have done that! I mean, you're a minister and all, and I wouldn't want to start any rumors or anything."

Brad rose and smiled down at her. "Don't worry. Laura's known me too long to jump to the wrong conclusions."

Sam's face cleared as she stood up as well. "Yeah, you're probably right. She did say you were a gentleman, and a gentleman wouldn't…well…you know."

"Wouldn't he?" Brad asked softly, moving closer.

Sam backed up in alarm, her heart accelerating to double time. "Brad…let's put things on hold till Friday, okay?"

It wasn't okay as far as he was concerned. He wanted to talk things out right now. In fact, he wanted to do more

than talk. But they'd agreed to wait until Friday, and Laura
was right—he was a gentleman. And a gentleman kept his
word.

"Okay," he capitulated. "I've got to get going, anyway."

Sam walked him to the door, and he paused on the tiny
porch, turning back to gently touch her hair, remembering
the way it had felt in his hands the night before. Exercising
great restraint, he took a deep breath and then bent down
and gently kissed her forehead, carefully avoiding the
puffy welt above her eye.

"Will you take it easy for the next few days, Sam?"

She nodded, trying to swallow past the lump in her
throat. "Uh-huh."

He gazed down at her, clearly reluctant to leave, and
finally let out his breath slowly in a long, heavy sigh.
"Well, I know one thing for sure," he said at last.

"What?"

"It's going to be a long week."

Sam wearily fitted her key in the lock and pushed the
door open. Not only was it turning into a long week, it
had also been a long night. There were times when she
found her work at the counseling center very rewarding.
And then there were other times, like tonight, when it left
her emotionally drained and depressed.

She dropped her purse on the hall table and stepped out
of her shoes, arching her back and tilting her head back
and forth to relieve the tension in her muscles. Was there
something else she could have done, or said, or offered
that would have made a difference? she wondered futilely.
It was the same question she always asked on nights like
this, and she came up with the same answer: maybe. But
she didn't have a clue what.

As Sam mechanically prepared for bed she wondered
how Jamie was doing, both physically and emotionally.
Her decision had been made under pressure, Sam knew.

The last thing her boyfriend wanted to deal with as a college freshman was a baby. And her parents were apparently of the opinion that a scandal would be worse than the alternative.

They were wrong, of course. Dead wrong. But they'd obviously convinced Jamie. Maybe, in the end, they'd threatened not to pick up her college tuition if she had the baby. Maybe they'd told her they would throw her out of the house. Only Jamie knew which pressure had finally pushed her to make a decision Sam knew she would live to regret. Because Sam also knew that the girl had had serious moral concerns. But Sam had seen the desperate, frantic look in her eyes both times they'd met and she knew that despite her best efforts, there was a good chance Jamie would go through with the procedure. Sam had done everything she could think of to prevent that from happening, even giving the girl her home phone number and encouraging her to call at any hour. But Jamie hadn't taken her up on the offer. She might call now, though, after the fact. Some of them did. And at that point all Sam could do was listen and share their anguish.

Sam lay awake a long time, staring at the dark ceiling. Jamie was probably doing the same thing right now. And if she was half as sensitive as Sam thought she was, similar nights lay ahead of her. Nights filled with regret and remorse and sadness. Maybe someday she would go on to marry, have other children, lead a fulfilling life. Most women did. But Sam suspected that even those who seemed able to put the decision behind them and move on still had moments of deep sadness and guilt.

As Sam finally drifted to sleep, she did something she hadn't done in a very long time. She turned to the Lord for help. Not for herself, but for Jamie. She asked him to watch over the girl in the difficult months—and years—ahead. She would need all the help and support she could get. Ending the life of an innocent child—by choice or through irresponsibility—often took only minutes. But it exacted a price that lasted a lifetime.

Sam thrashed on the bed, frowning in her sleep. She heard a child's anguished cry of fear and pain, followed by the plaintive utterance of a single word...*Mama*...that slowly turned into a scream of terror that went on and on and—

With a strangled sob, Sam awoke abruptly, her heart pounding, her breathing erratic. It was a familiar, if dreaded, scenario, and Sam knew what to do. She sat up quickly and turned on the light, forcing herself to take slow, deep breaths as she focused on the Monet painting strategically hung across from her bed. It was a coping mechanism she'd learned a long time ago.

She continued to breathe deeply, letting the beauty of the painting seep into her soul until the ugly images in her mind began to fade, and gradually her heart rate returned to normal and her respiration slowed. She was still shaky, though, her hands trembling as she reached for the sheet and pulled it up as she leaned back against the headboard.

Sam's eyes filled with tears. With every fiber of her being she wished she could forget that day, pretend it had never happened. Sometimes she managed to force the memory into a dusty corner of her mind, but always the nightmare would return, the images so vivid, the sounds so real, that for those brief moments before awakening she relived the horror in all its original intensity. Choking back a sob, she lowered her head to her knees and huddled on the bed, reliving once again that terrible time in her life....

"How could you let this happen? We've only been married two months! I don't want a kid, Sam. Get rid of it or I'm out of here."

Randy's voice was angry and his face expressed shock, but Sam was more shocked at the harshness of his words.

She didn't really want a child, either, at this point in her life. She was too young and too inexperienced and too frightened of the responsibility. Nor did she want to lose Randy. Since she'd alienated her parents by marrying him, he was all she had. There was no one else to turn to, and she had no job, no money, no place even to live without him.

Yet she couldn't bring herself to end the life growing within her, despite Randy's threats. The very thought of it was abhorrent to her. But as the days wore on and his threats intensified, she grew more uncertain and desperate. There just didn't seem to be any other option. Sleepless night blended into sleepless night as she struggled alone with her decision, and she grew pale from exhaustion and strain.

The night of horror began with Randy's angry parting words as he left for his band job.

"I told you to get rid of that thing, Sam. Make your choice now—it's me or it."

Sam watched him leave, the tears silently coursing down her cheeks. Wearily she lay down on the bed, staring at the ceiling in the latest of the impersonal, nondescript motel rooms that had become her home. Sleep. That was what she craved. Her body needed the rest and she needed the oblivion. But sleep had been a stranger lately.

Suddenly she remembered the pills Randy took. The blue ones and yellow ones; uppers and downers, he called them. He never seemed to have any trouble sleeping when he took the downers, she thought. It couldn't hurt to take one or two, could it? She needed the sleep so badly! She couldn't even think straight anymore, she was so tired.

Sam got up and filled a glass with water in the bathroom, then rummaged in his suitcase, finally withdrawing a small container. She hesitated for a brief second, then resolutely shook out two of the innocuous-looking pills and tossed them into her mouth, downing them quickly with a gulp of water.

Sam replaced the container and lay down, waiting for her eyelids to grow heavy. But instead, as the minutes ticked by, she started to feel strange. Lightheaded. Sensitized. Her nerve endings began to tingle, and she grew more alert rather than sleepy. As the feelings intensified, she frowned in confusion. This wasn't supposed to happen. Unless—

With growing, frightening certainty, she swung her feet to the floor and rummaged through Randy's suitcase again, once more retrieving the bottle of pills. She stared at it, then searched for the other bottle, pulling it out as well. With a sickening jolt, she realized that she'd taken the wrong pills.

Sam began to pace, frightened by the frenetic energy coursing through her veins and the erratic pounding of her heart. She had to find a way to tone down the effects of the pills, she thought in panic. Fresh air. That would help. Lots of fresh air. Maybe she should take a drive and just let the air rush against her face. Yes. That was a good idea. It couldn't hurt, anyway. Mike, the drummer, had picked Randy up in his van, so at least the car was here.

Frantically she searched for the keys, sighing with relief when her fingers closed over them in the pocket of Randy's jeans. She grabbed her purse and dashed for the car, rolling the window all the way down despite the light rain that was falling. Then she set out aimlessly on the unfamiliar roads of the small town.

Sam drove for almost two hours until gradually she began to feel better. As she waited at a red light on the outskirts of town, she decided it was time to return to the motel. She felt normal again—physically, at least. Maybe tonight she'd be able to sleep, she thought hopefully.

When the light turned green, she stepped on the accelerator, gaining speed as she crossed the intersection. And that's when it happened.

The subsequent sequence of events was a disjointed blur in her mind and was destined to remain so even years later.

A child's bike, suddenly darting in front of her through the deepening dusk.

The squeal of brakes.

A frantic attempt to turn the unresponsive steering wheel.

A dull thud against the bumper.

The sensation of slow-motion gliding as the car slid off the wet pavement and into a ditch.

The sharp impact of her head against the windshield as the car slammed into a telephone pole.

And then blackness.

Sometimes Sam wished that the story had ended there. That she'd never reawakened. But the horror had continued. Her next conscious memory was distorted faces, peering at her as she lay in the hospital, grotesquely moving in and out of focus. But the words were what would remain most indelibly burned into her memory.

The child's mother, leaning over the gurney as they wheeled her into the emergency room, as she shouted over and over: "You killed my baby! You killed my baby!"

The nurses, talking in low voices over the background noise of a child crying in pain somewhere else in the emergency room. "She has internal injuries. We can't save the baby."

The doctor, standing by her bed. "I'm sorry. We did everything we could, but there's a good chance you may never be able to conceive again."

And finally Randy, with his warped attempt at humor. "Well, you could have found an easier way to take care of the problem. But at least it's over."

Sam drew a shaky breath and reached for a tissue on her nightstand, focusing once more on the Monet painting. No, she thought in despair, it was never over. Not the next day. Not the next month. Not even seventeen years later. She lived with the oppressive guilt every day of her life.

It wasn't that anyone had blamed her. Witnesses said

the collision was unavoidable. But Sam knew differently. If she hadn't taken those pills, she wouldn't have felt the need for fresh air and gone for a drive with less-than-sharp reflexes. And she wouldn't have taken the pills if she hadn't felt so alone and in such deep despair. If only there had been someone to turn to, to talk with, she thought futilely. She had been so young and so desperate—and so very wrong. The bottom line was that because of her irresponsibility two innocent lives had ended that night. Those were the cold, hard facts. And they were irrefutable.

Sam knew she couldn't restore to those children the gift of life she had snatched away. All she could do was try to help other young girls who found themselves in her situation, let them know they weren't alone, that someone cared, that there were other options available that didn't include destroying a life. It was heartbreaking work, and she didn't always succeed. Like tonight. But sometimes she did, and in those successes she found consolation. She felt that in some small way it helped her to make reparation for her own wrong. Quite simply, the counseling center work appeased her conscience enough to allow her to go on living.

The dull, pounding ache in her head that was the typical aftermath of her nightmare intensified, and Sam rose and went to the kitchen in search of aspirin. As she filled a glass with water, her glance fell on the answering machine, and she noted that she had one message. She'd been so tired and upset when she arrived home that she hadn't even checked, an unusual lapse for her. Failing to return messages promptly was a no-no in the real estate game.

But it wasn't a business-related message after all, she realized, as soon as she punched the play button.

"Hi, Sam." The warmth of Brad's voice washed over her like a soothing balm. "I know you're not home, but I'm leaving for Dad's early in the morning and I was afraid I'd wake you if I called then. I just wanted you to know that I'm counting the days till Friday." He paused, as if debating his next words, then continued. "And I wanted to tell you that I miss you. See you soon."

The line went dead, and Sam leaned against the counter, overcome by an almost painful yearning. She missed him, too. On a night like this, it would have been so nice to turn to his strong, steady arms for comfort. But she doubted whether he would offer those arms if he knew the reason she needed them.

As she headed back to bed, Sam suddenly thought about her last Bible class, where the topic had been forgiveness. She'd been especially attentive that night. It had even given her a brief moment of hope. Until she realized that the concept, noble though it was, seemed too lofty for the human condition. In a perfect world, people might be able to practice that principle. But the world was far from perfect, and people were judgmental. It was a fact of life. Maybe the Lord could forgive her. Maybe. People were another story. Certainly not that child's mother. Even Brad, who was not only a minister but the finest, most decent man she had ever had the privilege of knowing, would have a very hard time dealing with what she'd done. If *she* couldn't accept it, find a way to forgive *herself,* how on earth could she expect anyone else to? No, it would be too much to hope for. Besides, even if the Lord could forgive her, as they taught in Bible class, she still didn't feel that she deserved a happy ending, let alone someone like Brad.

Wearily Sam climbed back into bed, the light still burning. After one of her nightmare episodes she could never bear to be alone in the dark. Brad had said he was counting the days till Friday, she recalled sadly. So was she. But while he looked forward to it with eager anticipation, she felt only dread. Because that was the last time she would see him. Calling off their relationship was the right thing to do, for both of them, she told herself resolutely. But it wasn't going to be easy.

Chapter Eight

Sam had hoped to have some time Friday before Brad arrived to mentally prepare for their discussion and to very carefully formulate her wording about why their relationship had to end. Breaking things off was going to be difficult, no matter what she said, but the right words might help.

However, things didn't work out quite the way she planned. In fact, it was a day of disasters, beginning with a flat tire, followed by a difficult client who insisted on seeing a house at precisely one o'clock and then arrived half an hour late, ending with a quicker-than-expected contract response requiring an unscheduled stop at the office to redo some paperwork.

By the time Sam arrived home, frazzled and exhausted, it was nearly four o'clock. The good news, she told herself consolingly, was that she still had time to prepare dinner. The bad news was that she didn't have time for anything else. As she hastily pulled on a pair of jeans and headed for the kitchen, she decided that she'd just have to wing her discussion with Brad and hope that the right words came when she needed them. Because right now dinner was going to require her undivided attention.

A few minutes later, after poring over the complicated instructions in the cookbook she'd dug out of the closet earlier in the week, Sam quickly came to the conclusion that she should have made time to familiarize herself with the recipes—beyond shopping for the ingredients—before Friday at four o'clock. Maybe, just maybe, she'd been a little too ambitious with the menu, she acknowledged reluctantly. Chicken *Cordon Bleu,* twice-baked potatoes and green beans *almondine,* not to mention homemade biscuits, would be something Laura could whip up in an hour. After reading the instructions, Sam wasn't sure she could do it in half a day, let alone the allotted two hours. She eyed the preparation times on the recipes skeptically, quickly concluding that they were for people who knew what they were doing, not novices. And she was *definitely* a novice.

A wave of panic washed over her, and she accelerated her pace, reaching into the refrigerator for the cheese. Thank goodness dessert was finished, she thought with relief, her glance falling on the English trifle she'd made the night before. However, because it had been deceptively easy to put together, it had given her a false sense of confidence about today's foray into the culinary arts. But that confidence was rapidly deteriorating.

Sam stared at the chicken recipe, her brow knit in concentration. It said to flatten the breasts, but how in the world did you do that? She tried pressing on them with the heel of her hand, but that had little effect. Would a hammer work? she wondered in sudden inspiration, rummaging around in her tool drawer. Yes, she thought triumphantly a moment later after giving one a whack.

The next step—layering the breasts with ham and cheese and then rolling them up—wasn't so easy. Maybe the breasts were still too thick, she thought with a frown, finally managing to get one of the uncooperative bundles into a semicylindrical shape. Why didn't these books have step-by-step pictures? she wondered in frustration. She brushed her hair back from her face with one hand and clutched the rolled-up packet of chicken, cheese and ham in the other as she checked the recipe. It said to dust the breasts in flour, dip in a beaten egg, roll in bread crumbs, then secure with a toothpick. Sam's frown deepened. If she tried to do any of those things they would fall apart. Maybe she could just sprinkle them with crumbs after they were in the pan, she thought hopefully. Sure. That ought to work, she decided, impaling the meat with a generous number of toothpicks. Besides, she'd already devoted way too much time to this recipe.

Sam moved on to the potatoes. She'd put them in the oven earlier, but when she removed them and tried to slice off a long end so she could scoop out the interior, the skin was too hard. She frowned and checked the recipe. Bake for one hour and fifteen minutes at four hundred degrees. That's what she'd done, wasn't it? She glanced at the temperature gauge on the oven. Apparently not. It read five hundred, not four hundred, she realized with dismay.

She looked at her watch and her panic intensified. It was already five-thirty, and Brad was coming at six. And she hadn't even started on the vegetable or salad yet. She put the chicken in the oven, then ruthlessly she crossed the homemade biscuits off the menu, concluding that English muffins would have to do instead.

Sam tackled the potatoes with renewed vigor. She finally managed to cut through the crusty skin, but in the process much of the shell shattered. Resolutely she forged on, scooping out the shriveled insides and adding the other ingredients before placing the mixture in what was left of the skins.

Finally she turned her attention to the green beans. The sauce sounded easy enough—just onion and slivered almonds sautéed in butter. She chopped the onion as rapidly as possible, dumped everything into a small frying pan, and set the heat on low. Maybe she could change clothes while the sauce cooked, she thought, distractedly running her fingers through her hair. Then she could throw the salad together at the last minute.

Sam headed for the bedroom, shedding her T-shirt as she went. What a day! And the most difficult part was still to come. At least now she had a minute to think about how she was going to break the news to Brad. She reached for the deep purple silk blouse she'd chosen, pulling it on rapidly, debating her approach. It might be best if she—

The harsh buzzing of a smoke detector made her jump, and she dashed toward the kitchen, her heart pounding. She paused for a brief second on the threshold, her eyes riveted to the smoke seeping out of the oven, then moved toward it and yanked open the door, only to be engulfed in a billowing gray cloud. Coughing, she tried to wave the smoke away as she peered inside, but it was difficult to see with her eyes watering so badly. As nearly as she could determine, it appeared that the cheese had leaked out of the chicken breasts and was now burning. In rapid order, she grabbed the pan and removed it, turned on the exhaust fan, opened a window and began waving a towel at the smoke detector to clear the air.

When the piercing alarm finally fell silent, Sam leaned back against the counter, her heart pounding. She surveyed the sad-looking chicken, desperately trying to figure out a way to salvage the unappetizing mess. Maybe if she scooped the cheese back in and—

Suddenly she sniffed and glanced suspiciously toward the stove. The almonds and onions in her butter sauce were turning black, and she flew across the room to remove the pan from the heat before the smoke alarm went off again. As she stood there holding it, her glance fell on the potatoes waiting to go into the oven. They looked pathetic, too. The skins had pretty much disintegrated, and the filling was already spilling out.

Sam thought she had felt panic before. Now she realized that had been mere concern. *This* was panic. She opened her refrigerator and looked inside in desperation, hoping that by some miracle a solution to her dilemma would appear. But no such luck. She had dessert, and she had salad, she thought, her eyes visually ticking off the ingredients—lettuce, tomatoes, mushrooms, parmesan cheese, red onion, Italian dress—Sam frowned. Where was the dressing? It had been on her list. She remembered that clearly. But as she frantically rummaged through the refrigerator, it became equally clear that it hadn't made the transition from list to reality. She must have forgotten it!

Sam stood numbly before the refrigerator, forced to admit the obvious—her dinner was a disaster. And Brad was expecting a home-cooked meal! The kind that Rachel used to make. Instead he was getting a culinary catastrophe. How was she ever going to face him? And what was she going to do about dinner? She didn't even have any microwave stuff left in the freezer! Maybe she could still call the gourmet shop and—

The ringing of the doorbell startled Sam, and she froze, her stomach sinking to her toes. With sickening certainty, she slowly checked her watch. Six o'clock. As usual, Brad was punctual. She looked longingly at the back door, and for the briefest moment she actually considered sneaking out and just disappearing. But of course she couldn't do that. Could she?

The bell rang again, and distractedly she pushed her hair back. She had to face him. There was no way out. Her heart pounding in her chest, she forced her legs to carry her toward the door. She hovered there, her hand on the knob, until a third ring forced her to respond. Taking a deep breath, she pulled it open.

Peripherally, she realized that Brad looked great. He was dressed in tan slacks and a blue-striped open-necked shirt, and his navy blue blazer sat well on his broad shoulders. He was also carrying a bottle of wine, which Sam figured they were both going to need before this so-called dinner was over.

Brad's smile of welcome slowly faded to a frown, then changed to a look of concern as he took in Sam's appearance. Her normally well-groomed hair hadn't even been combed, and there was a trail of bread crumbs across her face. Her silk blouse was attractive—but she was wearing it, untucked, over scruffy jeans. She was also barefoot. As Brad completed his quick but thorough scrutiny, alarm bells began ringing in his mind.

"Sam? Are you all right?"

She managed a shaky laugh. "Oh, sure. Why wouldn't I be? I mean, it's just a little dinner for two, right? Anyone should be able to handle that. Laura could. And I'm sure Rachel would have managed with no problem."

His frown deepened. "What are you talking about?"

"Your dinner. Or what was supposed to be your dinner. It's a disaster."

"Sam, let's go inside," he said carefully. She seemed on the verge of tears, but surely a recipe gone awry wouldn't make her almost hysterical. Not Sam, who took everything in stride.

She moved aside so he could enter, then shut the door behind him as he deposited the bottle on the table in the tiny foyer and then turned to her. He placed his hands on her shoulders, his eyes probing and concerned.

"Let's start over, okay?" he said, struggling to keep his voice calm. "Now what happened?"

Suddenly she felt tears welling up in her eyes. "Dinner. It's ruined," she said, sniffling.

"I don't mind if everything's not perfect," he assured her.

He didn't seem to understand. "Brad, it's inedible," she said.

"Oh, come on, it can't be that bad."

She nodded. "Yes it can. It is. Trust me on this. It's not a pretty picture in the kitchen."

"But what happened?" he asked, frowning in puzzlement.

"I don't spend much time in the kitchen. I didn't realize cooking was so time consuming or involved, so I guess I overextended myself with the menu. And I don't even have any microwave stuff in the freezer!"

Brad put his arm around her shoulder and drew her toward the couch. "Relax, Sam," he said easily. "It's not the end of the world. We'll make do. What turned out the best?" he asked encouragingly.

"Dessert. And it's not just the *best*. It's the *only* thing that turned out."

He kept his arm around her as they sat down, and though he was trying to remain calm, he was concerned and bewildered. He didn't understand why she was so upset. It wasn't like her to be thrown by something like this.

"Okay, then how about Chinese? I passed a place a few blocks from here."

"But I promised you a home-cooked meal."

"Can I tell you something, Sam? A home-cooked meal would have been nice. But food is *not* the reason I came tonight."

That was good news on the dinner front, solving one dilemma. But it only reminded her of the other, far more important one.

When she didn't reply, Brad removed his arm from around her shoulders and stood up. "I'll be back in twenty minutes," he said. "Will you be all right?"

She nodded. "Yes."

He hesitated uncertainly, not sure he should leave her alone in her present state. She looked up at him, saw the concern in his eyes, and managed a shaky smile. "Go on. I'll be fine," she said reassuringly.

He nodded. "Twenty minutes."

Sam heard the door click shut behind him and drew a long, shaky breath. He didn't seem all that upset about the dinner shambles, after all. But that was only because his attention was focused on another issue. And she'd better start thinking fast about how she was going to handle *that*.

Sam glanced down, and her eyes widened in surprise. She still had on her jeans! With a startled exclamation, she rose and made her way to the bedroom, quickly substituting a black skirt and leather flats for the jeans and bare feet. She was almost afraid to look in the mirror, and she did so tentatively, groaning as her worst fears were confirmed. Her face had been largely wiped free of makeup from the steam in the kitchen, there was a trail of bread crumbs across one cheek and her hair looked like it hadn't been combed since yesterday. She was going to have to work fast to make herself presentable before Brad returned.

By the time the doorbell rang, she'd not only dressed, combed her hair and repaired her makeup, she'd also finished setting the table—a job she'd abandoned earlier in the afternoon as the kitchen crises began escalating. She'd also discarded most of the evidence of her culinary disaster, wrinkling her nose in distaste at the unappetizing mess she'd created. Martha Stewart had nothing to worry about from her, she thought ruefully.

When Sam answered the door this time, she was calmer and much more in control. Brad noticed the difference immediately as he stepped inside, carrying two large white bags which were emitting tempting aromas.

"Feeling better?" he asked, turning to her with a smile still tinged by concern.

"Much," she assured him. "I can't even imagine what you must have thought when you arrived the first time," she said, feeling a faint flush of embarrassment creep across her cheeks.

"Worried," he replied quietly, his eyes searching hers as if to assure himself that she was all right. When he seemed satisfied, he nodded toward the bags. "Should we put these in the kitchen?"

"Uh-huh. Here, I can take one," she offered, reaching for a sack.

He followed her, pausing on the threshold to look around cautiously before entering.

Sam glanced back and laughed. "It's safe. I destroyed most of the evidence while you were gone."

Brad grinned. "Then let's eat. But first...how are you feeling? Are the stings any better?" he asked, his voice suddenly serious. "I meant to ask the minute I got here, but we sort of got sidetracked."

"Yeah, you might say that," she said with a wry grin. "Actually, I feel fine. Most of the stings have faded and the tenderness is slowing disappearing. How's your shoulder?"

"In working order," he said, flexing it to demonstrate. "It's still not very pretty to look at, but the color palette has changed from black and blue to blue and yellow. It doesn't hurt as much, either."

"Well, I have to say that when you ask someone out, you do show them a memorable time," Sam said with a laugh.

"So do you," he countered, nodding to the kitchen.

"Touché," she acknowledged. "But at least my disaster didn't involve injuries."

He grinned sheepishly. "True. Next time I ask you out, things will be better, I promise."

Sam's face clouded, and she turned away to hide her reaction, reaching into the bags to remove the food. "Why don't you go on into the dining room? I'll put this in bowls and be right there."

Sam hadn't turned away quickly enough, however. Brad saw the look on her face, and he didn't like what it implied. Clearly she was still skittish about the notion of a romance between them. But he wasn't leaving here tonight until he persuaded her to give it a try. And the first order of business was to find out *why* she was reluctant. It wasn't lack of interest, he was sure of that based on the smoldering look he'd seen in her eyes at the picnic. No, it was something else. Something quite serious, apparently. Nevertheless, he was convinced they could overcome it. Now he just had to convince her. But there would be time for that later, after dinner, when they'd both had a chance to relax a little.

"I'll open the wine," he said.

"That would be great."

By the time she brought the food into the "formal" dining area next to the living room, Brad was waiting to pull out her chair. "I got beef and broccoli and chicken cashew. I hope that's okay," he said as she sat down.

"Mmm. Great!" she replied, spooning generous servings of both onto her plate to make up for the lunch she'd skipped. "Let me tell you, this is much better than what we'd be eating if I tried to salvage the dinner I cooked," she said ruefully.

"That bad, huh?" he teased.

"Let's just say that cooking isn't my forte. I wish I'd learned how. You were lucky to have a wife who was good at it."

Brad chewed thoughtfully. This was the second time tonight that she'd mentioned Rachel. Maybe she thought he was comparing her to his late wife, and she felt intimidated and less suitable for him because she wasn't as "domestic." If so, he needed to diplomatically dispel that concern.

"Rachel was a good cook," he acknowledged slowly. "But I've found that everyone has their own unique talent. None are better or worse than the other. Just different. For example, you have a wonderful talent for drawing people out and making them feel happy. I can speak from personal experience on that one."

Sam flushed and glanced down. "Not very practical, though," she said.

He shrugged. "Depends on how you define *practical*. Joy and happiness are great foundations for coping with the trials and tribulations of everyday life. It seems pretty practical to me."

Sam felt a warm rush of pleasure at his words. Or maybe it was from the wine, she thought, speculatively eyeing her half-empty glass. She'd had a glass and a half already. Given that her usual drink was mineral water she'd never developed much tolerance for alcohol. But tonight she figured she needed a drink. Or two. Maybe it would mellow her out a little after the kitchen disaster, help her find the words to tell Brad she couldn't see him anymore.

The very thought of that discussion usually made her panic, but surprisingly, this time, it didn't. She just felt very relaxed and content. Must be the alcohol, she concluded. "The wine's good," she said with a smile, taking another sip.

"Yes, it is. I like to have it on special occasions."

"Is tonight a special occasion?" she asked.

"Maybe," he said noncommittally, his deep brown eyes watching her over the rim of his glass as he lifted it to his lips.

What a stupid question, she berated herself! Very deliberately and carefully she set her own glass down. No more wine for her. She cleared her throat—and tried to clear her too-foggy mind—before she spoke. "Well, how about if we have dessert and coffee in the living room?" she said brightly.

"Sounds good. Can I help."

"No!" she replied quickly. "I mean, thanks, but I can manage," she added, before escaping to the kitchen.

As Sam scooped out the trifle and waited for the coffee to perk, she took a deep breath. This was the moment she'd dreaded. How was she ever going to tell this wonderful man to get lost? And essentially that was what she had to do. He wasn't going to like it, even though she knew that in the long run it would be better for him. But making him understand that without revealing her secret would be tough. Yet telling him the truth wasn't an option. Because as hard it would be to lose him, it would be even worse to see the horror and recrimination in his eyes as *he* rejected *her* if she shared the terrible secret from her past with him.

Sam carefully poured the coffee and placed it on a tray, adding the bowls of trifle, cream, sugar and napkins as she tried to think of some way to delay her entry. But she'd have to deal with this sooner or later, and she might as well get it over with, she realized with a resigned sigh. Waiting wasn't going to make it any easier.

Brad was standing by the mantel when she returned, and he moved toward her and took the tray, setting it carefully on the coffee table.

"Dessert looks good," he said.

Sam tried to smile. "Well, the proof is in the tasting. I'm not making any promises." Even to her own ears her voice sounded strangely tight, and she hoped Brad wasn't picking up on her nervousness.

Her hope was in vain. He'd known this wasn't going to be an easy sell, and he'd been keenly attuned to her signals all evening, debating the best approach to use to convince her to give a romantic relationship a chance. He'd ultimately settled on the one thing he knew they had in common—physical attraction. That wasn't enough on which to build a long-term relationship—but it wasn't a bad starting place for his persuasive efforts.

"Well…shall we sit?" he said, when she remained on her feet next to the table. "Unless you want to eat dessert standing up?" he teased.

"Oh! No, of course not." She sat down on the couch, careful to allow room for a discreet distance between them. But Brad apparently had other ideas. He sat down very close to her, his arm brushing hers as he reached for his dessert. Sam's instinct was to scoot into the far corner of the couch, away from danger, out of the magnetic range of the attractive man sitting next to her. But she couldn't figure out a way to do that without being obvious, so she remained where she was, her back stiff, trying vainly to control the staccato beat of her heart.

"Sam?"

Brad was offering her one of the servings of trifle, and

she reached for it automatically. He picked up his as well, then leaned back and took a bite, chewing thoughtfully. Then he took another bite. And another. Finally he turned to her with a grin. "Well, the rest of your dinner may not have turned out, Sam, but this makes up for it. It's great! Go ahead, try some," he said, helping himself to a generous mouthful.

Sam did as he suggested, mostly because she couldn't think of anything else to do. She certainly wasn't hungry, although she had to admit that the creamy concoction was tasty. She continued to eat so she wouldn't have to talk, trying to buy herself a little thinking time while she figured out a way to break the news to the man sitting next to her.

She was only half-finished by the time he'd demolished his serving, topping it off with a sip of coffee before wiping his lips on one of the napkins. "You can make that for me anytime," he said, turning to her with a smile.

As he angled himself toward her, he jostled her arm, and Sam, who was just about to take another bite of trifle, missed her mouth. Fortunately the concoction stayed on the spoon, although a streak of whipped cream ended up on her cheek.

"Sorry about that," he said with a sheepish grin. "Here, let me."

He reached over and carefully dabbed at the sweet trail, and Sam literally stopped breathing. He was only inches away, and the magnetism she'd felt earlier was multiplied exponentially.

Suddenly Brad's hand stilled on her cheek, and the natural brown color of his eyes darkened perceptibly as they sought and held hers compellingly. Without releasing her gaze, he laid the napkin on the back of the couch and took her dessert out of her trembling hands, setting it on the coffee table in front of him.

Sam knew she should say something. Anything. She had to break the spell he was weaving with his passionately eloquent eyes before it was too late. But her voice deserted her, and she seemed incapable of fighting the powerful emotions that were sweeping over her like a relentless tide, igniting her body in their wake.

Brad reached over and stroked her hair, pushing it back from her face and letting it glide through his fingers. Silently he repeated the motion again. And again. And still again, until Sam thought her heart was going to explode in her chest.

"You have beautiful hair, Sam," he said softly at last, continuing to play with it.

"Thanks." Her voice sounded like a croak, and she cleared her throat. "It's the real thing, too. I'd never pick this color on purpose," she said nervously.

"Why not?"

"Why would anyone want red hair? It clashes with everything."

"Red? I wouldn't call your hair red," he mused, finally releasing her gaze to study the strands he held in his hand. "It's more...burnished. Like the color of autumn."

Sam struggled to take a deep breath. This wasn't working out at all as she'd planned. She thought they were going to have a nice, rational discussion about their relationship. She hadn't expected Brad to...well...do this. It was throwing her off balance, making it hard to breathe, let alone think.

"Um, Brad, I..."

He pressed a finger to her lips, effectively silencing what he supposed was going to be a protest. She gazed at him wide-eyed and swallowed convulsively, a pulse beating frantically in the hollow of her throat.

His gaze dropped to that very spot, and then he transferred his fingertip to the faded welt near her upper lip, letting it rest there gently. "Is this still tender?" he asked, his own voice strangely hoarse.

She shook her head as the touch of his finger sent a tremor rippling through her body. "No," she whispered.

"Good. Because I don't want to hurt you, Sam, but I'm not sure I can wait any longer to do this."

Very slowly, very deliberately, he leaned down and pressed his lips to hers, gently, tentatively testing her response, gauging her reaction. He was fairly certain that she would welcome his kiss—if she listened to her heart—but there was a chance he'd misread her attraction. This was the real test. He moved his lips over hers coaxingly, seeking a response, waiting for an unspoken invitation to continue.

As Brad's lips worked their magic, Sam suddenly felt as if she'd consumed the entire bottle of wine instead of just two glasses. She was dizzy and light-headed and drowning. And she was also fighting a losing battle with her resolve. She knew this was *not* the right way to go about ending their relationship. She needed to think rationally, and she was only going to be able to do that if she backed off, put some physical distance between them.

Logically, Sam knew that was what she should do. But it felt so good, and so right, being close to Brad. What could it hurt, just this once, to let herself enjoy a moment of tenderness with a man who seemed to care about her very much—as a person, not just for her physical assets, not just because he was looking for a good time or hoping for a one-night stand? Maybe it would be okay, she told herself, as long as things didn't get out of hand. And they wouldn't, not with Brad. That wasn't his style. So just this once, maybe she could let herself respond.

Except there was still a problem, she realized. It wasn't that she was uncertain *how* to respond. She'd been kissed by enough men in her time to have developed *some* technique. But this was a unique situation. Brad was…well…different. He was religious. How much response did he expect? She didn't want to come on too strong. Maybe he played this game by different rules. And if so, she didn't have a clue what they were.

Brad felt her hesitate, and reluctantly he backed off

slightly, enough to look down into her eyes. They were troubled, but he could also see the ardent spark glowing in their depths, could feel the trembling desire in her body as he held her in his arms. Yet she was holding back. "Sam? What is it?" he asked gently, his lips traveling across her forehead, leaving a trail of fire in their wake.

She swallowed. "I...I don't know how to kiss a minister," she whispered.

Brad's soft, throaty chuckle of relief did strange things to her metabolism. "I'll tell you what, Sam," he suggested, his voice husky with emotion, the leashed passion in his eyes making her breath catch in her throat. "Just try kissing a man." And with that he pulled her into his arms and lowered his lips to hers once again.

This time Sam threw caution to the wind. She could feel the hard, uneven thudding of his heart against her breast as he held her tightly, and a powerful surge of longing ricocheted through her body. If this was going to be her only chance to taste Brad's kisses, she might as well take full advantage of it. So she did exactly what he asked. She kissed a man. Thoroughly, completely, without reserve.

Brad had hoped for a response. What he got was an earthquake. Not that he minded. Far from it. It was just that the intensity of Sam's passion surprised him. The kiss that had started off gentle and tentative quickly became much more consumning as they both allowed the passion that had simmered below the surface for weeks to explode.

Sam moaned softly as Brad molded her slim, pliant body to his with strong, sure arms, deepening the kiss until their smoldering passion became a consuming flame. His mouth moved over hers with a fierce intensity, and Sam couldn't be sure whether the drumming pulse she heard was her own or his. But it didn't matter. The only thing that mattered for this moment in time was the oneness she felt with this man, whose surprisingly deep passion was turning her world upside down. She put thoughts of tomorrow aside as they explored the wonderful magic of the attraction that had pulled them together almost since the beginning, long before either was consciously aware of it.

When they at last drew apart, both were shaken and breathless, and Sam's face was flushed.

"Wow!" Her voice was hushed and awed, her eyes dazed, her lips still throbbing from the touch of his. "I didn't know ministers could kiss like that!"

Brad managed a crooked grin as he struggled to calm his own raging pulse. "Neither did I," he admitted. The response she had drawn out of him surprised him as much as it had obviously surprised her.

As Sam struggled to get her own pulse under control, she looked at him suspiciously. "Brad, are you sure you haven't, well, done more of this than you said?"

"No. In fact, to be honest, I was a little bit intimidated," he admitted.

She looked up at him in surprise. "Why?"

He shrugged and pulled her close again, liking the way her head nestled naturally into his shoulder. "Because I *haven't* done much of this. I wasn't kidding when I said my experience was limited. Rachel was the only woman I was ever intimate with, and other than that it was just a simple good-night kiss for the few other women I dated. Let me tell you, in my book this was *not* a simple good-night kiss," he said with a throaty chuckle. "Anyway, I guess I was afraid that I would fall short of…well, I know you've dated a lot more than I have, and…" His voice trailed off.

Sam pulled away slightly and looked up at him. "Brad, just for the record, I'd like to clear up some misconceptions you seem to have about my dating background," she said with a frown.

"Sam, it's not necessary. All that matters to me is what we have together. I've known you long enough to get a very good sense of the kind of person you are *now*, and whatever happened in your past dating history isn't relevant."

"But I'd still like you to know. Because my 'past dating history,' as you put it, wasn't nearly as wild as I have a feeling you think it was."

"You don't have to do this, Sam," he said, his eyes sincere and direct.

"I know. But I want to, okay?" She drew a deep breath. "Randy was the first man I was intimate with, and only after we were married. When he ran out on me, I didn't want anything to do with men for quite a while. For one thing, you can imagine what his leaving did to my newly acquired and very fragile self-image. But after a year or so, I started to feel very lonely. And I needed to find out if I was attractive enough to get dates, I guess. That's when I joined a singles group and started to socialize more."

Sam's eyes skittered away from his and she glanced down, playing with a button on her skirt. "There were a couple of times in those next few years when the loneliness got so bad that I thought intimacy would help, even if it was only for a night or two," she said slowly, her voice soft. "So I...I tried it. But I was wrong. It only made things worse. And after two episodes like that, I swore off one-night stands—and any other kind of stands. Besides, I guess some of my Christian upbringing stuck, because I just felt it was morally wrong."

She looked up then, her eyes connecting directly with his. "I've dated a lot, Brad. But that's all I do—date. Most guys aren't interested in dating indefinitely without a pay-off, so my dating roster changes frequently. But even casual dating has gotten old in the last year or so. To be honest, I rarely date at all anymore. So now you know."

Sam was right to assume that Brad had envisioned her social life to be much more...active. It was certainly the impression he'd picked up from Laura. But he couldn't doubt the sincerity in Sam's eyes. He would stake his life that she was telling him the truth.

"Will you forgive me if I say I'm glad that my impression was inaccurate?" he said. "It wouldn't have made any difference, because I think that the Sam I know is terrific. But I have to admit that it was hard to reconcile the image I had of your past with the woman you are now. I'm glad that I don't need to.''

"So the fact that I've had two…encounters…doesn't bother you?" she asked carefully, her voice soft.

"Sam," he drew her close again, cradling her head against his chest. "People have reasons for what they do. They make mistakes. They have regrets. We all do. You survived a very difficult, lonely period in your life in the only way you knew how at the time. And you learned from it. That's the best we can hope for in this imperfect, human world. What matters most to me is that the Sam Reynolds I know is a wonderful person. And I'm glad she's part of my life.''

He'd given her the perfect opening to bring up their relationship, she realized. But she simply didn't have the strength to do it, not when his lips were in her hair, and his hands were working magic again, and her heart was his willing partner.

Finally he drew back and smiled at her. "I'll tell you what, Sam. It's still early. I could pick up a video, if you like. Or better yet, we could just watch one of those old romantic classics from that collection you keep hidden in the office closet.''

Sam looked up at him in surprise, color stealing onto her cheeks at his teasing tone. "You saw them when you stayed that night, didn't you?"

"Uh-huh," he replied, his eyes twinkling.

"So my secret's out, I guess.''

"Yep. Sam Reynolds—a closet romantic. Literally. And a softie under that sophisticated career woman image." He put a finger under her chin and gently tipped her head up so she had to meet his eyes, which were warm and tender. "And I like you just the way you are," he added with an intimate smile before draping his arm around her shoulders. "Now, personally, I vote for Cary Grant. He's always been one of my favorites. What do you say?"

She nodded, her throat tight. "Okay."

And so they watched her old romantic movie, cuddling on the couch, missing some of the screen action as they played out their own romantic scenes. Then they had more dessert and coffee, prolonging the evening as much as possible, neither wanting this special moment in their relationship to end. But at last Brad reluctantly removed his arm from around her shoulders and looked at his watch.

"I have to go, Sam," he said with a sigh. "It's nearly two o'clock."

Her eyes widened. "You're kidding!"

"No. I wish I were."

He took her hand as they walked toward the door, lacing his fingers through hers. "How about dinner tomorrow?" he said.

"Not here, I hope," she said with a wry grin.

He chuckled. "No. I thought we'd go out."

"Good choice."

"So…is it a date?" he asked, stepping outside and turning back to face her.

When he looked at her like that, it was impossible to refuse. Besides, despite what had happened tonight, she hadn't changed her mind about breaking things off. Brad had said some nice things earlier about mistakes and regrets and doing the best one could in the circumstances. But a one-night stand, wrong as that was, was *not* equivalent to an irresponsible action that senselessly took two young lives. She doubted whether he would be as understanding about that "mistake." Ending their relationship was still the right thing to do.

"Yes," she said, forcing herself to smile.

"Great. I'll pick you up at six.?"

"That would be fine."

He reached for her then, and she went willingly, closing her eyes as she hugged him fiercely, the hard planes of his body solid and strong against her slender curves. And as his lips claimed hers in a warm, lingering kiss, she knew that saying good-bye to this wonderful man was going to be the hardest thing she had ever done in her life.

Chapter Nine

Sam glanced at her watch for the dozenth time and frowned. She was sure Brad had said six o'clock. It was now six-twenty. Restlessly she moved to the front window and pushed the curtain aside to stare at the gray shroud of rain that had been falling relentlessly all afternoon. She peered into the gloom, her eyes scanning the grounds and parking lot, but there was no sign of him. With a sigh she let the fabric fall back into place. This wasn't like him, she thought worriedly. Brad was *never* late.

Sam ran her fingers through her hair distractedly and wandered toward the kitchen, pausing on the threshold. Had she come in here for some reason? she wondered. If so, it escaped her. She shook her head and sank down at the dinette table, drumming her fingers on the glass top. Brad could have gotten caught in traffic, she reasoned. It did happen, even to punctual people. He'd probably be along any minute, she reassured herself, trying to remain calm.

By six-thirty, when she dialed his number and got only the answering machine, Sam wasn't calm anymore. By six forty-five, she started to panic.

She knew he hadn't forgotten their date. No way, not after last night. And if something else had come up requiring him to cancel or delay, he would have called her. That was just the kind of man he was. Which left only one possibility—an accident.

Sam began to pace. She tried to figure out the best course of action, but in her agitated state, her imagination was working overtime, and it wasn't easy to think rationally. She could start calling the hospitals, she supposed. Or the police. They might have an accident report. But what if Brad had injured himself at home? Maybe he'd fallen down the basement steps and was lying there unconscious!

With sudden decision, Sam rose and quickly scribbled a note to Brad, telling him she was going to the parsonage and to call her cellular number if he showed up. Then she grabbed her purse, taped the note to the front door and headed for her car. She knew this might be a wild-goose chase, but action was preferable to just sitting around. If she found no sign of him at the parsonage, she'd start calling the police and hospitals, she decided.

Sam drove quickly, pulling into Brad's driveway in record time. She'd never been inside the modest, one-story parsonage, but it stood right next to the church, and she'd seen it the day she gave the home-buying talk.

She slammed on the brakes and almost before the car came to a complete stop, threw open the door and raced up the steps, unmindful of her umbrella. Her heart thumped painfully in her chest as she pressed the bell. She waited impatiently, trying to ignore the string of frightening scenarios conjured up by her vivid imagination.

When the doorbell produced no response, Sam knocked and waited again, but still there was no response. She pressed the bell once more, with the same result. If Brad was in the house, he obviously couldn't get to the door.

She glanced around, debating her next move. The garage! That was it! Check the garage and see if his car was still here. Dodging raindrops, she dashed toward the detached structure and made her way to the side, cupping her hands around her face to peer in the smudged window. As her eyes adjusted to the gloom, her stomach dropped to her toes. The car was here. So where was Brad?

Sam looked back toward the house uncertainly, panic etching her features. Maybe she should break a window. Or would it be better to call the police first? But if Brad was hurt, it might not be wise to wait until the police arrived to get to him. Sam twisted her hands together and closed her eyes, leaning against the side of the garage. She hadn't yet developed the habit of talking to the Lord on a regular basis, but Bible class must be rubbing off on her, she thought, because in this moment of crisis she suddenly felt the need for higher guidance. Please, Lord, let him be okay, she prayed silently. He's such a fine and good man, and he's already had more than his share of pain and sorrow. Show me what to do to help him.

When she opened her eyes, her gaze drifted to the adjacent church, and suddenly, with a degree of certainty that startled her, she intuitively knew that Brad was inside.

Sam straightened up and slowly made her way toward the building, pausing at the door as a powerful feeling of dread engulfed her. She sensed darkness and desolation, could feel it as palpably as she felt the rough iron of the door handle beneath her fingers, and it frightened her. The sensation was weird and unsettling.

Sam didn't want to go in. But she couldn't just walk away. Because just as she sensed despair, and the vacuum of hopelessness, she also sensed that Brad needed her. And so, drawing a deep, shaky breath, she opened the door and stepped inside.

The vestibule was empty and silent as she closed the door softly behind her. Cautiously she moved forward to the double doors that led into the church proper. She gently eased one door open to slip inside, then let it shut silently against her back.

Sam stood unmoving, her shoulders pressed against the wooden door. When her eyes grew accustomed to the dimness, she scanned the church quickly. It seemed to be empty, she realized with a frown. But Brad was here. She was certain of it. She could *feel* his presence. She let her eyes sweep over the church once more, this time more slowly and carefully.

She almost missed him again. In fact, she would have if he hadn't reached up to run a hand wearily over his face just as her gaze swept past.

He sat in a pew near the front, off to one side, half-hidden in the shadows. With his head bowed and his shoulders slumped, his posture spoke silently but eloquently of defeat and sadness. A cold knot of fear slowly formed in Sam's stomach, then tightened painfully. Something bad had happened. Very bad. He'd obviously sought solace here, with the Lord. Maybe three was a crowd in a situation like this, she thought, suddenly uncertain. Maybe he needed to be alone and would consider her presence an intrusion. Should she quietly leave, wait outside until he emerged? she wondered.

A sudden ragged breath, sounding to Sam like a choked sob, echoed softly in the church and made her decision easy. Brad was hurting, and she wanted to help. It was as simple as that.

Instinctively she moved forward, pausing a few steps behind him to softly call his name. When he didn't respond, she tried again, this time a little louder.

"Brad?"

Her voice penetrated his consciousness the second time, and he lifted his head and slowly turned to look at her.

Sam's eyes widened in shock at his appearance. *Wretched* wasn't a word she dusted off very often, but it was the only one in her vocabulary that came anywhere close to describing Brad's face. His eyes stared back at her with a haunted look and his skin was stretched tautly, almost painfully, across his cheekbones. The deep grooves etched in his brow were matched by equally deep furrows on either side of his mouth. Sam found it hard to believe that this was the same man who had held her in his arms and laughed with her last night. He stared at her dazedly, as if he didn't even recognize her. The hand he passed across his eyes, as if to clear his vision, shook badly.

Trying to quell her panic, which was approaching epic proportions, Sam moved closer and sank down on the pew beside him. She reached out to touch his face. "Brad? What is it? What's wrong?" she asked urgently.

Slowly his eyes cleared, focused, and he stared at her in confusion. "Sam? Why are you here?"

"We had a date," she reminded him, speaking slowly. "When you didn't show up, I got worried and came looking for you."

"A date?" he repeated blankly.

"Uh-huh. For dinner. Remember?" she prompted, struggling to keep her voice calm.

He frowned, as if trying very hard to do just that, and then he closed his eyes and sighed, raking his fingers through his hair. "Dinner," he repeated. "Sam, I completely forgot. I'm sorry. Just let me change and—"

"Brad," she interrupted gently but firmly. "Forget dinner, okay? Just tell me what happened. Is it your dad?"

"My dad?" he repeated blankly.

"Is he all right?"

He turned and stared toward the chancel, nodding his head jerkily. "Yeah."

When he didn't offer any more information, Sam reached for his hand. "Then what is it? What's wrong? Can you tell me?" she asked, a tremor of fear running through her voice.

His fingers crushed hers painfully, but she didn't flinch. It was almost as if he needed a lifeline to grasp, and her hand was serving that function.

"I don't want to burden you with my problems," he said, and her heart ached at the raw pain in his voice.

"Brad, I care about you." She spoke slowly, deliberately, her voice intense. "I care a *lot*. I want to help if I can. Please...tell me," she pleaded.

"It's too late to help," he said dully.

"But it's never too late to talk. Come on, Brad. Please. Talk to me. Tell me."

He exhaled a long, shuddering sigh, and after a moment of silence he turned to her. "Remember I told you once that I tend to get too personally involved in the lives of my congregation? Well, tonight is the downside of that."

"What do you mean?"

He drew a shaky breath. "There's a middle-aged couple with a 'problem' teenage son. I've been counseling them for the past few weeks," he said, his voice so low she had to lean close to hear him. "Based on everything they said I eventually came to the conclusion that he was probably depressed—maybe clinically depressed—and that they needed to get him professional help. The only trouble is, I came to that conclusion too late." He wiped his hand across his eyes, and when he continued, his voice was uneven, laced with devastation. "He committed suicide this morning."

"Oh, Brad!" With her free hand, Sam reached over and touched his cheek. His whole body was shaking, and she could feel the grief emanating from every pore.

"What kind of minister am I that I couldn't prevent a tragedy like this?" he asked in anguish, his voice harsh with desolation, his grip on her fingers tightening.

Sam placed her free hand flat against his cheek and exerted gentle pressure, forcing him to turn his head so she could look directly into his devastated eyes. "Brad Matthews, don't you ever doubt the fact that you are a fine man and an equally fine minister," she said fiercely. "Your only problem is that you care too much. Surely this boy's parents aren't blaming you?"

"I don't know," he said, shaking his head. "But *I* blame me. There *was* a way to prevent this. I just didn't know what it was. And when they called today, looking for comfort, I failed them then, too. I couldn't find a way to explain what happened, why a young life was wasted. All I could do was go to them, tell them that I'm sorry and that we can't always understand the ways of the Lord.''

"Maybe that's what they needed to hear,'' Sam said gently.

He shook his head. ''A minister should be able to do better than that, find more words to ease their pain.''

"But you're also a man, remember? You told me that yourself. You're human, Brad. You did the best you could to help. That's all the Lord can ask. That's all this boy's parents can ask.''

"Maybe. But it doesn't bring him back,'' he said sadly. He was still clutching her hand, but his grip had loosened imperceptibly, and the tremors that had racked his body were subsiding.

"No,'' Sam agreed. ''But even when we don't understand why something happens we have to accept God's will.''

He looked at her wearily, and the ghost of a smile touched his lips. ''You're the one who sounds like a preacher.''

"Hardly,'' she said, her mouth twisting wryly. Then she reached up and smoothed the hair back from his forehead. "How long have you been sitting here?''

He shrugged. ''I don't know.''

"Well, I think you need to focus on something else for a while. Have you eaten anything today?''

He frowned. ''I had a bagel this morning.''

"That's what I thought. Now I'm not going to offer to cook or anything, so don't panic, but why don't we raid your refrigerator? I can whip up something simple, and I'll feel better if you have a meal. I think you will, too.''

"You don't have to do that, Sam.''

"Maybe I want to.''

"Are you sure?"

"Of course I'm sure. Come on. We'll make do."

An hour later, as they finished their simple meal of spaghetti and salad, Brad reached for her hand across the table. "I do feel a little better, Sam. Thank you. For everything."

"I didn't do much."

"You were here when I needed you," he said, rubbing his thumb across the back of her hand. Suddenly she winced, and he glanced down with a frown. Faint purple marks had appeared on her flesh, and he looked up at her in concern. "I did this, didn't I?" he said slowly. "In the church, when you took my hand."

She shrugged off his question. "Don't worry about it, Brad. You needed to hold on to a hand. Mine was convenient. I didn't mind."

He sighed. "I'm sorry, Sam. The last thing I'd ever want to do is hurt you."

"Brad, it's nothing. Really," she assured him. "Now how about some dessert? I saw ice cream in the freezer."

He shook his head. "Not for me, thanks. But go ahead if you want some."

"No. I'm full."

He took a sip of water and his lips quirked up ruefully. "You know, I'm beginning to wonder if we're ever going to have a normal date."

Sam smiled. Now was *not* the time to bring up their relationship. He'd had about all the stress he could handle for today. "I know what you mean," she said noncommittally.

"Well, given tonight's episode, I wouldn't blame you if you ate and ran. But I'd really like it if you could stay awhile. Maybe there's a good movie on TV or something."

"Just try to get rid of me," she said with a grin. She wasn't about to leave yet. Brad had suffered a terrific shock, and caring human contact was the best thing for him right now.

He gave her a grateful smile. "Thanks." He rose and reached for her hand, lacing his fingers carefully through hers. "Let's see what the tube has to offer."

They lucked out with a classic comedy, but the emotional trauma took its toll on Brad, and halfway through he fell asleep beside her, exhausted, his head dropping to the cushioned back of the couch.

For a long while Sam didn't move, content to sit close beside him, listening to his deep, even breathing and letting her mind rest. It had been an eventful two days, she mused, with nothing going according to schedule. She'd come here tonight to say goodbye to the man next to her. Instead she felt more linked to him than ever. It was almost as if, in the face of tragedy, they'd forged an even deeper bond, taking their relationship to a new, more intimate level. In many ways it was beginning to seem as if they really did need each other.

When the movie ended, Sam carefully reached for the remote and clicked off the set. She looked over at Brad, the harsh lines of anguish in his face now softened in sleep. With a sudden rush of tenderness she reached over and ever-so-gently brushed his hair back from his forehead. He sighed softly, and his head dropped to her shoulder. She really ought to go, she knew. It was getting late. But she hated to wake him just yet. He was so exhausted. She'd wait just a little while longer, she decided, tilting her head so she could feel his hair against her cheek.

As she sat there in the dim room she, too, began to grow drowsy. And as her eyes drifted shut, her last conscious thought was that this evening had certainly turned out differently than she expected. Falling asleep with Brad's head on her shoulder had definitely not been on the agenda.

A sudden pressure against his chest made Brad sigh, and he shifted slightly, coming partially awake. Subconsciously he was aware of a feeling of warmth, contentment and…for some reason the word *completeness* came to mind. He was just beginning to drift back to deep sleep when a soft, feminine sigh pulled him sharply back to reality.

Brad opened his eyes. The room was dim, illuminated only by a low-wattage lamp on a table near the door, giving the contents a fuzzy, slightly out-of-focus appearance. But one thing was very clear. Sam was wrapped in his arms, her head nestled against his chest, her glorious hair spilling over his arm.

As that realization penetrated his consciousness, Brad suddenly, abruptly, came fully awake. It had been more than six years since he'd awakened in a woman's arms, and he'd almost forgotten the intense, sweet joy of that experience.

Sam smelled good, he thought, inhaling the spicy fragrance that emanated from her skin, noting at the same time that she looked different in sleep. Younger. More vulnerable. And definitely appealing. Very appealing. His arm rested at her waist, and gently he traced her slender curves with his fingers, suddenly finding it difficult to breathe as a powerful, consuming surge of desire raced through his body.

Deliberately he stilled his hand. He had to get himself under control, he thought, his jaw tightening. Think rationally. He took a deep breath. Then another. That was better. First of all, he reasoned, it was late. Second, Sam needed to leave. Third, despite points one and two, he couldn't wake her up just yet. Not until he'd calmed down a little. Except that being snuggled up next to her soft curves wasn't helping in the least. Focus on something else, he told himself deliberately. Think about your sermon for tomorrow. Or maybe it was today already. Pretend Sam isn't even here.

Clearly, *that* was an unrealistic goal. But eventually he

would feel under control enough to face her. It just might be a long wait.

Sam was having a wonderful dream. She was wrapped in Brad's strong arms, her head nestled against his shoulder, the musky scent of his aftershave drifting in the air. She didn't want to wake up. But someone was calling her name. Persistently. So slowly, reluctantly, she opened her eyes—to find Brad's only inches from her own.

"Hi, sleepyhead," he said huskily, his lips curving up into a smile.

Sam frowned. Was she still asleep? Or was this real?

The gentle pressure of Brad's hand at her waist was real enough, all right, and suddenly the events of the evening came back to her in a rush. "What time is it?" she asked, her voice thick with sleep.

"I don't know. You're leaning on my arm, and it's asleep," he replied, his voice tinged with amusement.

For the first time, Sam became conscious of her position. Sometime after she'd fallen asleep she'd apparently turned toward Brad and cuddled shamelessly against him. Her face flaming in embarrassment, she quickly extricated herself.

Pushing her hair back from her face, she leaned over to search for her shoes, which she'd kicked off earlier in the evening.

"I'm sorry," she said, her voice muffled.

"Why?"

"I should have left when you fell asleep instead of..." She paused, fishing for the right phrase.

"Cuddling?" he supplied matter-of-factly. He didn't seem at all embarrassed, Sam realized in surprise.

"Yeah," she replied, tucking her hair behind her ear in a very uncharacteristic but endearing little-girl-like gesture.

"I'm glad you stayed, Sam," he said with quiet sincerity. "And there's nothing wrong with cuddling when two people care for each other." Then he glanced at his watch and gave her a wry grin. "Unfortunately, as a minister, I have to be concerned about propriety. Even if things *were* perfectly innocent, I doubt whether my congregation would appreciate discovering that a woman spent the night here."

She flushed. "I'm sure they wouldn't. I didn't mean to fall asleep, Brad. I was only going to stay a few minutes," she said apologetically.

"It's okay," he assured her. "Having you here helped a lot. To be honest, I wish you could stay the rest of the night."

Sam tore her gaze from his with difficulty and rose, smoothing down her skirt. So did she wish that, she thought as he stood beside her. But she left the words unsaid.

"Let me drive you home," he offered.

"But my car's here," she reminded him.

"Oh, yeah." He frowned. "I could drive you home in your car and then take a taxi back," he suggested.

She glanced at her watch. It was one in the morning, and he had an early service. "I appreciate the offer, Brad. But I can get home safely by myself. I have a phone in the car. Besides, you need to be awake in the pulpit tomorrow."

"You have a point," he admitted. "Still, maybe I'm old-fashioned, but I don't like the idea of—"

"Brad...I'll be fine," she interrupted gently. "I'll call you when I get home," she promised.

He capitulated with a sigh. "You win. But be careful."

"I will." She reached for her purse, then hesitated, frowning. "Brad...are you sure you'll be all right here by yourself?" she asked, gazing up at him worriedly.

He smiled sadly. "Yes, the darkest hours have passed. I'll be okay now."

They walked to her car in silence, and when she turned at the door to look up at him his eyes tenderly traced the contours of her face. The rain had stopped, but a fine, soft mist hung in the air, giving the world an ethereal quality. As he reached over to run a gentle hand down her cheek, Sam felt almost as if she had stepped into a scene from one of her favorite old romantic movies. And she *definitely* felt that way when Brad reached over and cupped her neck with his hand, then drew her close and lowered his lips to hers.

Sam didn't protest. She was past protesting. Her body was his ally. So was her heart. It was only her mind that fought this attraction. And her mind was not functioning too well at the moment.

Brad's lips moved over hers, gently, yet sensuously, drawing an ardent, breathless response from her. He pulled her closer, until her body melted against his. Sam's breath caught in her throat as his touch worked its magic.

By the time they drew apart, both of them were breathless.

Brad stared down at her, his eyes smoldering. He wanted Sam. To pretend otherwise would be foolish. For the first time in his life he truly understood the powerful temptations of the flesh. Brad had never experienced anything like the attraction he felt for Sam. Rachel and he had shared a quiet, deep passion. *Wild* was not a word that described the physical expression of their love. But it very definitely—and accurately—described his reaction when Sam was in his arms. The simmering, consuming need he felt for her was very hard to resist. Yet giving in to his desires went against everything he believed. It just wasn't his style.

Brad drew a long, deep breath and reached over to cup her face in his hands, gently stroking his thumbs over her cheekbones. Sam could feel him trembling. And this time it wasn't from shock and grief. He wanted her, just as much as she wanted him. But giving in to desires wasn't his way. She knew that, and she was grateful for his restraint, because in her present state she wasn't sure she would have had the strength to resist him if he'd pushed for further intimacy.

"I'll call you tomorrow," he said softly, his voice unsteady.

She nodded, not trusting her voice, and after one last, lingering kiss, she slipped behind the wheel.

As she pulled away from the parsonage, she glanced in the rearview mirror. Brad was illuminated in the mist by a streetlight, and the glow it cast around him added to the unreal, dreamlike quality of the scene. But it was real enough, Sam knew. Her lips were still tingling from the pressure of his mouth on hers, and her body was quivering with desire.

As she drove home through the mist, Sam thought about the similarity between their parting of moments before and so many of the old, romantic movies she collected. Of course, the movies had happy endings. Real life didn't, necessarily.

But for the first time, Sam felt a glimmer of hope. There were problems to deal with in their relationship, of course, obstacles to overcome. For a happy ending to become a reality, both she and Brad would have to make peace with her past, as well as her potential inability to have children. Both her age and her medical history were working against her on the latter, and she knew that he loved children and deeply desired a family. Accepting all of these things would require him to be very forgiving and to love her very, very deeply.

Sam knew it was a long shot even for a man like Brad. And she might be jumping to the wrong conclusions, she reminded herself. She knew Brad liked her. What she didn't know was just how serious he was about their relationship long-term. She suspected that he was the kind of man who would think this relationship out very deliberately and allow plenty of time for things to develop before jumping to any conclusions. *Impulsive* was not a word she associated with Brad. Love might not even have entered his mind yet. She couldn't be sure of his feelings, only hers. And the simple fact was that she had fallen in love with him.

Sam didn't know exactly when it had happened. All she knew was that it had. And she also knew that the love she felt for him was deep and irrevocable. But she was in no hurry to deal with those feelings. Time was good. It would give her breathing space to seek a way to resolve the guilt that had been part of her life for seventeen years. And it would give their relationship a chance to grow and deepen, provide her the opportunity to choose the perfect moment and the right words to tell him about her past. Not to mention the time to build up her courage.

Sam knew she was taking a chance. In the end, even if Brad came to love her, he might not be able to accept what she told him. It was risky. But for the first time in many years, she was beginning to believe that maybe she *could* have her own happy ending. And for the possibility of a happy ending, she was willing to take the risk.

Chapter Ten

"**S**urprise!"

Sam looked at Henry's stunned face, then at Brad, and smiled. They'd pulled it off, after all. Instead of the sedate seventieth birthday dinner with Brad, Rebecca and Sam that he expected, Henry was the guest of honor at a gala party in the Jersey American Legion Hall. The three-piece combo broke into "Happy Birthday," and fifty voices gave a rousing rendition of the song.

As the crowd moved forward to surround Henry, the three conspirators stepped back.

"I'd say he was surprised," Brad commented with a grin.

Rebecca laughed. "That's putting it mildly. This was a great idea, Sam. Left to our own devices, I'm afraid Brad and I would have come up with something much less imaginative. And definitely more boring."

"I doubt that," Sam demurred. "But surprises are a lot of fun. So I figured your dad might get a kick out of it."

Brad glanced at his father, flushed and laughing in the midst of the high-spirited crowd, and smiled. "I'd say your instincts were right on target."

The band struck up a fox-trot, and Sam turned to Rebecca. "Maybe you and your dad should have the first dance," she suggested.

Rebecca shook her head doubtfully. "I don't know if we'll be able to coax him onto the dance floor. He never was much of a dancer, even when Mom was alive. She always had to drag him out there. But maybe…" She directed a speculative look at Sam. "Why don't you try? He might dance if you asked him."

Sam hesitated. "Do you really think so?"

"Rebecca's right," Brad concurred. "You're the most likely person to get him out there."

Sam shrugged and smiled. "Okay. I'll give it a shot."

Three hours later, Rebecca gazed at Brad across the table and shook her head incredulously. "Do you believe this? Dad—line dancing! And did you see him in that conga line a little while ago?"

Brad chuckled. "Yep. Leave it to Sam. I told you, she's one amazing woman."

Rebecca smiled. "Speaking of which…anything new to report? It's been almost three months since we talked on Memorial Day."

The band shifted gears, and the melodic strains of "The Very Thought of You" drifted over the room. Brad looked toward the dance floor and rose. "I think it's about time I reclaimed my date," he said, glancing back at Rebecca, a mischievous glint in his eyes.

"You're not going to get off that easily, you know," she informed him pertly. "We'll talk tomorrow."

Brad grinned. "We'll see."

"Count on it," she called after him.

As Brad approached Sam and his father, his grin softened into a tender smile. She looked fabulous tonight, in an elegant black dress that enhanced her slender curves, the skirt slit to reveal an enticing glimpse of leg. He'd been wanting to dance with her all night, longing to feel her melt into his arms as she had at Laura's wedding, while they moved in time to a romantic melody. But Henry monopolized her after the first dance, and Brad was reluctant to interrupt. After all, it *was* his father's party. But enough was enough. He deserved at least one dance with his date.

Brad tapped on his father's shoulder and smiled. "Sorry to interrupt, Dad, but I think this dance is mine."

Henry stepped back. "'Bout time you danced with the prettiest lady here," he declared, giving Sam a wink.

The smoky look Brad sent her way made Sam's nerve endings sizzle. "I agree," he said, the husky timbre of his voice playing havoc with her pulse.

She moved into his arms, and he pulled her close as they swayed in time to the melodic refrain. With a contented sigh, she closed her eyes, enjoying the gentle but firm pressure of Brad's hand in the small of her back, his cheek against her hair, his fingers entwined with hers. It felt so right to be in his arms. So good. And so natural.

Sam thought back over the past two months, since the day she'd found Brad in the church, despondent over the young boy's suicide. That time of tragedy had been a turning point in their relationship, she realized in retrospect. Until then, Sam had fought her attraction to him, refusing to believe it could ever work between them. But that night, as she consoled Brad, a tender hope had been born. It was a fragile thing, requiring careful nurturing, but little by little it grew stronger as their relationship deepened and developed.

Slowly Sam had begun to believe that maybe— maybe—there was a future for them together. According to everything she was learning in Bible class, the Lord offered forgiveness to those who repented. And if the Lord could forgive her, maybe, just maybe, Brad could, as well. She even began to harbor a precarious hope that if he loved her enough he might be able to accept the possibility that theirs could be a childless union.

Sam knew she was juggling a lot of "maybes." There were issues she needed to resolve with Brad. And she would. Soon. But not tonight. Not when he was holding her so tenderly, his hand stroking her back, his lips in her hair. There would be time to face reality later. For tonight, for this moment, she just wanted to lose herself in the magic of his arms. And so, with another contented sigh, she molded herself even more closely against the hard planes of his body and refused to think about tomorrow.

Brad felt Sam move closer and glanced down at the top of her head. Her cheek was pressed to his shoulder, her glorious red hair resting softly against the front of his jacket. It was becoming more and more difficult to imagine his world without her, he realized. She was lively and energetic and fun, bringing joy and renewed life to his existence. She was also tender and compassionate and loving, and those qualities touched his heart, filling him with a deep yearning that grew stronger each day. He no longer wanted to part from her at the end of an evening together and return to his empty house—and empty bed. He wanted to fall asleep with her every night, his last conscious sensation her soft body snuggled against his, and wake up each morning to find her burnished hair spilling over his arm, her gorgeous green eyes merely inches away as they smiled sleepily into his. He wanted her to share everything with him, from his morning coffee to his last waking thoughts. In other words, he wanted her to share his life. Anything short of that was becoming less and less acceptable.

Weeks before, Rebecca had said he was in love. Brad had denied it then, but now he was forced to admit the truth. Rebecca was right. He loved Sam. And maybe it was about time he told her.

The music came to an end, and reluctantly he loosened his hold. Sam released a small sigh and stepped back slightly to look up at him, her unguarded eyes seeming to mirror his deepest feelings.

Yes, he decided. It was time he gave voice to what was in his heart.

* * *

"Okay, big brother, you've got fifteen minutes," Rebecca said with a glance at her watch. She poured herself a glass of orange juice then joined him at the kitchen table, where Brad was enthusiastically working his way through a gargantuan waffle.

"For what?" he mumbled between bites.

"To finish the conversation we started last night."

He looked at her innocently, twirling a bite of waffle in the syrup. "Which conversation was that?"

Rebecca took a sip of juice and pointed out the window, where Henry and Sam were in deep discussion next to the rose garden, apparently oblivious to the oppressive late-August humidity. "About you and a certain redhead. Who I like very much, by the way."

Brad smiled. "I like her, too."

Rebecca chuckled. "Yeah, I know. So why are you dragging your feet? Is it serious or not?"

Brad's hand stilled and he turned to look out the window, his eyes lovingly tracing Sam's profile. "It's very definitely serious," he affirmed quietly.

Rebecca reached over and touched his arm. "I'm happy for you, Brad," she said softly, all traces of her teasing tone vanishing.

"Thanks. I just hope she feels the same way."

Rebecca turned to look thoughtfully out the window. She had no doubt that Sam loved Brad. It was obvious. Yet she sensed some sort of tension, almost worry, in the other woman that she couldn't quite get a handle on. But maybe it was just her overactive imagination, she told herself. There was probably no reason for concern.

"Why so quiet all of a sudden?" Brad asked cautiously, wondering if Rebecca harbored doubts about Sam's suitability as a minister's wife. Sam wasn't stereotypical, that was for sure. Her flamboyant nature and less-than-active religious life had given him pause as well. They were issues he still grappled with on occasion. Yet he knew beyond the shadow of a doubt that he loved Sam. The rest he had put in the Lord's hands.

Rebecca suppressed her wayward thoughts and turned back to Brad. "Just thinking about what a nice couple you two make," she said, much to his relief. "And as for hoping she feels the same way—you won't know till you ask her," she pointed out. "But I wouldn't worry too much. The lady is definitely in love," she added with a smile. Then she swallowed the last of her juice and stood up. "Sorry to run like this. But Rose and Frances held the fort for me last night at the restaurant, and I don't want to impose too much."

Brad grinned, picturing the two maiden sisters who were combination hostesses, cooks and mother hens for Rebecca. "You were lucky to find them."

Rebecca smiled. "Don't I know it! They're a treasure! That's why I don't want to leave them in the lurch to handle the Saturday crowd alone. I'll just say goodbye to Dad and Sam on my way out," she said, pausing at the door. "And keep me informed," she added, smiling.

Brad watched as Rebecca joined Henry and Sam, giving each of them a lingering hug. She said something that made Sam laugh, and then, with a wave, she was gone. Henry and Sam went back to their gardening discussion, and Brad tackled his waffle again, spearing a bite and chewing thoughtfully. Rebecca was right. He wouldn't know how the lady felt till he asked her. And he would. Just as soon as the right opportunity presented itself.

"Well, I'd say the party was a success," Sam said as they approached St. Louis. "Your dad seemed to have a great time. And I like your sister. She's very nice."

"Yeah. I'm kind of partial to her," Brad replied with a smile. "She liked you, too, by the way."

Sam returned his smile. "I'm glad."

There was a moment of silence, and Brad suddenly sensed an undercurrent of excitement. He glanced at Sam curiously, in time to see her tuck her hair behind her ear—a gesture he'd come to recognize as a sign of nervousness or excitement. Something was very definitely up.

Sam drew a deep breath and turned to him. "I guess this is the weekend for surprises," she said with studied casualness. "I have one for you, too."

He looked at her and quirked an eyebrow questioningly. "You do?"

"Mmm-hmm. Just follow my directions when we get in a little closer."

He did as she asked, pulling to a stop a short time later in front of a contemporary ranch-style house.

She turned to him eagerly, no longer trying to restrain her excitement, her eyes sparkling with enthusiasm. "Well, this is it!" she declared.

He looked at her quizzically. "This is what?"

"Your house! I found your house!"

"My house?"

"The one you need, remember?" she teased. "I've been keeping my eyes open, but I just couldn't find the right one. This came on the market Thursday, and I took a quick look, even though it hasn't been officially listed yet. But I've got the key." She reached into her purse and withdrew it, dangling it in front of him enticingly. "Do you want to take a look?"

He grinned. "Absolutely."

For the next hour they poked through every corner of the house and the yard, and Brad had to admit that Sam's instincts were right on target. Even he hadn't known exactly what he wanted. Until now.

"So...what do you think?" she asked anxiously, when they'd completed their tour and stood once again under the vaulted ceiling in the living room.

He shook his head. "I don't know how you did it. But it's perfect."

A smile of relief brightened her face. "Thank goodness! I thought this was the sort of house you had in mind, but

I wasn't absolutely sure. And it's close to your church, too.''

"What do *you* think of it?" he asked.

"I think it's great!" she said enthusiastically. "It's modern—but not too much so. And it's bright and airy and spacious. I know it's a little more than you want to spend, but I really think it's worth it, Brad. This is a solid neighborhood, and the prices have steadily risen here. So it'll be a good investment.''

"I'll take your word on that. And it does seem ideal." He took a deep breath. "Okay. Let's make an offer."

"Great! I'll get the paperwork ready."

He glanced at his watch, a thoughtful look on his face. "I've got to take care of a few things this afternoon. How about if I stop by your place around seven? Would that work?''

"Sure. I'll be ready for you. I'll even chill a bottle of wine so we can celebrate.''

"That would be perfect," he said with a smile. And if things went well, he thought, they'd be celebrating a whole lot more than buying a house.

Brad nervously fingered the small velvet box in the pocket of his jacket as he waited for Sam to answer the door. He hadn't planned to move quite this quickly, but the opportunity he'd been waiting for had unexpectedly presented itself, and it was too good to pass up. What better time to ask Sam to marry him than when he was buying a house they would hopefully share? He'd spent the afternoon at the jewelry store, emerging lighthearted and excited with his purchase, but now that he was actually faced with posing the question, his confidence faltered. Maybe he'd misread Sam's feelings. Despite Rebecca's assessment, maybe Sam just liked him. Maybe that's as far as it went with her. What if she said no? he thought in sudden panic.

The door opened, and Sam's tender smile and warm, welcoming eyes allayed some of his doubts.

"Hi," she said, her gaze sweeping over his cream linen blazer, open-necked blue shirt and crisply pleated tan slacks. "You look nice," she added approvingly, her eyes returning to his.

"Thanks. So do you," he replied, returning the compliment with a warm smile. Then he reached for her, and she went willingly into his arms, her ardent, breathless response rapidly dispelling the rest of his doubts. His wavering confidence steadied.

When Brad released her after a lingering kiss, Sam smiled and stepped back, emitting a small sigh of pleasure. "Mmm. Nice. But you'd better keep your distance until we fill out the paperwork on the house. If you distract me too much I might add a zero to your offer or something," she warned with a laugh as he entered. She closed the door behind him, leading the way toward the kitchen. "I've got all the paperwork ready. It's on the table," she said, heading in that direction.

"Sam."

An odd note in his voice stopped her, and she turned to give him a questioning look. "What's wrong? Are you having second thoughts?"

He shook his head. "Far from it." He raked his fingers through his hair and gestured toward the couch. "Could we sit down for a minute?"

"Sure." She moved toward the living room, watching him with a worried frown as he sat down beside her and reached for her hand, cradling it between his. "What is it, Brad? Is the price too high? I know it's a little more than you wanted to—"

"The price is okay, Sam," he interrupted her.

She fell silent. Something was wrong, though she didn't have a clue what. She'd just have to wait for him to tell her in his own way.

Brad smiled at her tentatively, his thumb gently stroking

the back of her hand. "You'll have to forgive me if I seem a little nervous. But I've only done this one other time."

Something in his tone triggered a faint alarm bell in the back of her mind, and a knot began to form in her stomach.

"I know we've only been dating for five months, Sam. But as my father and sister told me, that's long enough when you meet the right person. And I have."

He gazed at her, and she stared at him, mesmerized by the soft glow of love reflected in his eyes. "Before you came into my life, there was a cold, empty place in my heart that desperately needed light and warmth. I found those things in you. And somewhere along the way, I also found something else. I found love."

He reached into his coat pocket and withdrew the small velvet box, flipping it open to reveal a sparkling solitaire.

"The simple fact is, I love you, Sam. I want to spend the rest of my life waking up next to you, laughing with you, sharing with you. I want us to grow old together surrounded by our children, with wonderful memories of a life filled with love and joy and discovery." He paused and took a steadying breath. "Will you marry me?"

Sam continued to stare at Brad, her eyes now wide with shock. This wasn't supposed to be happening. Not yet. Brad wasn't the impulsive type. He was the kind of man who should believe in a long courtship. She thought she had plenty of time to bring up the secrets from her past. But obviously she had thought wrong.

With all her heart Sam wanted to throw herself into his arms and say yes, to forget her past and think only of the wonderful future Brad offered. But that wouldn't be fair to him. He deserved to know exactly what he was getting. There were issues that had to be faced. And they had to be faced now, whether she was ready to address them or not. Carefully Sam withdrew her hand from between his and rose, nervously lacing her fingers together as she began to pace, trying to formulate the words that needed to be said.

Brad sat perfectly still, tuned in to every nuance of her response. While he had limited experience with proposals, this was *not* the reaction he had hoped for. He had expected surprise, yes. But not shock. And Sam was clearly shocked. She looked agitated and distracted, and the fact that she was putting physical distance between them was not a good sign. He felt his stomach clench, and his throat grew tight with tension. Had he misread her interest after all? He waited with trepidation for her to speak, but as the seconds slowly ticked by she remained silent, pacing nervously, her eyes almost desperate. Something was very, very wrong.

Finally Brad couldn't stand the silence any longer. "Sam?" he prompted, striving to keep his voice even, trying not to reveal his tension.

She ignored him, so he tried again. "Sam?" His voice was gentle, but a bit more insistent, and this time she paused, slowly turning to face him. Brad frowned at the fear and despair reflected in her eyes. "What is it?" he asked, suddenly afraid himself.

Sam drew a shaky breath, realizing she'd run out of time. She was backed into a corner and there was no escape. "It's just so…unexpected, Brad," she said, the explanation for her reaction sounding lame even to her ears.

"I realize that," he conceded, struggling not to betray his panic. "But I'm also getting the impression that it's unwelcome," he said cautiously.

"Oh, no! No! It's not that," she cried.

Brad couldn't doubt the sincerity in her voice or her eyes, and he breathed a little easier. His instincts had been right—she cared about him deeply. But something—apparently of a very serious nature—was holding her back. "Then what's wrong?"

"Oh, Brad!" She didn't even know where to start. Maybe it was best to begin with the lesser concerns. "Think about it. We're so different. How could this ever work?"

"We're not as different as you seem to think we are."
She was stalling, avoiding the real problem, and he knew
it. But eventually she'd have to tell him, and all he could
do was wait until she was ready.

"But…well…there are issues."

"Like what?"

"Like…I don't want to quit working," she said, grop-
ing for excuses.

"I don't expect you to," he assured her. "Lots of ministers' wives work. Besides, we could use the extra money.
Especially if we buy that house you found," he said teasingly, trying to lighten the mood of doom that now hovered menacingly over the room.

"I'm not the domestic type, either. And I can't cook."

"Trust me, I know," he replied, his mouth twisting into
a wry grin. "But I'm used to microwave food."

She frantically racked her brain for other excuses. "I
probably make more money than you do," she pointed out.

He shrugged. "Does that bother you?"

She stared at him, taken aback. "Well, no. But— Oh,
Brad, I'm not religious enough to be a minister's wife!"

"We'll work on it," he said easily. "I think that more
of your Christian upbringing survived than you realize. It's
just a matter of giving it a chance to develop."

Sam was out of excuses. This was the moment of truth.
She reached for a throw pillow, crushed it between her
fingers and hugged it in front of her like a shield before
turning to face him.

Brad frowned, his perceptive eyes missing none of her
distress. She looked pale, almost ill, and once more his gut
clenched as he braced himself for whatever was to come.

Sam drew a deep, steadying breath, and when she spoke,
her tone was no longer frenetic or agitated, but resigned.
"Brad, there are things you don't know about me," she
said slowly, her voice subdued.

"I know everything I need to know," he assured her,

but for the first time she detected a slight hesitation in his voice.

Sam swallowed convulsively and shook her head jerkily. "No. You don't." She walked over to the window and stared out silently for a moment, still gripping the pillow protectively. "But it's time you did," she affirmed quietly, taking another deep breath before she forced herself to turn and face him. "You know that volunteer work I do on Tuesday nights?"

He nodded. "Yes."

"It's at a counseling center. We work with young unmarried pregnant girls, giving them the support they need to carry their baby to full term instead of destroying it."

"That's good work, Sam. It's admirable," he said carefully, unsure where this was leading.

"No," she replied, her voice choked. She turned away, unable in the end to look at him. "I don't do it for altruistic reasons. I do it because…because of guilt."

There was a moment of silence as Brad absorbed her words, and though her face was averted, Sam could feel a slight withdrawal, a distancing, even though neither had moved.

When he spoke again, his tone was measured, his voice cautious. "Do you want to explain that?"

No, she cried silently. What she wanted to do was forget it! To erase it from her memory forever and be free to live her life without the shadow of guilt that darkened her days. But that was a futile wish. And it was time he knew the truth.

And so she told him. Of her pregnancy. Of Randy's threats. Of her indecision and desperation. Of the pills and the drive and the accident. She told him how her irresponsibility had caused two deaths and left her potentially unable to conceive. She spared him none of the details, placing the blame squarely where it belonged—on herself. Because this man, who had just offered her his heart, had a right to know the burden she carried—and would always carry—in hers.

Not until she finished, tears running down her face and her voice choking on the last few, choppy sentences, did she turn with dread to face him.

Their eyes met, hers filled with anguish, his with shock. They stared at each other silently across the room, now shrouded in gloom by the fading twilight. Brad's lips were compressed into a thin, grim line, and there were deep furrows etched in his brow. His eyes were no longer warm, but distant, horrified and dazed. It was exactly the reaction Sam had feared, and she reached up to wipe the back of her hand across her eyes, trying to stifle a sob.

"I'm sorry, Brad," she whispered brokenly. "I should have told you all this a long time ago, before…" Her voice trailed off. She had started to say, "before we fell in love," but the words lodged in her throat. "I'm so sorry," she repeated helplessly.

Brad didn't say anything. He just bowed his head and passed one hand wearily over his face.

Sam watched him, her heart breaking. She knew his reaction was what she deserved but she wished with all her being that it had been different. In the last few weeks she'd allowed herself to hope that maybe she could find her own happy ending, as Laura had. But now she was forced to acknowledge that her hope had never been more than a fragile illusion. One that was crumbling now before her eyes as she stood by helplessly, unable to do anything but watch.

Sam felt ready to crumble herself, and she suddenly knew that the one thing she couldn't handle was Brad telling her it was over. The words he would say would be forever burned in her memory, replaying over and over again in the lonely years ahead. She couldn't deal with that. It was better if she ended it herself.

Sam moved shakily toward the coffee table and picked up the velvet box in her trembling fingers, allowing herself one last look at the ring, the sparkling symbol of the dream that might have been. Then she closed the lid. The finality of the snap echoed hollowly in the heavy stillness that suddenly lay between them. She put the ring carefully into his hand and walked unsteadily to the door.

"I think it will be easier for...for both of us if we just...say goodbye, Brad." Her words were choppy, her breath coming in short gasps. "I hope someday you can find it in your heart to...to forgive me for not telling you all this sooner. I guess I hoped that...well, it doesn't matter now. Please...just leave."

Brad stared down at the ring box, almost as if he didn't understand how it had come to be in his hand, then walked toward her. "Sam, I..."

"*Please,* Brad," she repeated in a choked voice. "Just go. Please."

He stood only inches away from her, but the chasm between them felt so deep and wide it might as well have been an ocean. Sam opened the door and stepped back. He paused on the threshold to look at her, his eyes still glazed with shock, the porch light mercilessly highlighting the haggard planes of his face. He almost seemed like a stranger, she thought. The warmth and love and passion she'd grown so used to finding in his eyes had vanished. In their place she saw only...emptiness.

"Goodbye, Brad." Without waiting for him to respond, she gently eased the door shut and slipped the lock into place.

Sam sagged against the frame and closed her eyes as the tears ran unchecked down her face. It was over. She was alone. Again. Just as she'd been for the past seventeen years.

Except—maybe the Lord was still with her, she thought suddenly. And in her despair she turned to Him with a desperate plea. Forgive me for what I did to that wonderful man, she prayed fervently. I let him fall in love with me, knowing what would likely happen when he found out about my past. That was wrong. And, Lord, please...please forgive me, also, for what I did that night seventeen years ago. I've never asked for Your forgiveness before, because I never felt I deserved it. And I probably still don't. But I've carried the burden of guilt and sorrow for so many years. I don't think I can carry it any longer. Even if Brad can't find it in his heart to forgive me, I hope that You can. Because I need to feel Your love and forgiveness, and to know that I'm not alone. Please help me.

Laura frowned and replayed the answering machine one more time.

"Laura, it's Sam. I just wanted to let you know that I'm going out of town for a few days, in case you try to reach me. And would you do me a favor? Tell Brad that Leslie Nelson at my office will handle the contract for him. Thanks, kiddo. I'll call you when I get back."

Laura's frown deepened. Despite the straightforward content of her message, Sam didn't sound at all like herself. Her voice was...funny. Rough, ragged, like she'd been crying. And the message had been left at eleven-thirty. If she and Nick hadn't stopped for a late bite after the theater she would have been there to talk to Sam directly. Now all she could do was wonder—and worry.

"What do you make of it?" Laura asked Nick, who entered in time to hear the last play-through.

Nick shook his head, frowning. "I don't have a clue. But that sure doesn't sound like Sam."

"Do you think I should call Brad?"

Nick glanced at his watch. "It's twelve-thirty. I'm sure he's in bed by now."

She sighed resignedly. "You're probably right. I guess I'll just have to wait and talk to him after church tomorrow. I just hope he knows what's going on."

One look at Brad's face the next morning was enough to convince Laura that he knew exactly what was going on. There were dark circles under his eyes, as if he hadn't slept all night, and he had an uncharacteristic pallor. Obviously, Sam's problem was also Brad's.

Laura waited in the church after the service while Nick went down to the coffee room. The moment Brad emerged she rose. He saw her immediately and strode toward her quickly.

"Laura! I was hoping you'd wait. Do you know where Sam is?" he asked without preamble.

She shook her head helplessly. "I thought maybe you did. I had a message on the answering machine when we got home last night that she was going out of town for a few days. And she said to tell you to work with Leslie Nelson in her office on the contract, if that makes any sense."

He nodded impatiently. "Yeah, it does. The contract part, anyway. I'm getting ready to put a bid on a house. Listen, Laura, do you have any idea where she went?"

"No. None." She reached up and touched his arm, her voice etched with concern. "Brad, what happened? She sounded awful. And pardon me for saying so, but you don't look so great yourself. I have a feeling there's a connection there."

He raked his fingers through his hair and sighed. "You're right. There is. Sam and I...well, she told me some things last night...I guess I was just in shock or something.... I've been calling her, but I keep getting her machine. I don't know what to do...." He sighed again, his frustration almost tangible. "Frankly, Laura, I acted like an idiot," he admitted bluntly. "She needed me, and I wasn't there for her."

Laura couldn't follow Brad's disjointed rambling, but obviously something serious had happened between him and Sam the day before, which Brad now regretted. And if Brad was in this almost incoherent condition, Laura suspected that Sam's mental state was as bad, if not worse.

Laura desperately wanted to help, but she had no idea where to even begin looking for her friend.

"I'm sorry, Brad," Laura said helplessly. "I don't know what happened between you two, but Sam sounded devastated." She frowned worriedly. "I hate to think of her being alone, feeling like that."

"So do I," he said, his voice raw with pain. He reached around and wearily massaged his neck, his eyes desolate. "Look, Laura, if you hear from her, would you ask her to call me? Or find out where she is, at least?"

"I'll do what I can, although I have a feeling she won't call until she gets back. But if she's going to miss Bible class I'm sure she'll let me know," she added hopefully.

Brad stared at her uncomprehendingly. "Bible class?"

Laura bit her lip and frowned at her indiscretion. "I wasn't supposed to mention anything about that," she said slowly.

"Sam goes with you to Bible class?" Brad repeated incredulously.

Laura nodded reluctantly. "She has been for months. But she didn't want me to say anything."

Brad closed his eyes, and a muscle twitched in his jaw. All these months, while he'd been wrestling with the notion of getting involved with someone who didn't actively practice her faith, she'd been going to Bible class. Probably learning all about mercy and forgiveness and withholding judgment—the very principles he'd neglected to demonstrate last night, he thought bleakly.

He was a minister, a man who had dedicated his life to spreading the Lord's principles, who preached every Sunday about the importance of living the words in the good book—not just reading them. Oh, he talked a good show. But when push came to shove, when he'd been dramatically called on to put those principles into action, he'd fallen short.

Brad shook his head helplessly. "I can't believe how I failed her," he said, his voice shadowed with despair and self-recrimination. "She needed support and understanding, and I just shut down. I don't know how I can ever make it up to her."

Laura reached over and once more touched his arm. "Brad, do you remember the sermon you gave last Christmas Eve?" she asked gently. "About mending relationships and saying 'I'm sorry'? It gave me new hope when I needed it the most. And those two words really do make a difference. Maybe you just need to follow your own advice." She paused to pick up her purse, then turned to him again. "Call me if I can do anything to help, okay?"

"I will. Thanks, Laura."

Brad watched her leave and then sank down on the pew, his head bowed. It had taken him hours last night to sufficiently emerge from his shock to think coherently. He had spent the long, sleepless hours that followed pacing, trying to sort out his feelings. On the one hand, he was appalled by Sam's story. The deaths of two young children, one yet unborn, was tragic. And the tragedy *was* her fault. That was the undeniable fact. There weren't many things that tested Brad's tolerance, but irresponsible behavior that hurt others was one of them.

And yet—who was he to judge her? That was the Lord's prerogative, not his. All he knew was that Sam would no more purposefully hurt anyone than he would. Seventeen years ago she'd been a frightened teenager, driven by deep despair and desperation, coping as best she knew how. Yes, she'd made mistakes. But the tragic event that had taken two lives had been an accident. Yet, she'd shouldered the blame without excuses, and she'd paid for those mistakes every day of her life since. Did the Lord expect her to do so for the rest of her life? Hadn't she done her penance? Didn't the Lord offer forgiveness and a second chance for those who repented? That's what Brad preached. It was what he believed. But he hadn't expected his belief to be tested quite so dramatically—and so unexpectedly.

He had still been trying to come to grips with the first revelation when she dropped her second bombshell—that should they marry, theirs might be a childless union. Brad had been stunned. He loved children. And while his dreams of a family had died with Rachel, they had been born again in the past few weeks as he fell in love with Sam. Giving that dream up the first time had been tough. He had never expected to be asked to do so a second time. It was a tremendous blow, and he knew his resolve to marry Sam had faltered momentarily.

An image of her desolate, tear-streaked face last night as she said goodbye at the door flashed suddenly across his mind. She loved him, and had hoped he loved her enough to accept the tragic secrets from her past, so that together they could create a future that gave full expression to their love. His shocked reaction had clearly convinced her that those hopes were in vain.

But as he'd discovered during his long night of soul searching, they weren't. Because, despite the impression he'd given her last night, he did love her enough to accept her past. And even enough to accept a childless union, if that was to be their fate.

Brad sighed and wearily rubbed his forehead. The ways of the Lord were often difficult to understand. For some reason He was erecting obstacles in the path of this relationship, testing their commitment to the limit. Brad didn't know why. All he knew was that he loved Sam—with or without children, and regardless of the tragic event in her past. Because in her he'd found a love he'd never hoped to find again. She was so much a part of his life now, that he couldn't even imagine a future without her.

The challenge was to convince Sam of these things. Considering the haunted, empty look in her eyes when she said goodbye, it wasn't going to be easy. It had been a look of—*resignation* was the best word he could think of to describe it. As if she felt rejection was what she deserved, that she was somehow unworthy of love or happiness.

With sudden insight, Brad realized that that was *exactly* what she felt. He thought back to some of their earliest conversations. Once, he recalled, she'd admitted that she was lonely. But when he'd asked her why she'd never remarried, her reply had been trite. "Too picky," she'd said. Even then he hadn't quite bought that explanation. Her flippant tone had somehow seemed underlaid with sadness. And then there was the time he'd remarked that she was a good person. Her face had grown sad at his comment, and she'd told him to save his praise for someone who deserved it.

In the intervening months those conversations had receded in his memory. But now, as he reconstructed them, the pieces suddenly fell into place. With uncanny certainty, he realized that they formed the basis for a self-imposed punishment. She had sentenced herself to a solitary existence as a penance for her mistake. And his shocked, judgmental reaction last night had only confirmed the validity of that sentence.

Brad closed his eyes and made a heartfelt plea to the Lord. Please help Sam to feel Your forgiveness, to know that she's punished herself enough and that it's all right to allow love into her life, he prayed. And help me find a way to let her know that I don't hold her past against her, and that her love alone, even without a family, will be more than enough for me. Because I need her, Lord. I need her today. And tomorrow. And for always.

Chapter Eleven

"Laura? It's Brad."

"Did you hear from Sam?" Laura asked tersely.

"No. But I checked, and she's been calling into the office, so I know she's okay. Physically, at least. And she has to come back soon. Listen, I need your help with something. I need you to get Sam to Bible class Thursday night."

Laura frowned. "That could be a tall order, Brad," she said slowly. "I'm not sure she'll even be back in town. And if she is, I can't guarantee she'll go. She sounded really down in that message she left."

"I'm sure she'll be back," Brad said, with more confidence than he felt. "You know Sam. She won't neglect her work for long. But you're right about the class," he admitted with a sigh. "She didn't exactly see Christian principles in action the other night. I've left all kinds of messages on her machines at work and home, trying to apologize. She just isn't responding. But I have an idea that might work, if you can get her to the class."

"I'll do my best," Laura promised.

"Thanks. And sit in the front, okay? That way she won't be able to leave without causing a stir."

Laura nodded. "Okay. And Brad...good luck."

He sighed. "Thanks. I have a feeling I'm going to need it. Plus a little help from Someone upstairs."

"Hi, kiddo. Did you think I dropped off the face of the earth?"

"Sam! Thank heaven!" Laura said in fervent relief. It was Thursday afternoon, and no one had expected Sam to disappear for this length of time. Especially Brad, who grew more frantic each day. "We've been worried sick! Where are you?"

"I'm back. Home, sweet home. Just walked in the door, in fact. Listen, I'm really sorry about that weird message last Saturday night. I probably sounded like a fruitcake. But I was upset about something, and I just needed to get away—quickly. I didn't even stop to think about how it would sound to you. I hope you'll forgive me."

"Of course," Laura assured her. Obviously Sam wasn't going to mention Brad, so Laura didn't either. "Where were you?"

"Chicago." She'd taken the train up, not trusting herself to drive, and spent days just walking, thinking, grieving. In the end, she made some semblance of peace with her situation, though now her heart felt cold and empty. "I just got in, but I wanted to talk to you about Bible class tonight. I know it's my turn to drive, but I'm thinking about skipping. Would you mind?"

Laura took a deep breath. She'd worked this all out ahead of time, asking the Lord for forgiveness even as she fabricated her story. But it was for a good cause, she consoled herself. "Well, no. I can figure something else out, I guess," she said, with just the right amount of hesitation. "It's just that I agreed to lead one of the discussion groups tonight, and my car's in the shop. Nick has a dinner meeting, or I could use his. But I can check around for a ride. I was going to, anyway, if you hadn't called.''

There was silence for a moment, and Laura knew Sam was waging an internal debate—her friend's needs versus her own. Laura crossed her fingers and held her breath, hoping Sam's sense of responsibility was strong enough to overcome her reluctance to attend class. It was.

"Well, I don't want to leave you in the lurch," Sam said slowly at last. "Okay, I'll be by. The usual time?"

"Yes. Thanks, Sam. Listen, I don't want to pry, but…is everything all right?" Laura already knew the answer to that question. Even though Sam sounded more normal, Laura detected an undertone of strain in her voice, as if her light tone was forced. But Laura wanted Sam to know that she was willing to lend a sympathetic ear, though she suspected that Sam wasn't ready to talk yet. And her friend's next words confirmed that suspicion.

"I'll live, kiddo," she replied, but her voice sounded empty and sad. "Maybe one of these days I'll tell you all about it."

"Well, I'm here if you need someone to talk to."

"Thanks. I appreciate that, Laura. I'll see you tonight."

Sam hung up quickly and reached for a tissue. Two more seconds and she'd have lost it. It had taken all her self-discipline to make it through the practical part of their conversation without breaking down. She couldn't handle a personal discussion.

She filled the kettle and set it on the stove, gazing out the window unseeingly as she waited for the water to boil, her thoughts returning to last Saturday. It was a scene she'd replayed over and over in her mind these past few days, and with each review her sympathy for Brad had grown. Of course he'd been shocked by her startling revelations, coming totally out of the blue like that. He was only human, after all, even if he was a minister. And she had thrown a lot at him all at once.

But she knew he hadn't meant to hurt her. It simply wasn't in his nature. That's probably why he'd left so many messages during the week, checking to make sure she was all right. Not that she'd listened to any of them. As soon as she heard his voice, she hit the Erase button. It was easier that way. Because even if he was sorry for hurting her, his initial reaction had been the honest one—shock, recrimination and withdrawal. He blamed her, just as she blamed herself, for the deaths of those children. And the final blow had been her revelation that she might never be able to give him the family he wanted so badly. He was probably hurt, and maybe even angry, that she'd withheld that information from him. And he had a right to be.

The kettle whistled, and Sam poured the steaming water into a mug, absently dunking an herbal tea bag. The motion reminded her of the day she'd received Laura's postcard from Hawaii, five months before. That was also the fateful day Brad had called about needing a house. It seemed like years ago, she thought wearily. So much had happened in the intervening months. And yet so little had changed. She'd been alone then. She was alone now. Her brief fling with romance, and the soaring hope that now lay shattered, simply affirmed what she'd always believed. There would be no happy ending for her.

"Laura! Laura!" Sam hissed urgently, reaching ahead to physically restrain her friend, who was blithely heading toward the front of the meeting room.

Laura turned in surprise. "What's wrong?"

"Let's sit in the back," Sam said in a low voice.

"But Marion's up front. She's led a study group before, and she promised to save us seats so she could fill me in on the protocol before the lecture starts."

Sam sighed tiredly. It was too much of an effort to argue. "Okay. Fine."

Sam said hello to Marion, then sank into her seat. She

hadn't prepared for tonight's class, since she hadn't intended to be here. Maybe she'd duck out after the lecture, go have a cup of coffee or something, and come back for Laura later.

The moderator stepped up to the podium, and the room grew silent. "Good evening, everyone. Welcome. It's my pleasure tonight to introduce our guest lecturer. Reverend Williams can't be with us, but we are fortunate to have as a replacement Reverend Brad Matthews. He's a wonderful speaker, as you'll soon discover, and I'm sure his talk will provide us with plenty of ideas for our discussion groups. Reverend Matthews' topic tonight is forgiveness."

Sam felt the color drain from her face as Brad entered the room from a side door and moved to the podium. For a moment she actually felt dizzy, and she forced herself to take several deep breaths.

"Sam? Are you all right?" Laura leaned over and eyed her friend worriedly.

"Did...did you know about this?" Sam asked, still fighting a wave of blackness. She turned to her friend, and one look at Laura's guilty, flushed face gave her the answer. Sam's gaze swung to Brad, who was now opening a folder from behind the podium. This was a conspiracy, she realized. Laura had lured her here falsely, made her sit in the front of the room so she couldn't leave without causing a stir and calling attention to herself. And Brad had put Laura up to it. Sam stared at her friend, the shock in her eyes giving way to uncertainty and then hurt. How much did she know?

Laura could easily track Sam's changing emotions in her unguarded eyes, could imagine her train of thought, and she reached over to touch her friend's arm. "Brad just asked me to get you here," she said quietly. "I don't know what happened between you two, but I do know that he's been a basket case all week. And you didn't sound much better on that message you left. I'm sorry if I did the wrong thing, but I hoped maybe this might help."

Sam was saved from having to respond by Brad's opening comments. She glanced longingly at the distant door, but there was no escape. She was stuck, plain and simple. She felt Laura squirm uncomfortably beside her, and a twinge of guilt tugged at her conscience. Laura had only done what Brad asked, and her heart had been in the right place. Sam couldn't hold that against her. Laura had no way of knowing that there was no simple fix for the problems she and Brad faced. Sam touched her arm, and when Laura looked over, Sam forced her lips up into the semblance of a smile. "Don't worry, kiddo," she whispered. "I know you meant well."

Laura squeezed her arm. "Thanks," she said gratefully, relief flooding her eyes.

Sam glanced back at Brad. Tonight he was in clerical garb, the first time she'd seen him dressed in his "work" clothes since the wedding. He made a nice appearance, she thought, studying him surreptitiously. He had a certain presence that radiated strength and solidness, inspiring confidence and trust. But his face seemed different than it had a few days before, she reflected. Older, somehow, and weary. There were lines at the corners of his eyes, and the shadows underneath spoke of sleepless nights and worry. Even the glint of silver that brushed his hair on each side seemed more prominent than before. Last Saturday's scene had obviously taken a heavy toll on him, she thought guiltily. And she could have prevented it if she'd had the courage to reveal the truth earlier in their relationship, before love complicated their lives. She could only hope that he quickly realized the truth—that he was better off without her. Maybe he already had.

But then why arrange this elaborate ruse to get her here tonight? she wondered with a puzzled frown. It wasn't as if he was giving her any special attention. In fact, except for a brief glance in her direction when he entered, as if to assure himself that she was there, he hadn't made eye contact with her once. Which was fine, of course. She preferred it this way. It would be much more difficult to keep her emotions in check if he looked at her with those probing, insightful eyes of his.

But still the question remained: Why did he want her here tonight? Sam didn't have a clue.

Brad launched into his well-prepared talk, and Sam was struck by the mellow, soothing quality of his voice, which she'd first noticed at Laura's wedding. Now, as then, she found it restful and comforting. Of course, his topic was another story. As she'd discovered, the notion of forgiveness was good in theory. But practical applications were another matter. Some things, obviously, just couldn't be forgiven.

As Brad neared the end of his talk, Sam began to plan her escape. She figured he must be hoping to waylay her after the lecture, and she didn't intend to give him the chance. As soon as he finished, she would head for the exit door to her right. She started to lean over to tell Laura that she'd be back later to pick her up, but Brad suddenly closed his notes and looked directly at her. His intense eyes locked onto hers with a riveting gaze, and the words died in her throat.

"Tonight we've talked about the Biblical context of forgiveness and the theory behind it," he said. "And as we've seen, this topic receives a great deal of attention from Scripture writers. But before I close, I'd like to focus for a few moments on the practical applications of forgiveness."

Sam swallowed with difficulty, and she suddenly found it hard to breathe. She stared at him, frozen in position, as she listened to words that seemed directed at her alone.

"Forgiveness is a concept that all of us embrace as Christians. I preach about it frequently, in fact. It is an admirable quality that we all strive to practice. But because we're human, we often fail.

"We know what the Scripture says. Matthew tells us not to judge, so that we may not be judged. And he tells us that we must forgive not seven times, but seventy times seven. In his letter to the Ephesians, Paul reminds us that we should be kind to one another, and merciful, forgiving each other as the Lord generously forgives us. And when he wrote to the Colossians, he repeated that message. In Ezechiel we read about the new life that comes to those who repent and do what is right and just. And he offers us hope, promising that none of our wrongs will be remembered if we practice virtue.

"My friends, those are powerful words. They capture one of the most beautiful elements of our faith—the recognition that people are human and do make mistakes, but that the Lord offers forgiveness and a 'second chance' to those who repent.

"As we strive to practice our faith, let us also remember that judgment belongs to the Lord. That while we can judge whether a *behavior* is right or wrong, only the Lord can judge a person. Because only He knows what is in our hearts. If we have judged someone, and hurt them by doing so, let us resolve to mend that hurt. Let us find the courage to say 'I'm sorry' and ask for their forgiveness. If the Lord is willing to give us a second chance, can we do any less for each other?

"And while we're forgiving each other, let us not forget to forgive ourselves. Sometimes that's the hardest kind of forgiveness of all to practice. Maybe we carry a burden of guilt over something from our past, which continues to color our lives today. Let us go to the Lord with that guilt, and let us place it in His hands, along with our request for forgiveness. I promise you, He won't turn away.

"I know that forgiveness isn't easy to practice, especially when someone you love fails you, or hurts you, or doesn't truly hear your plea for understanding. But don't turn away. Don't cut that person off. Give him another chance. Forgive him for not being there when you needed him most. For failing to demonstrate his love. Give him the chance to say 'I'm sorry.' Remember that broken relationships *can* be mended. All it takes is forgiveness born of love. And love is the key. Because, as the Bible tells us, love never fails.''

Sam sat numbly as the audience responded to Brad's words with enthusiastic applause. He continued to hold her eyes, as if trying to read her reaction. She knew his beautiful words of healing, spoken from the heart, had been meant for her. Was it possible that he had accepted her past, after all, that he still loved her? she wondered incredulously. Somehow it seemed too much to hope for. She gazed at him uncertainly, questioningly…and at the warmth and reassurance in his eyes a tiny flame of hope stirred among the cold embers of her heart.

The moderator stepped forward to thank Brad, and he reluctantly turned away to shake the woman's hand. Sam blinked rapidly and groped for a tissue in her purse, trying to calm her frantically beating pulse.

Laura leaned over and whispered in her ear. ''Sam, don't worry about giving me a ride home. Nick's picking me up later. We arranged it ahead of time.''

Sam nodded mutely, too overwhelmed with emotion to speak.

Laura gave her arm an encouraging squeeze and joined the crowd moving toward the door. Sam remained seated, her eyes on Brad, who was still talking to the moderator. Eons passed before the woman finally shook his hand and exited.

For a long moment Brad gazed at her in silence from the small stage. Then he slowly moved toward her, lowering himself to an adjacent folding chair when he reached her. Sam's eyes lovingly tracing the strong line of his jaw and his firm but tender lips, connecting at last with his eyes to bask in their tender warmth. He angled himself toward her, draping an arm across the back of her chair, and Sam had a sudden urge to reach over and smooth away the deep lines of fatigue in his face. She stifled the impulse with difficulty, clasping her hands tightly together in her lap instead, waiting apprehensively for him to speak.

"Thank you for coming tonight, Sam," Brad said quietly.

"Laura didn't give me much choice," she replied softly, glancing down. The rapid rise and fall of her chest clearly indicated her unsteady emotions, but she was powerless to control her physical reaction to this unexpected turn of events.

"Don't hold it against her. It was my idea."

"I figured as much."

"When you wouldn't return my calls, I couldn't think of any other way to tell you how I felt."

She ventured a glance at him. "It sounded like *you* were apologizing to *me*," she said hesitantly.

"I was."

"But...but I'm the one who should apologize. I should have told you a long time ago about my past."

"Why didn't you, Sam?" he asked gently. There was no recrimination in his voice, only curiosity.

She looked down again. "I guess because I...I was afraid you'd reject me. I never felt worthy of your love, and I figured once you found out about my past you'd feel the same way." She looked up at him, her eyes pleading for understanding. "I meant to tell you, Brad. Honestly I did. But the more involved we became, the less I wanted to lose you. And so I just kept waiting...and waiting...until finally it...it was too late," she said, her voice breaking.

He reached over and stroked her cheek, and Sam quivered beneath his tender touch. "It's not too late, Sam," he said gently. "At least, I hope not."

She looked up at him, the flame of hope in her heart beginning to blaze more brightly. "What do you mean?" she asked cautiously.

"I mean I love you," he replied with simple, straightforward honesty. "I did last Saturday, before all this happened. And I do now."

"But how can you? After what I did?" she asked uncomprehendingly. "And it...it didn't seem like you did last Saturday. You were so...distant...that night."

He sighed. "My only excuse is that I was in shock. I was having a hard time coping with everything you told me. It was like information overload or something. And I was judgmental, which was wrong," he admitted. "Only you and the Lord know what was in your heart seventeen years ago. You were a desperate teenager, pregnant with a child your husband didn't want and with no one to turn to for help. I didn't know you then, Sam. I can only grieve for your pain and the burden of guilt you've carried all these years. But I know you now. And I know that you're one of the most sensitive, considerate, caring people I've ever had the privilege to meet. And I think you were that kind of person back then, too. I think that's why you were so devastated by what happened."

He reached for her hand, cradling it between his. "That's why you never married again, isn't it?" he said gently. "Because you felt that by denying yourself the happiness and joy of love, you could in some way make amends for what you did."

"Yes," she confirmed, her quavering voice barely audible as she lowered her head in shame.

"Well, let me tell you what I think, Sam," he said, his own voice steady and sure. "You spent seventeen years alone and lonely, atoning for what you did. I suspect the Lord would ask no more than that. And neither would I."

Tentatively Sam raised her head and stared at him. His gaze was direct and unwavering, and she couldn't doubt the sincerity of his words. But there was still another issue.

"What about...what about the family you always wanted, Brad? I can't promise you that."

"I know. I thought about that a lot," he admitted. "I love children, Sam. I've never made a secret of that. I think a loving family is the greatest gift the Lord can bestow. You and I happen to know, going in, that the odds are against us. But even if they weren't, there's no guarantee that we'd be blessed with children. Rachel and I weren't. There was no reason that the doctors could detect. It just never happened. We finally accepted it as the Lord's will.''

He paused and looked down, running the tips of his fingers over the back of her hand for a moment before continuing. ''The fact is, Sam, my love for you isn't contingent on whether you can have children. I'd like children, yes. But if that means giving you up, there's no contest. Maybe we'll have children. Maybe we'll adopt. I don't know. I do know that I love you, and with or without children I believe we can have a full and rich life together.'' Brad paused, reached into his pocket and withdrew the familiar small velvet case. Sam's heart stopped, then raced on.

''I got the house, Sam,'' he said.

She nodded, her eyes locked on the case in his hands. ''I know.''

''You do?''

''Leslie told me.''

''Ah. I should have guessed. Well, it's a great house, Sam. But I really don't want to live there alone.'' He paused, and Sam tore her eyes away from the case to gaze up at him. The smile he gave her was warm and tender and filled with the hope of spring, even though the month was August. ''I tried this once before without much success, but I'm nothing if not persistent,'' he said with a crooked grin. He flipped open the case, and Sam stared down at the solitaire sparkling against the velvet lining. ''The offer is still open, Sam, if you'll have me. Will you marry me?'' he asked huskily.

She gazed up at him and nodded mutely, overcome by a flood of emotions. Joy. Gratitude. Relief. Awe. And love. Mostly love.

Brad smiled and removed the ring from the case, cradling her hand in his as he slipped the solitaire on her finger.

Sam gazed down at it for a moment, but the dazzle of the sparkling stone paled in comparison to the radiant glow on her face when she looked back up at him. "I love you, Brad Matthews," she said, her voice choked with emotion as her eyes caressed the contours of his face.

"The feeling is definitely mutual," he replied, his own voice none too steady. And as his lips closed over hers, in a tender kiss that spoke more eloquently than words of commitment, caring and the promise of a future shared, Sam's last, lingering doubts vanished. Here, in his arms, was where she belonged. For always.

"I guess we're on, Sam," Henry said nervously, adjusting the unfamiliar bow tie.

Though her own nerves were quivering, she smiled reassuringly and linked her arm in his. "I guess we are."

"You sure do look pretty," he said shyly.

Sam glanced down at the cream-colored lace sheath. The scalloped hem ended modestly just above her knees, and the long sleeves were demure. But the neckline—cut straight across, the scalloped edge revealing an enticing glimpse of creamy skin on her shoulders—gave the dress "Sam pizzazz," to use Laura's term.

"Thanks, Henry. So do you. That tux suits you."

"Do you think so? I never wore one before."

"It's perfect."

The music suddenly changed, and Sam drew a deep breath, her fingers tightening on the small bouquet of cream-colored roses and holly sprigs in her hand. "Well, this is it."

The doors opened, and they moved forward slowly into the candlelit church. Christmas was still two days away, but Brad's congregation had pitched in to complete the decorating in time for the wedding. Poinsettias adorned the altar, and fir trees draped in twinkling white lights stood on each side, adding a magical touch to the scene. Sam's gaze skimmed over the sea of smiling faces, coming to rest on Rebecca and Laura who stood in front to the left. Their elegant, gored, forest-green velvet dresses, with cowl necklines and low-cut backs, complemented the festive setting, as did their bouquets of red roses and holly.

Sam's gaze connected with Laura's, and for a long moment of linked eyes—and hearts—a wealth of understanding passed between them. Both had come so far in such a short time. Nine months before, when Sam had made her way down this aisle as Laura's maid of honor, she would never have believed that it would soon be her turn to walk down the same aisle as a bride. And yet it had happened. Thanks to Brad.

Sam turned then to gaze at the man who would soon be her husband. Her husband, she repeated in silent wonder, still finding it hard to believe. Lovingly she let her eyes drink in his tall form. Not surprisingly, he looked wonderful in his tux. Handsome. Distinguished. *Stalwart.* It was an old word, but it fit him.

It was his eyes, though, that held her spellbound. Tender, caring, softened by love, and—simmering in their depths—just a hint of the passion he'd held carefully in check all these months. A passion that he would soon be able to allow free rein, Sam thought with a sudden, delicious tingle of anticipation.

As Henry relinquished his hold, Brad smiled down at her and tucked her arm in his, protectively covering her hand with his own. And as they moved forward to take the vows that would unite them as man and wife for all time, Sam's heart overflowed with joy. The holiday might still be two days away, she thought, but she had just received the most wonderful Christmas present of all—her very own happy ending.

Epilogue

Fourteen months later

Brad gazed tenderly at Sam's face, serene in sleep, and reached over to gently press his lips to her forehead. She stirred slightly at his touch, and he smiled in anticipation as she burrowed a little more deeply into the pillow, then emitted a small sigh. He never tired of watching her awaken. First there was the flutter of her burnished lashes against her creamy cheeks. Then came the slightly unfocused confusion in her vivid green eyes. Finally there was the smile that warmed her face as her eyes cleared and connected with his, a smile filled with deep, abiding love that never failed to make his breath catch in his throat. Not a day went by that he didn't thank the Lord for sending this special, cherished woman into his life.

"Hi there, sleepyhead," he said softly, lightly brushing a stray wisp of hair off her forehead as their gazes met.

"Hi," she mumbled sleepily, rubbing her eyes with the backs of her hands in a little-girl-like gesture, endearing because it was so at odds with her usual sophisticated demeanor.

A sudden rush of tenderness swept over him, and his throat constricted as he delicately stroked her cheek. The gray tinge of fatigue that had earlier shaded her face was gone, he noted thankfully, leaving in its place an almost luminous glow. "How do you feel?" he asked.

She considered the question thoughtfully. "Good," she said at last, a contented smile softening her face. "And happy. And very grateful."

"My thoughts exactly," Brad replied huskily. "And I might also add, very blessed." Then he withdrew a single, perfect, long-stemmed rose from behind his back and handed it to her. "Happy Valentine's Day, darling," he said tenderly.

Sam smiled mistily, overwhelmed as always by the bountiful love in his expressive eyes, and inhaled the sweet, rich fragrance. "It's beautiful, Brad," she whispered. "Thank you."

"There are twenty-three more over on the table," he told her, nodding toward an overflowing vase.

Sam's eyes grew wide. "Oh, Brad! That's such an extravagance!"

"Well, only a dozen are for you," he admitted.

"Oh?" she said, quirking an eyebrow.

"Yes," he confirmed solemnly. He took her hand between his. "I must confess, Sam...there's another woman in my life now. The other dozen are for her."

"And what might this other woman's name be?" Sam asked, her lips curving up into a sweet smile.

"Emily." He said the name wonderingly, as if savoring the sound of it on his tongue.

A tender light suffused Sam's face. "And where is Emily?" she asked softly.

Brad reached behind him and carefully lifted a tiny pink bundle, which he placed in Sam's outstretched arms. "She's right here. Waiting patiently for her mommy to wake up."

With one finger, Sam carefully touched the tiny but perfect nose, stroked the fuzz of reddish hair, stared down in awe at the wide blue eyes that gazed up at her so trustingly. She had never been this happy in her whole life, or overcome by so many emotions. Her throat tightened, and a tear spilled out of one eye to trail down her cheek.

Brad reached over and delicately traced its path with one fingertip, then wiped it away with a featherlight touch. "No more tears, Sam," he said, his voice firm but gentle. "Our time for weeping is past. This is our time to laugh—and to love." Then, one hand resting on their new daughter, the other on Sam, he reached over to tenderly claim the lips of the woman who had brought him joy beyond measure.

Sam closed her eyes, and in the moment before the magic of his kiss drove all thoughts from her mind, she was overcome by a profound sense of joy and fulfillment and gratitude. And by something else as well—the peace of true forgiveness. It was as if a burden had suddenly been lifted from her heart, and for the first time she felt truly free from her past.

And as Brad's lips closed over hers, her heart soared. For here, in this circle of love that the Lord had blessed her with, she had at last found her redemption.

* * * * *

Dear Reader,

I've always enjoyed reading romances, so as a writer I suppose it was inevitable that I would eventually pen my own romantic tales. I especially enjoy writing inspirational stories, because they allow me to focus on the three things that last—faith, hope and love.

A Groom of Her Own was a special pleasure to write because it embodies all three of these elements. Sam's faith gives her the courage to hope, and the love she and Brad share is strong enough to free her from her past. As this story illustrates, nothing is impossible with God and love really does conquer all. If that isn't inspirational, I don't know what is!

The tremendous power of love is a recurring theme in romances, and it appears again in the third and final book of my Vows series, *A Family of Her Own,* which features Brad's sister, Rebecca. It is a story of vulnerability and of innocence lost, and how love transforms the lives of three very special people.

I hope to the Vows series touches your heart. And as you journey through life, may your path always be paved with faith, hope and love.

Irene Hannon

Coming in May 1998

Irene Hannon's heartwarming Vows series
continues with Book #3, the story of
Rebecca Matthews

in

A Family of Her Own

Just turn the page for an exciting preview....

Chapter One

Rebecca Matthews stifled a yawn and reached for the cup of coffee in the holder under the dashboard. It had been a long day and she was bone weary. She glanced at her watch, and groaned. Ten-thirty. Make that a *very* long day, she amended ruefully. Maybe she should have taken her brother up on his offer to stay the night.

Unfortunately tomorrow's schedule wouldn't bend to accommodate staying the night in St. Louis, or even her late-night arrival home. She'd still have to be up no later than six to prepare for the Friday lunch and dinner crowd at her restaurant.

Still, the trip had been worth it, she consoled herself. When Brad called earlier in the day to say that he and Sam were at the hospital, she'd whipped off her apron and left the restaurant in the capable hands of Rose and Frances. That was twelve hours ago. But if it had been a long day for Rebecca, it had been an even longer one for Sam, she thought sympathetically. Her sister-in-law had endured a drawn-out, difficult labor. And poor Brad had been a wreck. But at seven thirty-five, when Emily Matthews had at last deigned to make her entrance, her parents' pain and concern had quickly been supplanted by joy.

Rebecca was happy for Sam and Brad, but love—at least of the romantic variety—wasn't something she knew much about, she reflected sadly. And she probably never would. Since she opened the restaurant three years ago, there had been little time to indulge in self-pity or dwell on her loneliness, but today, when she'd viewed at such close proximity the circle of love shared by Brad, Sam and their new daughter, it had been very hard to hold back her tears as she cradled the tiny new life in her arms, knowing that it was unlikely she would ever repeat the experience with her own child as a loving husband stood by her side.

At thirty-three, Rebecca was still young enough to have the children she'd always wanted. That wasn't the problem. The problem was finding a husband with enough patience to deal with her problem. But patience was a virtue that seemed to be in short supply these days. And any man who was remotely interested in her would have to possess an awful lot of patience.

Rebecca sighed again. She hadn't met a man yet who was willing to date her more than a couple of times without expecting some physical closeness. While Rebecca's Christian principles didn't allow for casual intimacy, she realized that at some stage in a developing relationship kissing and touching were appropriate. And expected.

But Rebecca couldn't handle that. Even if she liked a man, her only emotion when faced with physical contact was fear, not desire. And no man she'd ever met could deal with that. In fact, she'd stopped trying to find one who could. It was easier this way. Less humiliating. Less stressful. But certainly more lonely.

Yet seeing Brad and Sam together these last few months and now watching them with their new daughter, made Rebecca yearn for the same things for herself. Maybe, just maybe, the Lord would send her a man who would be able to fan into life the flame of desire buried deep in her heart, who would patiently teach her how to respond and dispel her fear, she thought with a little surge of hope. Surely there had to be a man out there somewhere who could help her find a way to express the love she'd held captive for so long in her heart!

With sudden resolve, she promised herself that if a man came along who seemed worth the effort, she would make one more attempt to explore a relationship. It wouldn't be easy, she knew. But maybe, with the Lord's help, she could find a way to overcome her fear and create her own circle of love. And if nothing else, it was a wonderful fantasy, she thought wistfully.

But right now she better focus on reality, not fantasy, she reminded herself firmly. The fog actually seemed to be growing denser—and more dangerous. It might be better to get off the interstate at the first St. Genevieve exit and take the back road into town, she reasoned.

The exit sign loomed out of the mist unexpectedly, and Rebecca took the exit ramp slowly, with a bizarre sense that the world as she knew it had ceased to exist. Carefully she turned onto the deserted secondary road, her headlights struggling to pierce the gloom as she crept along. As she drove through the swirling mist, an eerie feeling swept over her. She knew there were homes scattered along the road, but they weren't visible tonight. She had no points of reference with which to mark her progress, and she felt disoriented and vulnerable.

Rebecca gasped as her headlights suddenly illuminated a figure walking slowly along the road, almost directly in front of her car. She swerved sharply to avoid it, then glanced in the rearview mirror in time to catch one final glimpse of the spectral apparition before it was swallowed up in the gloom.

Good heavens, what had she seen? she wondered in alarm, her heart pounding as adrenaline raced through her veins. She forced herself to take several deep calming breaths and eased back on the accelerator, frowning as she mentally tried to recreate the image that had briefly flashed across her field of vision.

It was a man, she realized, wearing a white dress shirt and a tie, and carrying a suit jacket. Had he been weaving slightly? Or was that just a trick of the swirling fog? she wondered. And why would he be walking along the road at this hour of the night in this weather? Her frown deepened and she lifted her foot off the accelerator even farther, slowing the car to a crawl.

There were only a few possible explanations for the man's behavior. Either he was a lunatic, he was drunk or he was in trouble.

The first two possibilities frightened her. She wasn't equipped to deal with them. Not alone on a deserted road. But if he was in trouble or hurt—she thought about the story of the good Samaritan, who came to the assistance of the stranger on the road, and bit her lip thoughtfully. There was definitely a parallel here. Her Christian principles just wouldn't allow her to turn her back on someone in trouble. If he needed assistance, she had to provide it. But she wasn't going to take any chances, either. She'd just wait until he appeared and then use her best judgment to determine how to proceed.

Rebecca carefully pulled her car over to the side of the road, double checked that all her doors were locked and that the windows were tightly rolled up, and waited.

Suddenly the man appeared out of the mist immediately to her left, and Rebecca drew a startled breath. He was less than ten feet away, walking right down the center of the road. In the unlikely event that a car appeared, he would be a sitting duck, she realized. But he seemed oblivious to the danger. He also seemed oblivious to her car. In fact, he didn't seem to notice anything. And he was definitely weaving, she realized. His gait was unsteady, and his head was bowed.

Rebecca lowered her window a mere two inches and called to him. "Excuse me...do you need help?"

The man's step faltered momentarily, and he raised a hand to his forehead, but after a moment he continued to walk without even looking in her direction.

Rebecca frowned and quickly put the car in gear, following along slowly beside him. She lowered her window a little farther and tried calling even more loudly. "Hey, mister!"

The man stopped again, and this time he glanced confusedly in her direction. Rebecca studied his face, and though it was mostly obscured by the billowing wisps of fog, she could tell that he was fairly young. Late thirties, maybe. He was also tall. Probably six feet. And he looked strong. Very strong. Which frightened her. She would be no match for someone of his size, and on this deserted road anything could happen, she thought fearfully.

But suddenly, as the opaque veil between them momentarily lifted, she realized that her fears were unfounded. The man was clearly injured. His face was gray, and there was a long, nasty-looking gash at his hairline. He was obviously in no condition to walk, let alone attack anyone. She'd be willing to bet that at the moment her strength far surpassed his.

Feeling a little less frightened, she lowered her window even more. "What happened?" she called.

"Accident," he mumbled, gesturing vaguely behind him.

Rebecca hadn't seen a car, and she looked at him suspiciously. "What kind of accident?"

"Deer," he replied, his voice slurred. He didn't appear to be able to manage answers of more than one word.

Suddenly he started to walk down the road again, but after only two shaky steps his legs buckled and he fell heavily to his knees, palms flat on the pavement.

Without even stopping to consider her own safety, Rebecca unlocked her door and dashed toward him, stopping abruptly when she reached his side to stare down helplessly at his bowed head and sagging shoulders. What was she supposed to do now? Tentatively she reached down and touched his broad shoulder.

"Look, you can't stay here," she told him urgently. "You're in the middle of the road. It's dangerous."

Her words finally seemed to penetrate his consciousness, and he tilted his head to look up at her. His brown eyes were clouded and dazed, and he seemed to be having a difficult time focusing.

"Dizzy," he mumbled.

"Look. I'll help, okay?" she offered, tugging more forcefully on his arm.

This time he made an effort to stand. And as he struggled to his feet, she realized just how tall he was. At five-five she wasn't exactly short, but he towered over her by at least six or seven inches. And he was well-built. And obviously strong.

A wave of panic washed over her, and for a moment her resolve to help wavered. But when she loosened her grip, he swayed, and she was left with no choice but to guide his arm around her shoulders. Stay calm, she told herself sternly. Think logically. The man is hurt. He does not represent any danger.

She took a deep breath, repeating that mantra over and over again as she slowly guided him to the car. He leaned on her heavily, his breathing labored, and she stole a glance at his face. He looked awful, and she wondered if he might have other injuries besides the deep gash at his hairline. Please, Lord, help me get him to the hospital as quickly as possible, she prayed.

When they reached the car she propped him against the front of the hood and backed up, eyeing him worriedly. "Stay put, okay?" she said slowly, enunciating every word. "I'm going to unlock the car door."

Rebecca had no idea if he understood her words—or even if he heard them.

Just as she stepped away from his side, he stumbled, wildly flinging out an arm to try and regain his balance.

Unfortunately, Rebecca was right in the path of his knuckles.

The backhanded blow caught her on the chin, and she staggered back, grabbing at his arm to keep from falling. But that only threw him more off balance, and before she knew what was happening he fell against her, pinning her to the hood of the car under his body.

Dazed from the blow, aware only that she was suddenly immobilized and at his mercy, Rebecca panicked as a wave of primitive fear swept over her. With a strangled sob, she struggled to get free, writhing beneath the man's weight. But he was heavy. So heavy! She could hardly move. But she had to get free! She had to! Summoning up all her strength, she shoved him far enough away to tear her body from beneath his.

The stranger seemed stunned by her action, and he staggered back, his eyes glazed. He wavered, then dropped to one knee, groaning as he raised his hands to his bowed head.

Still reeling from the man's blow, Rebecca reached up and gingerly felt her tender chin. Her chest was heaving as she drew in one ragged breath after another, and she braced herself against the hood, not sure her trembling legs would hold her up. In fact, her whole body was shaking, she realized. As she struggled to control her irrational reaction, she watched the man touch the gash at his hairline, then stare in confusion at the blood dripping from his fingers.

With a sickening jolt, Rebecca realized that the impact of his fall must have opened the cut again, and a pang of guilt swept over her. Dear Lord, what was wrong with her? The man was hurt, for heaven's sake! He was in no condition to attack her even if he wanted to, which was unlikely. He hadn't hit her on purpose. She needed to get a grip.

Rebecca took several more deep breaths, then knelt beside the stranger and scanned his face. The man needed medical attention. Immediately.

She drew a deep breath and lifted his limp arm, tucking her head underneath and draping it around her slender shoulders. She needed to get him into her car before he passed out.

"Okay, can you try to stand?" she asked. "I'll help. Just lean on me." Rebecca made an attempt to rise, but it was like tugging on a dead weight. He didn't budge. "Come on, mister, just try. Please!" she pleaded.

This time when she urged him upward he took the cue, struggling to stand as Rebecca tried to assist him. Once he was on his feet he swayed, and she planted her feet solidly, struggling to maintain her own footing. She glanced up worriedly, noting the deep grooves of pain etched in his face and the thin, compressed line of his lips. Despite the chilly air there was a thick film of sweat on his brow, and his breathing was labored.

"We're almost to the door," she said encouragingly, trying to keep the panic out of her voice. "It's just a few steps. You can make it."

Half dragging, half pulling, she got him into the car, expelling a shaky breath as she shut the door. She retrieved his suit jacket from the middle of the road where he'd dropped it, tossed it into the back seat, and slid behind the wheel. As she put the car in gear, she glanced over at his semi-prone form. She wasn't even sure at this point if he was conscious. But at least he was still breathing, she thought with relief, noting the even rise and fall of his chest.

As she drove carefully through the swirling, silent fog, she stole an occasional glance at her unexpected passenger. Although his color was ashen, his clothes stained and rumpled, and his hair disheveled, she could tell that he was handsome in a rugged sort of way. His dark brown hair was full and slightly longer than stylish, almost brushing his collar in the back, although it was neatly trimmed. Her eyes traced his strong profile and firm jaw, which seemed to speak of character and integrity. Yet there was a worn look about his face—a sort of deep weariness that had nothing to do with his injuries. For some reason she had the impression that he was a man who had seen it all and now viewed the world with scepticism and cynicism. Despite his look of world-weariness, however, there was a feeling of leashed power about him. Even in his present condition he seemed to radiate energy and vitality and...sensuousness.

Rebecca was taken aback by that impression. Yet it was true. The man exuded an almost tangible virility. She stole another glance at him.

Rebecca's gaze snapped back to the road. She was letting herself get way too fanciful. The man was a stranger! None of her speculations were grounded in reality. For example, just because he looked like he had character and integrity didn't mean he did. Looks could be deceiving. She knew that from experience. Caution was more prudent than curiosity in a situation like this, she warned herself.

Yet she couldn't help but wonder about him. Why had he been driving on this road alone so late at night? She ventured another quick glance at his left hand. No ring. That didn't mean anything, of course. He might be one of those married men who preferred not to wear a ring. But for some reason she had a feeling he was single—and unattached. Surprisingly, a little tingle ran down her spine at that possibility.

Which was silly, she told herself sharply. In a few minutes they'd be at the hospital and, her duty done, she could finally go home and catch a few hours of much-needed sleep. She'd probably never see the man again. And that was just as well. For some reason he unnerved her, even in this comatose state. He was just so...male.

Rebecca knew that wasn't a very articulate explanation for her reaction, but it was accurate. His mere presence seemed somehow...dangerous...and threatening. Threatening to what, she wasn't sure. Certainly not her physical safety, not in his present condition. It was almost as if he was a threat to her emotional safety, to her peace of mind. Which made no sense at all. She didn't even know the man. And she never would. In a few minutes she'd leave him at the hospital, and that would be the end of this little adventure.

But oddly enough, that thought didn't give her much comfort.

* * * * *

This March Love Inspired celebrates
the joys of parenthood with
three wonderful stories
about babies and families.

Don't miss any of these heartwarming books:

CHILD OF HER HEART
by Irene Brand

A pregnant woman's devotion to her unborn
child brings her unexpected love on the
road to motherhood.

A FATHER'S LOVE
by Cheryl Wolverton

A wealthy businessman finds twin babies on his
doorstep and enlists the help of a pretty nanny, who
teaches him about faith, fatherhood and forgiveness.

WITH BABY IN MIND
by Arlene James

The fourth book in the Everyday Miracles series
tells the story of a dedicated nurse and a gruff
bachelor who are united by an orphaned
child...and restored faith!

Welcome to *Love Inspired*™

A brand-new series of contemporary inspirational love stories.

Join men and women as they learn valuable lessons about facing the challenges of today's world and about life, love and faith.

Look for the following March 1998
Love Inspired™ titles:

CHILD OF HER HEART
by Irene Brand

A FATHER'S LOVE
by Cheryl Wolverton

WITH BABY IN MIND
by Arlene James

Available in retail outlets in February 1998.

LIFT YOUR SPIRITS AND GLADDEN YOUR HEART
with *Love Inspired!*™

Steeple
Hill™

LI398

This March watch for the next story about the lives and loves of the residents of Duncan, Oklahoma, as *Love Inspired* brings you another

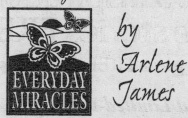

by Arlene James

EVERYDAY MIRACLES

Every day brings new challenges for young Reverend Bolton Charles and his congregation. But together they are sure to gain the strength to overcome all obstacles—and find love along the way!

You've enjoyed these wonderful stories:

THE PERFECT WEDDING
(September 1997)

AN OLD-FASHIONED LOVE
(November 1997)

A WIFE WORTH WAITING FOR
(January 1998)

Now meet Parker Sugarman, a bachelor who desperately wants to keep custody of his orphaned niece. But Parker needs a wife, and so proposes marriage to his good friend Kendra. He knows she'll be a wonderful mother. But will Kendra's faith be strong enough to help Parker become the perfect family man? Look for:

WITH BABY IN MIND

available in March from

Love Inspired

IEM98-3

Take 3 inspirational love stories FREE!

PLUS get a FREE surprise gift!

Special Limited-time Offer

Mail to Steeple Hill Reader Service™
3010 Walden Avenue
P.O. Box 1867
Buffalo, N.Y. 14240-1867

YES! Please send me 3 free Love Inspired™ novels and my free surprise gift. Then send me 3 brand-new novels every month, which I will receive months before they appear in bookstores. Bill me at the low price of $3.19 each plus 25¢ delivery and applicable sales tax, if any*. That's the complete price and a saving of over 10% off the cover prices—quite a bargain! I understand that accepting the books and gift places me under no obligation ever to buy any books. I can always return a shipment and cancel at any time. Even if I never buy another book from Steeple Hill, the 3 free books and the surprise gift are mine to keep forever.

103 IEN CFAG

Name	(PLEASE PRINT)	
Address		Apt. No.
City	State	Zip

This offer is limited to one order per household and not valid to present Love Inspired™ subscribers. *Terms and prices are subject to change without notice. Sales tax applicable in New York.

ULI-198   ©1997 Steeple Hill

WELCOME TO *Love Inspired* ™

A brand-new series of contemporary inspirational love stories.

Join men and women as they learn valuable lessons about facing the challenges of today's world and about life, love and faith.

Look for the following February 1998 Love Inspired™ titles:

A Groom of Her Own
by Irene Hannon

The Marriage Wish
by Dee Henderson

The Reluctant Bride
by Kathryn Alexander

Available in retail outlets
in January 1998.

LIFT YOUR SPIRITS AND GLADDEN YOUR HEART with *Love Inspired*™!

Steeple
Hill™

LI298

Welcome to *Love Inspired*™

A brand-new series of contemporary inspirational love stories.

Join men and women as they learn valuable lessons about facing the challenges of today's world and about life, love and faith.

Look for the following April 1998 Love Inspired™ titles:

DECIDEDLY MARRIED
by Carole Gift Page

A HOPEFUL HEART
by Lois Richer

HOMECOMING
by Carolyne Aarsen

Available in retail outlets in March 1998.

LIFT YOUR SPIRITS AND GLADDEN YOUR HEART

with *Love Inspired!*™

Steeple
Hill™

LI498